S.J. MARTIN

The Papal Assassin's Wife

Paramour. Poisoner. Protégé

First published by Moonstorm Books 2022

Copyright © 2022 by S.J. Martin

All rights reserved. No part of this publication may be reproduced, stored or transmitted in any form or by any means, electronic, mechanical, photocopying, recording, scanning, or otherwise without written permission from the publisher. It is illegal to copy this book, post it to a website, or distribute it by any other means without permission.

S.J. Martin asserts the moral right to be identified as the author of this work.

First edition

This book was professionally typeset on Reedsy. Find out more at reedsy.com

Contents

1	Chapter One	1
2	Chapter Two	9
3	Chapter Three	17
4	Chapter Four	26
5	Chapter Five	34
6	Chapter Six	38
7	Chapter Seven	47
8	Chapter Eight	57
9	Chapter Nine	69
10	Chapter Ten	76
11	Chapter Eleven	82
12	Chapter Twelve	91
13	Chapter Thirteen	102
14	Chapter Fourteen	110
15	Chapter Fifteen	119
16	Chapter Sixteen	127
17	Chapter Seventeen	139
18	Chapter Eighteen	147
19	Chapter Nineteen	153
20	Chapter Twenty	164
21	Chapter Twenty-one	170
22	Chapter Twenty-two	178
23	Chapter Twenty-three	188
24	Chapter Twenty-four	195

25	Chapter Twenty-five	207
26	Chapter Twenty-six	221
27	Chapter Twenty-seven	233
28	Chapter Twenty-eight	244
29	Chapter Twenty-nine	252
30	Chapter Thirty	263
31	Character List	272
32	Glossary	275
33	Author Note	278
34	Maps	280
35	Read More	284
	About the Author	286
	Also by S.J. Martin	288

1

Chapter One

Genoa – Feb 1088
Piers De Chatillon had decided exactly whom his new wife would kill…he just hadn't told her yet! He raised his eyes to the soaring roof of the impressive St Syrus Basilica in Genoa as the choirs began their choral psalms. The only other sound was the chinking chains of the thuribles as the altar boys swung them back and forth, the incense wafting over the heads of the large, silent, assembled crowd.

He brought his attention back to the altar. The Archbishop of Genoa, Conrades Di Mezzarello, an old family friend, stood at one side of the altar looking suitably awed because Chatillon's uncle, Pope Urban II, was about to conduct the wedding ceremony. This explained why not only was the basilica crammed full of standing people but hundreds, if not over a thousand, were standing in the spring sunshine outside. All waiting for a glimpse of, or hoping for a blessing from, the Holy Father.

Piers De Chatillon, a wealthy French noble, powerful Papal Envoy and renowned assassin, was waiting for his young bride to arrive. Isabella was the beautiful but tempestuous daughter of the Signori Guglielmo Embriaco, the influential leader of the Maritime Republic of Genoa. The basilica was packed with Genoa's nobility, and many other guests and friends from all corners of Europe, who wished to see Chatillon marry. Many never expected to see this happen so they came from Rome, Milan, Paris and even the wild wind-lashed coast of western Brittany. Such was the reach and influence of this man.

For Piers De Chatillon was no ordinary Papal Envoy. He'd always been somewhat of an enigma: an arch manipulator, a consummate politician and diplomat used by popes, kings and princes alike but also a ruthless killer who would, for a price, remove any problem. There was no doubt that he was feared, but he also attracted wary respect and even admiration from those that knew him well. Then there was the small group who considered him their comrade and friend and would freely give their lives for him.

Even in his late thirties, he was a striking figure, tall and darkly handsome with a lithe but muscled warrior build, achieved through hours of practice with sword and staff. However, intelligence shone out of those piercing, almost black eyes. When you suddenly came to his attention, and he caught your gaze, it could be unnerving, and would often force you to avert your eyes. Yet when necessary, or when it was useful, he could be charm incarnate.

Beside him stood three men. On his left was Edvard, his Vavasseur, servant and friend, a defrocked monk who had been at his side for the last sixteen years. On his right was Morvan De Malvais, a tall, handsome Breton Horse Warrior. Today Morvan was dressed in a rich velvet tunic instead of the usual trademark laced leather jerkin with his crossed swords on his back. They had confronted each other, daggers drawn, prepared to kill the other, in a dark alleyway in Ghent years before, but they had finally become firm friends. Morvan was forever indebted to Chatillon, for when warrior monks kidnapped Morvan's young son, Conn, it was Chatillon who tracked them down in the Italian Alps and followed them to Avignon. Young Conn, although physically and mentally scarred, was now back safe with his family in Brittany.

The third man was older but was one of Chatillon's early mentors as a young man in Paris—Gervais de la Ferte, the powerful Seneschal of France whose daughter Ette had married Morvan De Malvais. When Chatillon was only sixteen, Gervais had watched him kill an older, experienced young man in a duel. He had predicted back then that the young Piers would grow into a dangerous man, and he'd been proved right. However, they had remained firm friends, often working together for the French King Philip or Gervais availing himself of the many services that Chatillon offered, for Piers had the biggest network of informers and messengers in Europe. If you wanted information, then Chatillon would deliver it to you—for a price. If you wanted someone killed or merely incapacitated temporarily then he was your man.

A hush from the whispering congregation heralded the entrance of Isabella and her family into the basilica.. Chatillon turned and watched the group approach. The immense crowd parted before them as Isabella and her father walked slowly towards the altar. Behind them came Chatillon's ward, the young girl Marietta De Monsi, the daughter of a friend and lover who had died in his arms. He had promised the dying woman that he would become the girl's guardian until she came of age and inherited her mother's wealth. Marietta looked very pretty, her hair decorated with flowers and a smile on her face.

'Too late to run now,' whispered Morvan into his friend's ear, and he received a swift punch to his ribs in return.

Signori Guglielmo Embriaco was an impressive figure, and he was delighted with this match for his daughter, which would bring even more prestige and influence to his family. Also, he was grateful to get his stubborn and rebellious daughter off his hands to this powerful Papal Envoy. She must have turned down at least a dozen suitors. Now in her twenty-fourth year, she should have been married years ago, but she'd refused all of her parents' choices. This time, he'd put his foot down and threatened to send her to a convent if she didn't accept Piers De Chatillon. To his surprise and to his wife's astonishment, Isabella accepted this offer of marriage because Piers both attracted and fascinated her. She had seen the apprehension in people's eyes as he approached, and more importantly, she discovered quite quickly that he was not a man she could control, which excited her.

Isabella looked beautiful, her eyes modestly lowered; she was dressed in an over gown of light blue silk with matching ribbons wound in her hair. Morvan gave a low whistle of approval as she reached her future husband's side in front of the altar. She raised her deep brown eyes briefly to Piers, and he smiled. She was indeed very beautiful, with her heart-shaped face and mane of golden and honey-coloured hair but with the unusual dark-winged eyebrows that framed her large eyes. As he gazed down, Chatillon thought she was perfect for the role he had in mind for her, both as a wife and as a skilled courtesan. She was almost a blank canvas, and he'd mould her to become a diplomat and a woman any man would want in his bed. But she would become more than that, for he would

CHAPTER ONE

ensure that she would be trained to become an expert poisoner.

As Isabella stood beside the dark, handsome man who was to be her husband, she felt a frisson of excitement, and her stomach fluttered at the thought of being alone with this man in his bedroom tonight. His warm hand, with its elegant, but strong fingers, reached down and lifted her hand to his lips, in greeting, as her father, bowing his head to Pope Urban and then to Piers De Chatillon, stepped back. The ceremony was a blur, as all she knew was the presence of the man beside her, and she cast surreptitious glances up at him, which he sometimes met, smiling reassuringly. Even the awe at having the Pope conduct the ceremony couldn't override her excitement at becoming this man's wife.

She came from the most powerful family in Genoa, so she was used to wealth and influence, but Piers De Chatillon was different. She'd seen how wary and careful the Genoese nobility were in his presence, and how they watched their words. This man had power; he was wealthy and respected, owning houses and estates all over Europe. Despite that, she admitted, it was the alarm in some people's eyes when confronted with Chatillon that she found almost intoxicating, for she could see that some of them truly feared him.

Pope Urban wrapped his stole around the wrists of the couple, binding them together as he gave his final blessing and smiled down at his nephew. He was delighted that Piers had finally decided to marry, and if God wished, they would have children to carry on the De Chatillon name and inherit the vast estates. He'd worried that Piers would never get over the awful murder of his former love, Bianca; although he'd dozens of liaisons, he'd never loved anyone again as he had loved her. Perhaps now, with Isabella, that would change, and he would find happiness; he truly hoped so.

The ceremony over, they stood back to give precedence to the Pope, but Odo smiled and waved them forward. 'This is your day, you go ahead, and I'll follow on with my friend, the Archbishop.'

They bowed and then turned, walking slowly towards the double doors at the far end of the basilica, while congratulations and bows came from all sides. Chatillon felt a sense of satisfaction as he made his way through the crowds, and he glanced down at Isabella and smiled. He was pleased to see there was no forced maidenly modesty about her now. She held her head high; pride at landing a catch that had placed her above all of the Genoese society in influence was writ clearly on her face, as she inclined her head gracefully to the crowds.

As the crowd surged forward to see them, Chatillon's eye was caught by a tall, dark figure leaning against a pillar at the back on the far side of the nave. He was in the shadows, but Piers could see he was not dressed in the colourful holiday garb of the guests and crowd at the wedding. The Signori had declared a day's holiday for all, and the people of Genoa were taking advantage of it. As they kept walking towards the entrance, Chatillon glanced back. He had many enemies, too numerous to name, making him always watchful. As the man crossed a patch of sunlight, he could see the shoulder-length dark hair and the worn laced leather jerkin of a warrior. He was very tall and well built, but he was moving now in the shadows on the edge of the crowd, which had pushed forward to see the Pope, so Chatillon lost sight of him.

Was it another horse warrior? he wondered. *Could it even be Luc De Malvais, Morvan's older brother? Had he changed his mind and made the long journey from Brittany to be here?*

Piers looked back again, scanning over the heads of the crowd to try to locate the man because he was uneasy about him, but he'd disappeared. There was something familiar but also unsettling about this warrior, and Chatillon always took great care, with so many out there ready to take revenge on him or even to attack his uncle, the Pope. He turned to try to catch the eye of Morvan De Malvais behind him, but he was much further back, walking with his pretty wife Ette behind the religious procession of the Pope and Archbishop, so there was no help there. He looked for the towering figure of his Vavasseur, Edvard, but could not locate him either.

As they emerged through the huge carved doors into the bright spring sunshine of the square, the crowd outside loudly cheered the newly married couple. As expected, the servants of the Signori Embriaco scattered handfuls of largesse across the crowd. Dozens of silver coins were thrown, with the people scrabbling at their feet to find them. However, it was soon over despite a few vicious fights about ownership. The crowd fell silent as the trumpets blared and Pope Urban II emerged onto the basilica's steps. Chatillon and Isabella stood to one side as he spoke and blessed the crowd before he was escorted away, to the Embriaco Palace, to the sounds of the crowd's echoing cheers.

The other noble guests from the basilica were now streaming out into the square behind them, and their servants pushed the crowd back. Chatillon looked for Edvard but still couldn't immediately locate him, and then he made out his impressive bulk standing on the far side of the square. He immediately noticed that Edvard's arm was raised, and he seemed to be remonstrating with someone. Chatillon was sure it was the tall, dark man from the basilica, probably an assassin sent to ruin this day.

He muttered an excuse to Isabella, and his hand went to the hilt of his dagger as he pushed his way impatiently through the crowds towards where he'd last seen Edvard. He could see fleetingly through the crowd that Edvard seemed to have the man against the wall of the Lateran Palace, but Piers couldn't distinguish who it was. As he hurriedly made his way, people tried to stop him to congratulate him, and beggars clutched at his rich clothes, but he pushed them impatiently aside. Piers drew his dagger. He realised his heart was thumping as, finally breaking through the crush, he sprinted across the small open space before the Lateran palace. His dagger raised, he forcefully pushed his friend Edvard sideways to try to save him. Edvard staggered away in surprise as Chatillon found that the tall warrior had grabbed his raised wrist in a vice-like grip. His gaze met the dark, narrowed eyes. Too late, Chatillon realised who it was....

Chapter Two

Chatillon let out the breath he had been holding, for he couldn't quite believe whom he was seeing. He blinked in quick succession, for looking back at him was Finian Ui Neill, an Irish lord and warrior who had shared many trials and fights with him in the past. Finian had saved his life in Prague many years before, and he had sworn to return to fight at Chatillon's side one day. That had been fourteen years ago, and they hadn't seen hide nor hair of him since—Chatillon even thought that the Irish lord might be dead.

Finian released his wrist. 'Is that any way to greet an old friend who has travelled hundreds of leagues to be here at your wedding?' he asked in that deep Irish lilt, a wide grin on his face. Chatillon reciprocated with an embarrassed smile, and sheathing his dagger, he put a hand out to pull a smiling Edvard to his feet.

'Finian, you're a sight for sore eyes—fourteen years and not even a message to tell us you're still alive, and then you turn up out of the blue at my wedding,' said Chatillon with a laugh as he shook his head at his friend. Finian clasped his friend's arm and looked into his face. The last fourteen years had been kind to Chatillon despite his near-death experience in Prague. He still had almost black hair with only a slight hint of grey at the temples.

'I'm afraid I've been somewhat occupied of late in trying, unsuccessfully, to lay the family blood feuds to rest in Ireland,' Finian said as he looked away from them across the square. Chatillon saw the sudden pain in his friend's eyes and slapped him on the shoulder.

'We will talk and catch up tomorrow. Meanwhile, you are, of course, our guest. Edvard will look after you. Morvan De Malvais is here with his wife, Ette. I believe you fought alongside him and his brother Luc for a while in Brittany, so he will also be pleased to see you.'

At that moment, with two armed servants, Isabella appeared at his side, annoyed and concerned but she was now looking with interest at the new arrival. 'My father is waiting for us with the carriage, we must go,' she whispered. Chatillon nodded, and clasping arms with Finian, again, he bade farewell for now to his friend.

The wedding feast was a joyous occasion but went on for hours with toast after toast. Piers had little time for conversation with his friends as he was seated beside his uncle, the Pope, and had to give him the thanks and attention he deserved. Sitting beside them, Isabella could hardly eat any of the rich food for the apprehensive knot in her stomach.

She was not naïve or totally innocent. She'd lost her virginity to Alfredo, a distant cousin, a few years before, and Chatillon was certainly aware of this, as he had discovered her perfidy. However, Alfredo had been a mere boy, while Piers De Chatillon was an experienced lover, who had no doubt made love to dozens of women if her older brother was to be believed. The way Chatillon's eyes roamed over her body, with that amused smile, sent a shiver of anticipation and apprehension down her spine.

'I think we should leave our guests shortly,' he said, raising her hand and gently biting her fingertips. 'I find I cannot wait much longer to have you naked in my bed,' he murmured. She looked up into those intense dark eyes and felt her body responding; a wave of unexpected sensation spread between her legs. He smiled into her eyes, saw the excitement and apprehension, and laughed softly. It was a very long time since he'd made love to an innocent and inexperienced woman. He felt himself hardening as he thought about what he would show her and teach her tonight. He stood up.

'Honoured guests and your eminence,' he said, bowing to his uncle, the Pope. 'Thank you for the pleasure of your company today, but my wife is impatient to get me into bed.' As he expected, everyone laughed while Isabella coloured up into a delightful blush.

After a short carriage ride, they walked up the stairs of his beautiful large castello, built into the cliffs overlooking the harbour of Genoa. Isabella had been there once before as his guest. She knew it belonged to his former lover Contessa Bianca Da Landriano, and was one of the many properties she'd left him. However, the lovely Italian Contessa had been murdered nearly eight years before by an assassin. Isabella was unconcerned about his past, and the castello would now become her home in Genoa.

Piers led her up to their bedroom and closed the door firmly behind him. He pulled her round to face him and held her face in both of his hands. He kissed her deeply for some time. She'd never been kissed like that, as he possessed her mouth and sent thrills through her body. She came up wide-eyed and breathless. He held her at arm's length for what seemed an age as his eyes swept over her body, and he ran his hands down the sides of her arms, lightly caressing her.

Releasing her, he turned away and poured them a glass of white wine. It came from the hills above the city and had been cooled in the deep cold wine cellar, built into the cliffs behind the house. He gently rolled the chilled wine around his mouth as he regarded his young wife. 'Come here and sit,' he said, indicating the long divan that ran alongside the wall, on the other side of the small table. Isabella perched on the edge of the couch, watching the dark, enigmatic man opposite her. Chatillon gave a small laugh; it was like a pigeon watching a hawk, he mused. However, to Isabella, it was not fear of him that consumed her, but more apprehension about the unknown and what her future life would bring both in and out of the bedroom with this man.

He watched the emotions chasing across her face and smiled. 'You are very beautiful, Isabella. I could see the envy on men's faces as we progressed through the basilica into the square.' She smiled back at him. This was safe territory, as she knew her effect on men. 'Your beauty, charm and intelligence will be very useful to me, for not only will you be my wife, I also intend to turn you into a consummate diplomat. I've other plans for you, which I think you'll enjoy, but more of that later. After your adventures with the spineless boy Alfredo, we both know you're not some timid virgin. Now you can show me what you've learnt, and then I'll show you what I expect from you in the bedroom.'

Isabella's eyes widened in alarm, for Alfredo's desperate

fumbling in a local barn had shown her very little. She'd only let him have his way for the pure excitement of breaking all the rules. She was so bored with her life in Genoa, and it had brought the thrilling danger of being caught. However, she'd never found his mauling and probing pleasurable, and it had been over in minutes as he'd spent himself on the grass.

Chatillon watched the uncertainty and panic as her hands clenched around the wine glass. He decided to take pity on her. 'I am correct, am I not? Your cousin Alfredo did deflower you?' She nodded, and suddenly she felt ashamed of what she had done. This was her husband and she couldn't meet his eyes. 'How long did this go on for, months? A year?'

She took a large mouthful of wine and looked away again as she replied, 'It only happened with him twice, once in the old watermill and once in a barn. I will admit that it was I who pushed Alfredo into it; I wanted to force my father to let me marry him because he was so easy to bully and control.'

To her dismay and embarrassment, Chatillon burst out laughing, and Isabella could feel her anger rising as his laugh echoed around the large, lavishly furnished bedchamber. She banged her Venetian glass goblet down onto the table and stood as if to leave, her eyes flashing. He was on his feet in a trice and had her wrist in a vice-like grip. 'I've heard all about your temper and stubbornness, Isabella, but do you think I'm someone you can control? I am sorry if you're offended by my laughter, but it was, in fact, a compliment to your ingenious strategy, which I'm afraid I spoilt by offering for your hand. If you had married him, you would have been very bored, though. I promise you, Isabella, you'll never find yourself bored with me.'

She felt somewhat mollified by this. 'You are hurting my

wrist,' she murmured.

He released her wrist. 'Think yourself lucky, Isabella, for if you had broken my prized Venetian glass, I would have lifted your gown and put you over my knee, and I wouldn't have been gentle.' She looked at him in disbelief, for no one had ever dared to lay a hand on her, for she was Isabella De Embriaco.

'Enough of this. Tonight is our wedding night, and I intend to show you the meaning of pleasure.' He stepped forward, and turning her around, he lifted the long tresses forward over her shoulder and unlaced the ties at the back of the gown that went down to her waist. He dropped his lips onto the nape of her neck, an area he knew excited a woman. His hands moved around to the front, and he caressed her breasts before slowly releasing the blue silk gown to drop at her feet. She now stood in a fine, almost transparent chemise dyed the same light blue as the gown.

He turned her around and, taking her hands, pulled her over to the chair where he sat down. She expected him to remove her chemise, but instead, he pulled her between his legs, his strong thighs holding her there. He brushed his fingers lightly back and forth across her hardening nipples, lowering his head to lick and bite them through the thin linen. She gasped with pleasure, as she'd never experienced such excitement that seemed to race down through her body. His mouth was still on her breasts, as his hands caressed her body, moving from her waist to grip her buttocks and then moving down the outside of her thighs. He placed his knee between her legs to open them, as he put his head back and stared intently up at her. 'Tonight is all about you, Isabella, about your pleasure. Tomorrow, I'll teach you how to do the same for me.'

She gazed down at this handsome man whose lips and hands

seemed to be everywhere on her body. Then she closed her eyes as his hand stroked gently back and forth on the linen chemise between her legs. 'I often find that doing this makes the experience far more sensual and enhances the sensation, especially when the material is damp. Come here!' he said suddenly. Standing, he pulled her against him, and she could feel the effect she was having on him, as his hard erection pressed through his braies against her hip. Taking her hand, he led her to the divan. 'Lie down,' he ordered in a voice resonant with desire. He slowly peeled off his clothes until he stood naked in front of her. Years of sword fighting and riding had kept him in prime physical condition, and her eyes followed the dark hair on his broad chest down across his stomach to his muscled thighs and swollen manhood.

He climbed onto the divan and knelt between her legs as he caressed her body again. She put her head back and closed her eyes, loving every moment of pleasure but in her mind still seeing his naked muscular body in front of her. Suddenly he kissed his way down between her legs, and she gasped and arched her back in pleasure, crying out as he took her to new heights. She lay panting. Her eyes wide, she raised her head and looked at him, as he knelt up between her legs and, reaching over, picked up his glass and took a mouthful of wine. 'That's the first of many, Isabella. Let's get you out of that chemise, so I can stroke every part of that body and cup those beautiful breasts.'

She smiled at him, and her hand stroked his face, following his jawline. She wanted this to go on for a long time, and now she found that she was bold enough to whisper that she wanted him deep inside her.

Chatillon laughed. 'Not yet Isabella, but soon I promise....'

he said in a voice hoarse with desire.

Chapter Three

Chatillon made love to Isabella again the next morning before greeting his guests downstairs. He looked back from the doorway and smiled at the rosy naked body of his wife. She was curled up on top of the embroidered cover with her eyes closed and a contented smile on her face. She had taken to his lovemaking enthusiastically, and he hadn't enjoyed himself this much in bedsport for some time.

He descended the stairs, a smile on his face, to see a group of his friends breaking their fast in his hall.

'I would have a smile on my face with her in my bed,' laughed Morvan, who then grunted with pain, as his elfin wife Ette elbowed him hard in the ribs and glared at him. Everyone laughed, and Chatillon seeing Edvard standing near the door, waved him over to sit and join them. Edvard often joked that his unusual position in the household as a servant, mentor and friend meant that it was like being in purgatory; you were definitely not in hell, but you were allowed so many glimpses of heaven.

'I believe you have to leave today, Morvan?' said Chatillon

tearing some fresh bread and cutting a chunk of cheese.

The Horse Warrior nodded. 'We cannot stay longer, I am afraid, as we have to be back in Brittany for my son, Conn. I dare not leave him for too long. My brother Luke and his wife Merewyn look after him most of the time, but he understands that I am his real father. So now we spend more time together, especially in the stables. He is very interested in the bloodlines of the warhorses, so we look at them together and plan the breeding programme. However, there's no doubt that Conn has been damaged by his years of captivity with the warrior monks. He still has nightmares, and such sadness often lurks behind his eyes at times that it is heartrending. We know it will take time and lots of love.'

Chatillon, having been there when the boy was found, inclined his head in understanding, he was amazed the child had even survived.

'I heard about this, even in Ireland, the stolen child of the Horse Warriors. My ears pricked up because as you know I spent a year or so in Morlaix with them, and knew the family, but I never saw this child, he must have arrived later. Why did they take him?' asked Finian. Morvan hesitated, indecision on his face as they had hidden Conn for so many years. Chatillon seeing his dilemma answered for him.

'Briefly, Finian, Conn is the illegitimate child of Morvan and Constance, the daughter of King William. So as you can imagine, the child was seen as a useful pawn for Pope Victor, who you knew as Cardinal Dauferio. Even King Philip of France was asking questions about this child, trying to find out who his parents were. It goes without saying that Gervais, here, will not share Conn's parentage outside this room.' said Chatillon glancing at his older friend with a narrow eyed look that spoke volumes.

Gervais de la Ferte swiftly nodded in agreement, for like the others around the table, he realised that this child could still be a target for many years to come because of his bloodline. The illegitimate grandson of King William could be a definite asset to those with ruthless ambitions.

'The child was stolen when he was very young and carried off to live in a remote mountain hermitage by the warrior monks. To say he had a harsh life, lacking in love or affection, is an understatement. He was trained to be a warrior, as were another six unfortunate boys, taken from their families. Cardinal Dauferio saw these boys as the future sword of the church. Each boy was trained in a brutal regime to kill from the age of four, and each one carries a full tattoo of a cross on his back. Fortunately, I discovered where he was being held, and the Malvais brothers and their stepfather Gerard went to rescue him. Unfortunately, during the rescue the monks killed Gerard, who as you know was a much-loved father figure to the Malvais brothers. Now Conn is safe and he is where he should be, with his family.'

The room was silent for a while as Finian and Gervais took in what they had heard.

'So what are your plans, Chatillon and what of young Marietta, your ward?' asked Ette to lighten the mood of the wedding breakfast.

'We will spend a delightful week here enjoying our honeymoon; Isabella's mother has insisted that Marietta live with them as she adores the girl. After all, despite the tragedy of her mother's death, Genoa is the child's home. She has friends and a tutor here in the city. Isabella and I agreed she should have a base here rather than being pulled back and forth with us across Europe. Then we leave for Paris as I've business with King Philip. We've achieved our aim of ensuring that Robert Curthose became Duke of Normandy. We now need to secure our alliances with him.' he said, looking up as a servant entered. The man went straight to Edvard and whispered in his ear. Edvard pushed his chair back and drained his goblet.

'Problems?' enquired Chatillon with a raised eyebrow.

'Two pigeons have arrived. I'll go and decipher the messages.'

'Probably more congratulations!' announced Gervais smiling.

In no time, Edvard was back with a concerned frown. 'A message from Paris, Sire. King Philip wants the Seneschal to return immediately.' Gervais De la Ferte looked puzzled as he pushed his chair back and wondered what was so urgent.

'The second one is from Rouen. It is from the new Duke of Normandy, Robert Curthose. He is asking for your support and that of Pope Urban as he's about to invade England!' There was a shocked silence around the table, and they all looked at Piers for his response, but Chatillon gave a rueful smile as he shook his head. He was not at all surprised.

'Surely he'd not be that foolish, Piers, especially at this time of year with the gales and storms in the Channel?' said Morvan.

'You know Robert better than most, Morvan, as you served both him and his father, King William, for years with the Horse Warriors.' Morvan was silent for some time as he thought this through.

'Yes, he became my friend, but it always depends on who is advising him at the moment; those around him who have his ear have always influenced Robert. You, of all people, should know that Chatillon,' he said archly. Chatillon laughed at his audacity and turned to Gervais.

'Well, that's our trip to Paris postponed. Isabella will be disappointed. Although I may well send her to you in a month's time, as the house there needs refurbishing. I am sure you'll look after her for me, Gervais, and please introduce her to the French court.'

His daughter, Ette, snorted with disbelief at this information. 'You are intending to trust your young and beautiful wife to my father?' she asked in wide-eyed amazement that made the whole table laugh and her father shake his head in mock horror, for Gervais did have somewhat of a reputation for the ladies, to say the least.

Chatillon continued. 'First we will go to Rouen, which I believe is about to become Normandy's capital if my informers are correct. I do hope so—it is nearer and more accessible than Caen. Once there, I'll try to steady the ship of Robert Curthose and his ambitions. My informers also tell me that his uncle, Odo, the Bishop of Bayeux and Earl of Kent, is with him. Robert has released him from the prison his father incarcerated him in several years ago. Bishop Odo has likely influenced Robert to invade England as he never liked William Rufus and Odo will want to be back in a position of power in England.'

Finian frowned down the table. 'I'm afraid that being buried in the wilds of Ireland for so long, I don't understand. I thought that Robert was satisfied with the Duchy of Normandy. I believe this was what he always wanted and what he repeatedly fought his father for, to become Duke.'

'To a certain degree Finian, but Robert made the mistake of not going to his father's deathbed, whereas William Rufus and his younger brother Henry cleverly did. I'm told that seeing how close his father really was to death, William Rufus didn't stay for long; instead, he took a horse to the coast of Normandy and waited for a message from Rouen. As soon as he received the news that King William was dead, he took a ship to England to seize the treasury at Winchester and take the throne before his eldest brother could.'

'So Robert, as the eldest son, now believes that William Rufus has stolen the throne of England from him,' Finian observed.

'He is certainly not the only person who thinks that, Finian. A large group of influential nobles think the same thing. Many wealthy and powerful families own land on both sides of the English Channel, in England and Normandy. They are interested in seeing England and Normandy united again under one king, so they do not find themselves serving two masters. It wouldn't surprise me if they supported Robert's claim,' added Chatillon.

'Gervais, Edvard will see to your packs and servants, and we will send messengers ahead to book your inns on the road. I know how much you hate ships and water during the winter months.'

Gervais laughed; he'd nearly drowned in storms and shipwrecks in the North Sea and the Mediterranean. Both times, he had been rescued but believing his luck could not hold for the third time, he swore he'd never set foot on a ship again.

'Morvan, Ette, farewell and bon voyage, for I believe you sail at noon if the wind from the east holds. I'm going to see my uncle, who, is staying with Archbishop Conrades, but Odo plans to return to Rome tomorrow. So I need to go and alert him to the plans of Robert Curthose. Finian, I'll return here for dinner, and we'll talk then.' With those words, Piers bowed and left them.

An hour later, he was sitting with the Pope and Conrades in

the splendid Bishop's Residence; the Archbishop offered to leave as he could see immediately that Piers had news, but the Pope waved him back into his seat.

'So, Piers, what has you coming hotfoot over here when you should be with your lovely bride?' he asked.

'News from the west, your Eminence. Duke Robert Curthose is about to attempt to take the throne of England, and he has asked for your support.'

Pope Urban raised his eyebrows but then sat for some time with a thoughtful expression before he responded.

'As you know, Piers, Lanfranc, the Archbishop of Canterbury, was a close personal friend, correspondent and adviser of King William. I received a long missive from him before I left Rome to come here. Lanfranc had no idea that the King had been badly injured in battle and died. No one had thought to contact the top prelate in England to inform him of this momentous injury and death. He was shocked and devastated when he heard that William was dead. He was just as shocked to discover that suddenly William Rufus was the heir to the throne of England. He refused to believe that King William would ever split his empire in this way, so Lanfranc would not accept William Rufus as king. However, Rufus had already seized the Royal Treasury, so after several weeks of argument and deliberation, Lanfranc finally gave in, when Rufus promised he'd follow the Archbishop's advice and counsel. The Archbishop crowned William Rufus at the end of September. When Robert Curthose heard of this, he reacted with disbelief, and he released not only his uncle Odo from prison but also Duncan, the eldest son of King Malcolm of Scotland, which could cause further problems.'

They absorbed this information as the fire crackled until

Chatillon spoke. 'I expect it is your wish to support Robert Curthose in his endeavours against his brother, as we've spent years and a fortune in gold, ensuring that he became the Duke of Normandy and was under our influence. We were successful, so it wouldn't be in our interests to cut him loose now.' Again, there was silence as the Pope weighed the pros and cons of this invasion for the Holy See before he answered.

'Go to Rouen and assess the situation, Piers. We all know that Robert can be somewhat reckless. Find out who is flocking to his banner and which nobles are supporting him. If you're satisfied, I'll provide funds for additional ships.'

Bishop Conrades leaned forward to interject at this point. 'Where is the youngest son in all this? Henry, isn't it? Always had his nose in some book or tract when I saw him. I remember thinking he'd go into the church being so studious. Which brother will he support?'

Pope Urban nodded sagely. 'A good question. How old is Henry Beauclerc now, and which way will he jump, Piers?'

Chatillon gave a wry smile. 'He must be nearly twenty years old, and from what I've seen of him, he's a very clever young man who was left a considerable amount of money, but the only lands mentioned were his mother's lands in England which he hasn't received from William Rufus to date. I'm sure this will rankle with him, as he's a proud and ambitious young man. He will likely side with whichever brother offers him the most. Rumour had it that he personally counted every gold coin of the five thousand he was given on his father's death, to check it was all there.'

The Pope smiled at the thought of this avaricious young man. He always appreciated men who could be bought, and such men had smoothed many paths for him in the past. 'Make it your task to learn more about him, Piers. Now you must return to the beautiful Isabella and keep planting those seeds. I expect several nephews and nieces to carry on the Chatillon name. You are the last of the line, I depend on you.'

Chatillon laughed and made his farewells.

Chapter Four

Isabella had said farewell to their wedding guests and she now gathered the household servants together, to outline her expectations of them in the castello. Listening to her, Edvard smiled, for she'd take the weight of household management off his shoulders. At the last count, there were a dozen houses and manors across Europe along with the huge Chatillon estate outside Paris. She'd certainly be kept busy managing the Stewards and staff of the Chatillon properties, for although some were excellent, others needed a good kick to get them off their lazy backsides. Watching her, Edvard was sure she'd do that.

When Piers arrived home, Isabella was sitting on the wide stone balcony chatting happily with Finian and Edvard, and he joined them to watch the sun setting in the west. As the mist descended, it coloured the hills in the distance in soft mauve. It was a beautiful sight.

Isabella turned and smiled at him, and he pulled her out of her seat to his side. 'So, my love, instead of Paris, we leave for Rouen in two days; I presume you'll arrange with Edvard everything we need for our journey?'

She smiled, enjoying the responsibility of now being his Chatelaine but also pleased that she had Edvard to guide her, for there was so much she didn't know about Piers. Chatillon ran his fingers gently down to the base of her spine, and she shivered at the sensation. Her eyes met his, and he could see the excitement and anticipation in hers.

'We will now leave you for an hour or so, gentlemen, but I'm sure you'll understand.' Finian grinned, and Isabella blushed as Chatillon gripped her hand and pulled her firmly towards the stairs.

They all met again at dinner, and Isabella positively glowed from her husband's lovemaking. Finian was suddenly overtaken by a wave of sadness that was almost a physical pain. Watching him, Chatillon saw the Irish warrior's mouth tighten, and his eyes close for a few seconds.

He leaned towards Isabella, who had finished her meal. 'I need you to leave us, Isabella, as we've things to discuss, but I promise I'll come and find you in an hour or two.' She inclined her head, smiled and bade goodnight to them all.

Chatillon filled up their wine glasses and raised his in a toast.

'To old friends, lost friends and new pathways ahead.'

They all drank deeply, and Chatillon sat back regarding the Irish warrior. 'Well, Finian Ui Neill, you were a lost friend who has returned. I think it is time for you to tell us what you've been doing for fourteen years. We know that you were riding with Luc De Malvais and the Breton Horse Warriors for several years, but I presume you were foolish enough to return to Ireland, where there was still a huge price on your head for murdering the King of Leinster.'

Finian took a mouthful of wine before replying. 'You and I

are both classed as master swordsmen, Chatillon and I hate to admit it, but you're probably better than me, but only slightly.' Edvard and Chatillon smiled at this. 'However, I tell you, I would never take on or challenge Luc De Malvais. I've never come across a warrior like him. Riding into battle, often against overwhelming odds, he shows no fear and is terrifying to watch. I've seen men retreat and run at the mention of his name, or at the sight of him on that huge evil black warhorse of his. I learnt a lot from them in those years.'

Chatillon said nothing at first, simply inclining his head in agreement. He sensed that Finian was playing for time. He anticipated that the news Finian was about to impart would be difficult for him to relay.

'There are three people I would choose to fight by my side in a difficult situation, and Luc De Malvais is certainly one of them. He still terrifies me! You are the other two I would choose, my friends,' said Chatillon, raising his glass to them.

The Irish warrior took another gulp of wine while Edvard glanced at Chatillon in concern and met his eyes.

'Just tell us what happened, Finian,' said Chatillon softly, reaching across the table and gripping the warrior's forearm, in comradeship.

'Yes, you are right, I went back to Ireland, for although my uncle, King Conchobar, was murdered, his son Mael mac Conchobar succeeded him, and he protected my father and mother.'

He paused, and Chatillon asked, 'Well, that was your main worry laid to rest, your mother's safety, so why did you not leave again immediately?'

'My cousin Mael, who I was foolish enough to trust, imprisoned me to end the blood feud with the O'Briens. They were continually ravaging the lands of Meath. He kept me locked away for several months while negotiating with Turlough O'Brien, as he intended to hand me over to him. They fed me well but kept me in chains while my parents pleaded for my life to no avail. So we all travelled to the outskirts of Dublin because Mael had enthusiastically agreed to a trial by combat. For over an hour, I fought against the champion of the O'Briens until both of us were almost on our knees, he was good and I thought for a while that he would kill me. Then I remembered the trick you taught me, Piers, and I made the sword fly from his hand. I will never forget the open-mouthed astonishment on his face as I leapt forward and thrust my dagger into his throat.'

'So that was the end of the blood feud with the O'Briens?' asked Edvard, and Finian nodded.

'Yes, we returned to our kingdom of Meath, but this time I rode at the front with the King as I was now his acclaimed champion. How things can change,' he said bitterly.

Chatillon leaned forward again, putting his elbows on the table and steepling his fingers. 'So why is there so much sadness on your face, Finian Ui Neill, if this problem was resolved?'

'For several years, life was very good, and I fell in love. We rode to visit the northern Ui Neills in Tullyhogue. We needed to strengthen our alliances, as Mael didn't trust the O'Briens to keep the truce. There, I met Niamh from the Owen clan—the most beautiful creature I've ever laid eyes on but as wild as the very hills where they lived. She'd been half-promised to one of the MacDiarmat brood, but her father thought that a wealthy cousin of the King of Meath was a better option, so we were married. I took her back to Meath, and we were blissfully happy. We were given an old crumbling fortified manor outside the capital at Trim, and I began to improve and extend it into a real home for us. Within a year, we had bought our first horses to breed from, to create the big warhorses I rode in Brittany. We had two beautiful children there, a boy of seven and a girl of five with her mother's tumbling auburn curls. However, the peace didn't last. There had been several attacks to the south of Meath, so we put together a raiding party to catch them and chase them over the border.

'It was a trap! The MacDiarmat clan were waiting for us, and King Mael was badly injured. We managed to escape and got the King back to the fortress at Trim, but he was losing too much blood. More of the MacDiarmat clan were waiting for us as we galloped towards the fortress. The O'Briens had ended the blood feud, but the MacDiarmats had never forgotten that I had killed their king and stolen a woman intended for them, so they were taking their revenge.'

He stopped as Piers refilled his wine goblet. Both men were hanging on his words, fearing there was worse to come.

'Go on. Did you defeat them?' urged Chatillon.

'Eventually, yes. They attacked us as we rode for the gates, but we were fighting for our home and our women. We killed all but the three that escaped on horses they had hidden in the woods. We carried the King inside, where my mother and his wife tried to save his life but to no avail. We stayed beside him for several hours as he fought for his life, gasping for breath as he'd been lung stabbed, and the red bubbles of blood were coming from his mouth. We all knew it was over for him at that point. It was early dawn when I left Trim and rode north to my home.'

Again, he stopped, and he dropped his head into his hands.

Chatillon moved his chair and put a hand on his shoulder.

'The MacDiarmats who escaped hadn't ridden south to their homes in Leinster. They rode north, killed my guards and crept over the gates of my home in the night when the other men were asleep. They moved into the house, cut my children's throats and they all raped Niamh before stabbing her. She was still alive when I reached her, but she lay in a spreading pool of her blood. She clutched at my hand and whispered my name, and I sat there on the floor and held her in my arms as she died, my children's bodies lying beside us. I feel such guilt, Piers. I should never have left them there. I should have taken them to safety in the fortress at Trim, but I thought they would be safe at home with half a dozen of my men.'

The silence in the room was deafening for several moments as Chatillon and Edvard took in what they had just heard. The shock was clear on their faces.

'No man ever deserves to find his family like that, and you thought you had left them well guarded.' whispered Chatillon, and he pulled his friend's head onto his shoulder as the tears ran down Finian's face.

'Tell me you found them, the murdering bastards,' said Edvard, his voice almost breaking with emotion.

Finian couldn't speak; he was so distraught at the memory and the pictures in his head of what he'd found. He had shut it all out. He had raged but never broken and cried as he'd not spoken of it all, until now, and the floodgates had opened.

He raised his head. 'I found them camped about ten miles away, they were heading back south. I killed one outright but injured the others. I'm not proud of what I did, but I made them suffer. I tied up and emasculated the other two and left them to bleed out on the ground. Edvard nodded satisfactorily at this and took Finian's left hand in a tight clasp.

'You are here with us now, Finian Ui Neill. You are like a brother to us after what we've been through together. You have a home with us, wherever we are, for as long as you wish—forever, I hope,' said Chatillon.

Finian raised grateful eyes to both of them, and taking back his hands, he wiped his eyes on the sleeves of his tunic. He felt that some of the weight of guilt had been lifted just by telling his friends what had happened, but it would never be forgotten.

'You need to go up to that beautiful wife of yours, Chatillon. I'll be happy to sit with Edvard and discuss other things. He can tell me of your exploits with the Malvais brothers and the warrior monks, for as I learnt to my cost, danger always seems to dog your steps.'

Chatillon stood looking down at the Irish warrior. It was a tale that had shocked him to the core, but he was pleased that Finian had chosen to come to them. He bade them goodnight and slowly ascended the stairs.

Isabella sat waiting expectantly by the fire, anticipation clear on her face. However, Chatillon didn't go to her; he walked across the room without a word and placing both hands on the stone mantle he gazed at the flames.

'Is something amiss?' she asked.

'I'm the first person to admit, Isabella, that I've little or no empathy for my fellow man. I find it a wasted emotion. Very little ever touches me, and I can kill men or women without a second thought or regret. However, listening to Finian Ui Neill tell the story of the slaughter of his wife and children in Ireland has touched a deep chord within me. The worst thing is that I can do little to help him, or take away his sorrow, apart from being here as a friend to listen and console.'

She could see the paleness of his face, and she stood and placed her hand over his. 'Sometimes friendship is all a man or woman needs to deal with a tragedy like this. Just knowing that someone is there who cares,' she said.

Isabella gazed at him, realising that this was a Chatillon rarely seen by anyone. He looked down into her face and recognised that she was being genuine, and he was grateful.

'Come Isabella, let us go to bed and make love slowly and gently. I think tonight's revelations call for love and affection.'

Chapter Five

Robert Curthose stood with his uncle Odo, Bishop of Bayeux, who had formerly been one of England's richest and most powerful men. They were in the Great Hall of King William's impressive but bleak fortress in Caen. King William had been displeased at his brother Odo's attempts to make himself Pope. So when Odo went so far as to plan a military expedition to Rome without his brother's knowledge or permission, it was the last straw, and King William had Odo arrested. Odo was grateful to his nephew Robert for releasing him from prison in Rouen after five years of comfortable but confining incarceration.

As the eldest son and heir, Robert had always had a good relationship with his uncles. Odo, an astute and powerful man with much support amongst the Norman nobility, believed that Robert Curthose should be King of England.

His other uncle, Robert, Count of Mortain, was also unhappy with the division of Normandy and England and was about to join them in Caen, to support him.

Robert paced up and down until Odo remonstrated with him.

'God's blood, nephew, have a seat. He will be here soon. His ship has only just docked. This agitation isn't helping any of us!'

Robert stopped and turned to face him. 'I need to know if my uncle Mortain has persuaded the waverers, the fence-sitters, to join us. At the moment, I've got the support of most of the nobility of Normandy and England, but I need their names and loyalty confirmed.' Odo guided him to a chair and pushed him firmly down into it.

'Be assured, Sire, the country will rise for you as you're the rightful heir and the eldest son. William Rufus is nothing but a usurper.'

Robert rested his chin on his fist and regarded his uncle, who was usually cautious. He felt reassured by Odo's calm demeanour. He gazed around the bleak hall at Caen fortress; the early morning sunshine shone from the high windows on the bare walls. This had been his home with his father, his mother Queen Matilda, and his younger brothers, for many years. His father's tastes had always been simple and martial, and this fortress was the home not of a family but of a warrior king who had no time for fripperies.

'As we discussed, uncle, I've decided to move the capital of Normandy back to Rouen almost immediately. I have no desire or wish to live here in this grim, cheerless fortress.'

Odo glanced around; it was a large and impressive hall, but Robert was right. William had preferred an austere Spartan style which Queen Matilda had softened with tapestries and fabrics in their rooms above. But when he compared it with other sumptuous European courts he'd visited, it was bleak indeed.

'As you wish, Robert, I have made the Steward aware, and

he will arrange for our belongings and some furnishings to be transferred. I'm sure that the Burghers and merchants of Rouen will be delighted, for they lost the prestige of having the Duke in residence. After all, it was the capital of Normandy for hundreds of years before your father moved the capital to Caen, and they presented petition after petition to your father to move it back, to no avail.'

At that moment, the Steward loudly announced the arrival of Robert, the Count of Mortain. Odo's slightly younger brother strode into the hall. He'd always been one of King William's greatest supporters and a major landholder in England. Robert, watching him approach, remembered that his father had always described him as not the wisest man in the world but loyal and solid, and that was what Robert needed now—loyalty.

Mortain clasped arms with his older brother and then with Robert, before his booming voice echoed around the walls. 'Well, Odo, the time you spent in the English court before Yuletide paid off, for support to remove the usurper, William Rufus, from the throne has certainly grown. Nearly a dozen powerful families have sworn allegiance to Robert, and several bishops, including Archbishop Lanfranc.'

Odo clasped his hands in delight. 'I knew they would support the rightful heir, but let's not fool one another; most of them have a purpose in this, owning land on both sides of the channel. They don't want to serve two overlords. They will also be expecting rewards for their service and support.'

'That doesn't overly worry or concern me, for once we've pulled William Rufus from the throne, I will have access to the Royal Treasury and take the lands of any families who support my brother. Don't unpack your bags, uncle; we will ride to my fortress at Rouen. I refuse to spend another night in this place.' He strode out, running lightly down the steps and calling for his horse. The nobles in the court, and his two uncles, scrambled to follow him.

As they reached the horses, Robert of Mortain raised a questioning eyebrow at his older brother. 'Too many memories here in Caen and, I think, some sadness for his mother's death.' whispered Odo.

'I wondered if it had more to do with guilt. His father may be dead, but William's presence is still felt here. I keep expecting him to come striding in, and of course, Robert must feel some regret at not being at his father's deathbed,' suggested the count.

Odo shrugged. 'I, too, am finding it difficult to believe that King William went so quickly, and as usual, he leaves nothing but chaos and flux behind him!' Robert laughed as a chill February breeze swirled the dead leaves around the courtyard.

Mounting up, they galloped after Robert to take up residence in the larger and older castle of Rouen. It would be a long journey, and Odo pushed Robert Curthose for an overnight stay at the inn in Tottenville. His older bones did not appreciate ten hours in the saddle any longer.

Moreover, Odo wanted time for their servants to catch up with them. He enjoyed his own comforts and possessions around him after long years as a prisoner. Tomorrow, they would arrive in Rouen. He found that he held no grudge against the Castellan who was in charge of the castle where William had imprisoned him. The man was only following orders, and the food had been good.

Chapter Six

It was twilight when the broad cog anchored at the edge of the wide bay that led in to the distant port of Marseilles. To Isabella's disbelief, Finian swore to them he could see the twinkling lights of the town in the distance—she could see nothing but blackness. He gave a crow of triumph when a sailor who had climbed to furl the sails confirmed it. The crew were wrapping the sails and anchoring to wait for the morning tide that would take them in.

'You always had excellent eyesight, Finian. You could see riders that were often a mere spot in the distance to the rest of us. I remember Bianca's man, Joseppi, who didn't like you anyway, used to get angry when you could spot outriders in the distance that he couldn't see.'

'Ah yes, the taciturn and unpleasant Joseppi. Where is he now, Chatillon? Is he still commanding Bianca's men?'

'Unfortunately not Finian; the warrior monks killed him in a skirmish in Genoa, they beheaded him. I had sent him to guard a friend, and he died alongside her servants, defending her. I disbanded Bianca's mercenaries, keeping the best and youngest to add to my own. You are now commanding the remainder of them. You may recognise one or two from our days in Prague.'

As the dusk deepened, Finian couldn't help a glance behind, and he scanned the horizon for sails to the south. They were considerably later than expected as they had been followed and chased across the sea by Saracen pirates. 'I presume there's no sign of them?' asked Chatillon watching him.

'It's difficult at this time of night as the dusk and mists merge on the horizon, but I can see nothing alarming out there, and there are no mast lights,' he answered.

Isabella had heard the Captain say it was unusual for these Saracen pirates to attack in the winter months, so another thought occurred to her. 'Did these men target us for a reason, Piers? Did they know about the chest of money you're carrying from the Pope for Robert Curthose?' she asked her husband.

' No, I think it was purely by chance. This is a larger-than-usual merchant cog, which is unusual in the winter with the rougher weather, and they could see by her water line how heavily laden she was. They think she's packed full of rich pickings such as the last trading goods of the season.'

Isabella was only partly reassured, as they had been very lucky to escape from the pirates, mainly because a sudden storm whipped up by the Mistral wind, racing off the land, had given them respite from the pursuit. Their experienced Captain had raced for the coast, using the wild wind behind them to drive them in and find a sheltered bay. The tension and fear had been palpable amongst the crew, as they had rounded the rocky promontory of Antibes and crept into a cove, anchoring beneath the cliffs. It was a wild and rocky berth for many hours as the ship was pitched and tossed by the vicious gusts, and many of Chatillon's men were sick. He was pleased to see that Isabelle fared well. She seemed to be a natural sailor. He watched her as she clung to the gunwale in the worst of it, exhilaration clear on her face; she was excited and seemed fearless.

By the next morning in the sheltered cove, the wind had dropped slightly, and the skies had cleared, but it was cold. Isabella had stayed on the bow platform under the covered heavy canvas awning, wrapped in the fur rugs that Edvard had provided.

Meanwhile, the men nervously scanned the horizon as they emerged slowly from the cove. Seeing that the coast was clear, they had set sail for Marseilles. There was no sign of the large Saracen galley that had chased them.

The Santa Maria was a much larger than average merchant cog with a high stern platform. Fifteen of Chatillon's men were with them, with their horses and equipment, all under the charge of Finian, who seemed much happier now that he had some purpose in life.

Chatillon came out to join Finian at the rail. 'We need to reach Rouen with all haste. As soon as we land, we must head for Lyon. Pushing hard, we should reach it by nightfall.'

'It must be nearly forty leagues! Will Isabella keep up with that pace?' he asked.

Chatillon smiled. 'She's much tougher than she looks and is an exceptional horsewoman. She used to gallop off on her own, easily losing her escort, to escape the confines of the Embriaco household and the watchful eyes of her parents and brothers,' laughed Chatillon.

Isabella raised her eyes at the laughter. Seeing the shape of the two men against the darkening sky, she smiled. There was still a chill in the wind, and she pulled the rug further around her shoulders. The heavy canvas flapped over her head. She could have moved further back for more shelter amongst the bags and packs stored behind her, but she quite enjoyed the feel of the wind on her face. The crew and men were settling down for the night around the deck, unrolling their thin pallet beds. The anchors had been dropped, and the boat rocked roughly at times on the high swell. She could still hear some of their men retching, while others diced on the deck by the light of a covered lantern.

She began to feel drowsy and considered stretching out on the deep pile of fur covers and rugs behind her. She knew that Piers and his friend Finian would talk for a while yet. She liked the Irish warrior and was pleased that Piers had him and Edvard at his side. She glanced over at the big man, already laid on his pallet, hands behind his head, eyes closed. He was something of an enigma, this ex-monk who had dedicated his life to being at Chatillon's side, without a backward glance. He seemed to make their lives run smoothly and effortlessly, and she was learning so much from him.

Suddenly, there was a small flash of light on the southern horizon, then another. She stared at the spot for some time but saw nothing more. She glanced over at Finian and Piers, but they were leaning on the gunwale facing the land. Well away in the distance lay Marseilles, a good few hours sail into the harbour. She turned and stared back out to sea. What had it been? A flash of lightning from the storm that was moving away? Another ship making for Marseilles? Whatever it was, she couldn't see it now. She snuggled down, pulling the covers up to her chin. An hour later, Chatillon climbed in beside her, pulling her warm body into his arms.

'You're very cold,' she murmured.

'I can think of a way we can warm each other up,' he said, untying his braies and moving his hands up under her heavy wool gown. She gurgled with laughter as they tried to make love quietly. She squirmed with pleasure as his hands caressed her, and couldn't help a small gasp escaping as he entered her. Afterwards, she smiled in amused contentment, for they had been like conspirators taking pleasure in each other. She slid her hands under his tunic and stroked his broad chest. She knew she was falling in love with her handsome husband. Tucking her head under his chin, she began to drift off.

Chatillon lay content, listening to her breathing and enjoying the closeness and affection she was showing him, he had never expected or indeed needed this before. Suddenly, her breathing changed as she moved and murmured, 'There was a light!'

Chatillon raised his head slightly to look down at her. He couldn't see her face in the dark; was she awake or was she dreaming, he wondered.

'I saw a light, and it flashed twice out at sea,' she repeated. He untangled her arms and legs from his body and gently lifted her head.

'Where? When, Isabella? Wake up. What did you see?'

She told him, and he quickly pulled back on his braies, tied on his chausses and pulled up his soft leather boots. 'Stay here, I'll be back shortly' he said.

As he emerged bare chested from the deep canvas awning onto the deck, all was quiet. The shapes of the sleeping crew and his men littered the deck. He could hear the horses moving around under their canopy towards the stern, but all was still elsewhere. He moved to the far gunwale and scanned the horizon. It was dark, and as he gazed south across the sea that was still moving with a deep swell, he could see nothing. He let out the breath he'd been holding when he felt a hand on his arm and whirled around, automatically going for his dagger.

'You are far too twitchy, my friend,' said a deep Irish voice beside him. Chatillon laughed softly and with relief.

'Years of practice and experience, Finian, you know that.'

The Irish warrior could only just make out the outline of his friend's face in the faint light of the lantern hanging from the mast. 'What is it? Something must have brought you out away from the warm body of your wife?'

'Isabella has just told me that she saw a light out at sea; it flickered twice.'

Finian scanned the distant darkness. 'It may have been a far-off storm. Sometimes you get those double flashes; they are common in the wild weather of the Irish Sea. I thank God every time I reach the shore over there.'

Chatillon gave a snort of laughter, but neither man moved. They both stood and stared outwards as Edvard, always a light sleeper, joined them. They explained what had happened, and he grunted in understanding. He could feel the tension emanating from his friend, and he scanned the dark seas but could see nothing out there.

'Let us hope they all drowned in the storm as they deserve,' said Finian bitterly, having experienced their cruelty.

'You were captured as a young man, were you not?' asked Edvard.

Finian nodded. 'In the Bay of Biscay, when I was about eighteen years old, my cousin Padraig and I were helping out on a large fishing boat. As usual, the Saracens came out of nowhere, raiding the coasts of Portugal. I was lucky and I escaped after only a few months on the oars, but they certainly left me with scars.'

'It's very rare for men to escape from the galleys; how did you manage that?' asked Chatillon.

'It was during a raid. We were pulling at full speed, but the other ship turned and came at us bow first. We smashed into her and badly damaged the bow of our ship, which was holed below the water line. Within minutes, she was listing badly, and they were moving barrels and goods to the stern to try to lift the bow. Everyone could see that she'd still sink in no time, so we knew we had to get off her, but our feet were shackled and chained. We would go down with her unless we were freed, but the pirates, caring only for themselves ignored our cries. I waited my chance, and as one of the overseers, a big man, went past us carrying a box, I managed to strangle him with my chain looped around his neck. I grasped the keys from his belt and freed myself and others around me. However, the Saracens could see what was happening and drew their swords to stop us. There was no time to lose, and those of us who could swim leapt over the side and were rescued by the trading boat. The other wretches, including my cousin Padraig, were too high up in the bows, no one could reach them in time. The ship went down bow first, so they must have died in her, still chained to the oars.'

Edvard shook his head in astonishment, for although this Irishman got into dangerous situations he seemed to have many lives.

'You were lucky, Finian—not so for the other few dozen still in chains—but I do believe that people can make their own luck,' added Edvard.

'The horses seem to have finally settled; they are always

terrified in storms,' said Chatillon softly.

Finian nodded but then froze because a faint sound was coming across the water, a soft, repetitive sound that he recognised. He suddenly gripped Chatillon's arm tightly.

'Wake the men quietly, and I'll go to the Captain. A galley is coming at us in the dark, and she is coming at speed. She will try to ram us amidships, and we must raise one anchor to swing the cog lengthways. Edvard, try to clear us some space to fight on the middle deck.'

They leapt to the tasks; Chatillon shook his men awake and told them to arm themselves for an imminent attack. Finian pulled the burly Captain out of his bed, explaining what was afoot.

The sound of the oars splashing into the water could clearly be heard now, as the long sleek Saracen galley moved swiftly towards them.

'Douse the lanterns!' shouted Finian as he helped the crew pull in the bow anchor rope, and the Captain, at the helm, swung the steorbord around. Slowly the big heavy cog began to move. To Finian, it seemed agonisingly slow, they would never do it in time.

Chatillon had returned to the awning. Strapping on his sword and sliding his dagger into his belt, he woke Isabella telling her to hide under the high pile of fur rugs and not to come out no matter what she heard. He promised he would return for her.

He stood with a half dozen of his men in front of the awning on the high bow deck. Their feet were braced for the impact of the galley, for hit them, it certainly would, in one way or another.

Finian was on the stern deck with the Captain and his crew of five. They were rough men from Marseilles, and he knew that they could certainly handle themselves. Most of them carried clubs and staffs with a dagger tucked in their belt. Finian had learned from Edvard, the hard way, the damage a well-wielded staff could do. He looked down into the belly of the ship; most of the space was taken up by the horses under an awning, but he could see the darker shape of Edvard, who had about ten men moving boxes and barrels, roping them to the sides, so there was more space to fight.

All they could do then was wait. Finian heard the splashing sound stop, and he knew they had shipped oars to attack.

'Here they come!' he shouted, planting his feet firmly and drawing his sword.

Chapter Seven

A crunch and the sound of splintering came sooner than expected as the silent, deadly galley, three times the size of the cog, hit the rear of the leeboard side. Fortunately, now having only one anchor, the ship swung away as the galley scraped down its side doing minimal damage. The gunwale of the cog remained intact, and only the upper hull was splintered. Within seconds grappling irons were thrown from above, which pulled the ships closer together, and Saracen pirates were swinging and leaping aboard, swords drawn.

Finian grinned with satisfaction as he saw the surprise on their faces when they saw what faced them. They thought they were dealing with a large loaded trading cog manned by a minimal crew. They expected a rich cargo and, if they were lucky, a few passengers to ransom. The crew they would enslave, the boat they would sink. Instead, they found a large contingent of armed fighting men waiting for them. Many were cut down as their feet touched the decks, which soon became slippery with their blood.

The one thing the Saracen pirates did have was numbers—it

was a fully manned ship. Each galley could have upward of over eighty men, although a third would be galley slaves, driven and whipped to fight. After the initial attack, Chatillon, Finian and Edvard found themselves outnumbered and fighting for their lives. Finian saw at least two of the crew go down. The Captain was behind him on the stern deck, roaring and belaying about him with a huge heavy club that took away any nearby men attacking him.

Isabella, hidden deep under the fur covers, clutched the dagger Piers had given her and listened to the clashing blades. The cries, shouts and screams assailed her ears. She was frightened—who wouldn't be—but she was also afraid for Chatillon and their friends. The fighting seemed to go on for an eternity until she could take no more. She had to take a look and see what was happening. She gently unfurled the fur covers from her head and looked out of the opening of the awning.

The noise was now even more fearful, but she noticed that the loud cries of attack had dropped to grunts and growls as men pushed and fought against each other, sweat dripping from their brows. She crawled slowly to the awning's edge and looked out onto a hellish scene. There was some light coming from the galley's large swinging lanterns, which had been lit when they attacked. This cast a garish, lurid light over the blood-soaked decks. Bodies lay scattered, some crawling with nightmarish wounds, many dead. One Saracen sat with his back to the gunwale, trying unsuccessfully to hold in his entrails. Isabella swallowed and turned away.

She could see that Finian on the stern deck and Chatillon not far in front of her were holding their own and cutting down any adversary. Edvard, mid-deck, was whirling his staff above his head, and there were repeated sounds of him cracking skulls with blows that lifted his victims off their feet. But still more Saracens came as they swarmed over the gunwale, weapons in hand, to drop to the deck. She watched a bare chested Chatillon jump nimbly down onto the main deck to meet this new wave of attackers. She leant further forward and glanced up at the galley beside them. It was twice as high as the cog, and their leader stood on the fore deck shouting orders. She watched the cruel-featured Saracen. He had a very dominant presence, and she could see a deep scar running down his face as he turned towards the lantern. There was a tall, younger man beside him who must be his son, for the resemblance was uncanny—the same cruel, thin mouth, pointed chin, and a short black, trimmed beard. He was wielding a lash and shouting at the men below, who cringed away in fear. A large black man was following his orders, and she realised, as the man pulled chains out of the wooden blocks, that they were releasing the galley slaves to fight. She threw the fur covers aside and stood, clinging to the centre awning pole as the cog rocked back and forth. She watched as the men were pushed to the gunwale of the galley and handed short wooden clubs to fight, the lash falling on their backs with vicious strokes as they were forced over the side to attack the cog.

Isabella saw the fear, the hopelessness, and the anger on some of their faces. She looked across and saw Finian on the stern deck leaning on his sword for a second to catch his breath. She shouted over at him, trying to be heard above the noise, and she pointed at what was happening. Isabella could see his dismay at this new wave of attackers.

'Turn them Finian!' she shouted.

The Irish warrior stared at her while raising his sword, ready to attack, not immediately understanding what she meant.

'The slaves! They don't want to fight; for God's sake, turn them!' she yelled at the top of her voice.

Finian grinned and jumped down to join Edvard on the main deck. As the men were driven over the side, he jumped on a box, put up his hands and shouted, 'Join us, and we will free you. Help us kill your captors.'

She could see their uncertainty, and some of them glanced fearfully behind, the phrase *caught between the devil and the deep blue sea* running through her mind as she watched them with her heart in her mouth. Fortunately, a big, badly scarred man at the front understood, and he turned and began joyfully laying into the Saracens whilst shouting at the others to do the same. Not all followed or listened to him. Many galley slaves still died on the swords of Finian and his men, but well over half turned on their captors.

Isabella breathed a sigh of relief as she saw that the galley slaves were now making a difference. She was so absorbed in what was happening in front of her that she didn't see her two guards die on the fore deck behind the awning as their throats were cut. She saw Chatillon glance up at her, grin, but then firmly indicate she should get back inside.

The young Saracen with the lash had heard her shouting. He couldn't believe his eyes as he gazed at the blonde beauty in a thin linen chemise that clung to her body in the wind and left nothing to the imagination. He pointed her out to his father, who grinned when he saw her.

'Go and get her, Malik. She will fetch a mountain of silver in the markets with that hair, probably more than several cargoes.'

His son stood for a second, his eyes narrowed. 'Yes, but not immediately, for we will both enjoy her first.'

His father laughed as his son grabbed a rope and swung expertly over onto the fore deck behind the canvas awning. Bending his knees, he landed lightly, and his soft leather boots made no noise as he made his way forward with a dagger in one hand and a cord in the other. Fortunately for him, it was dark there, shadowed from the large galley lanterns by the high awning. Young Malik, in no time at all, quietly dispatched the two guards at the side who were busy watching the melee below. He crept down the side of the awning, moving behind Isabella while she was looking away towards the galley. The cacophony of noise from below hid the sounds of his approach as he stepped over the packs, treading softly across the fur covers she'd discarded.

Isabella had moved only slightly back inside, obeying Chatillon, but she was reluctant to drag her eyes away as she watched him see off another attack, his chest shining with sweat. She could see now why they talked about his swordsmanship in awed tones. None seemed to be able to stand against him. She saw he had a grin on his face as he fought, and she smiled, dropping her hands to her sides as it appeared the tide was turning in their favour.

At that moment, two things happened swiftly: a noose of thin cord was dropped over her head and pulled tight on her throat while a hand was clamped over her mouth, and she was pulled back onto the pile of fur covers. Her hands came up to claw at the tight restriction to her throat to no avail as she was turned and thrown face down. Her hands were pulled roughly back behind her as he knelt on her lower back to hold her down and he looped the rest of the thin cord around her wrists. Her attacker pulled the cord tight, so her wrists were pulled cruelly up her back and pain streaked down her arms. She began to squeal as she realised she couldn't move her wrists downward to release the strain, or it would choke her. He pushed her face hard into the covers, until she thought she would suffocate.

'Be quiet, or I will slit your throat here and now,' he hissed as he turned her back over.

Pain shot through her arms again, now pinioned up her back, and the cord tightened as she gasped for breath. The man straddled her body, a knee on either side. His fingers loosened the cord on her throat slightly, and as he turned sideways, she recognised his profile. He stared down at her with a grin as his hands began to explore her body, squeezing and hurting her breasts.

'Shall I take you while your man is fighting for his life down there? I think that thought would excite me even more,' he said, lifting her chemise and moving his hands up her thighs.

Isabella began to scream, but he hit her hard and covered her mouth again. He tore a strip from the bottom of the thin linen chemise and gagged her. 'I will enjoy making you pay for that later,' he said, pulling her onto her knees and dragging her across the fur rugs to the back of the awning. Drawing his dagger, he cut a hole in the canvas and dragged her roughly through and threw her roughly onto the planks of the fore deck. She lay there, her knees grazed and paled as she saw two of their men, their bodies twisted on the deck with their throats cut. He pulled her, gasping and coughing through the gag, over to the gunwale where he'd tied the grappling rope. Malik forced her to kneel on a wooden box against the side.

Untying the rope, he hauled hard to pull the bows of the two ships closer while keeping Isabella pinned firmly between his thighs. Suddenly, a horn blew, and the remaining Saracens fighting on the cog made for the sides; two of them even dragged a prisoner with them, a wounded crew member. His father, seeing that his son, Malik, now had the woman captive, was cutting his losses. He sent men to the gunwale to pull her up and catch her, knowing his son would swing her across.

Chatillon had heard Isabella's scream, but when he glanced up at the awning, he could see nothing, and was occupied in fighting a huge black-bearded brute of a man who was armed with a vicious curved sword. As he forced the man back, the Saracen slipped on the deck, and Chatillon delivered a fatal blow, piercing his chest. He stood back for a second to breathe, his chest heaving and now splashed with the man's blood. He heard the horn blow, knew what that meant and smiled. He stepped forward and glanced along the gunwale shouting at his men to cut the ropes and free them from the galley when his eye caught movement on the fore deck, and his heart stopped.

The Saracen had pulled Isabella to her feet on the box, ready to pick her up and throw her across to his waiting men. Chatillon, sword in hand, raced up the narrow wooden steps to the top of the bow deck, cursing as his feet slipped on the blood and he fell back to his knees. The man now had Isabella firmly grasped to his left side, his hand gripping the cord around her throat. His right arm had a rope from the galley tied firmly around his right forearm. He stepped up on to the box with her and stretched his arm out, ready to swing across, helped by the waiting men above. His father shouted encouragement and then a desperate warning as he saw a man hurtling towards his son.

All Chatillon could think of as he raced forward was that he'd be too late. They were moving to leap, and Isabella was in the way as he leapt high in the air, reaching across to sever the man's right arm at the elbow. The young Saracen screamed and let Isabella thump to the deck. He turned to face his attacker as Chatillon stepped forward and thrust his sword through his throat.

A scream of absolute rage came from the galley behind him as the Saracen leader watched his son Malik crumple and die at the hands of this man. As the galley moved slowly away, the roar of anguish from the Saracen leader continued. Chatillon ran to his wife, and drawing his dagger, he cut the cord at her throat and wrists.

Finian appeared beside him and, picking up the dead man's body by the arms, threw it over the side as the Saracen Leader gripped the gunwale and watched. Chatillon, holding Isabella tightly in his arms, glared at him as his galley moved away. There was no doubt that this attack had cost the pirate dear in more ways than one. Even in the dark, Piers could clearly see the figure on the fore deck dressed in white who shouted across the water, 'I swear I'll find you and kill you, whoever you are. I will have vengeance for my son Malik.'

The galley oars finally began to bite into the water, and the pirates moved swiftly away.

'Another one to add to the long list of your enemies,' said Finian as a concerned Edvard joined them.

'We could see what was happening, but we were too far away to get there in time,' said Edvard regretfully..

Chatillon kissed away the tears streaming down Isabella's face as the shock of what had happened registered. 'You are safe now. I swear I will never let that happen again. Finian or Edvard will always be with you when I am not,' he whispered.

A few hours later, they set sail again for Marseilles. The bodies of their enemies had been thrown over the side. Some of the wounded Saracens were still alive, but no quarter was given to them. Some able-bodied prisoners were in chains. Their own men were being tended by Edvard and a recovered Isabella, who bravely insisted on helping. Finian and Chatillon stood and watched them as the bodies of their own dead were laid out and stitched into shrouds of old sailcloth.

'Isabella is a very brave woman and she is certainly a perfect wife for you. I've said this before, but life will never be boring at your side, Chatillon. Danger and death are two companions that seem to dog your steps from what Edvard has told me,' commented Finian.

Chatillon gave a wry smile. 'I promise you I don't look for it, Finian, it just seems to find me,' he said as the unhappy Captain approached them.

'I lost two crew members, and another was taken, prisoner. They saw him being dragged screaming onto the galley.' The man complained bitterly about the loss for several moments as it was a good crew. They commiserated with him, promised him recompense for his loss, and he went on his way slightly mollified.

The Irish warrior shook his head. 'Well, the Saracens will know who you are now they have a prisoner. Please do not take their threats lightly, Piers. They are a race who make Irish blood feuds look tame in comparison.'

Chatillon turned his dark eyes on his friend and wearily inclined his head. Then he looked Finian up and down in the dawn light as he leant on his sword; they were both blood-spattered and grey-faced with exhaustion, but thankfully neither was wounded. He stood pensively for a moment.

'Do we know who he is?' asked Chatillon.

Finian shook his head. 'No, but we've two pirates who

will tell us.' He grinned, and Chatillon smiled. Finian's bloodthirsty enthusiasm at times amused him, although he was nowhere near as ruthless as Edvard when it came to extracting information from prisoners or enemies.

'We may have to stay in Marseilles longer than anticipated. We will all need a good night's rest before we ride for Rouen. Tell Edvard to arrange accommodation for us. I recall that a large inn on the outskirts is commodious, with good stabling; he will know the one.' Finian agreed and went to have that conversation.

Chatillon stood on his own for a while. He was pleased to see the boat was now edging into the large port of Marseilles, full of bobbing, sheltered boats of all sizes and descriptions. His stomach suddenly clenched at the thought of what had nearly happened to Isabella. He knew what went on in the slave markets of the Barbary Coast, and he'd not have been able to live with himself if she'd been taken. He was suddenly filled with raging anger, and his knuckles turned white as he gripped the gunwale. He had told himself he was not in love with her—it was very early days, and he didn't love easily. However, he found he had great affection for her; she was his wife, and he would protect her with his life.

Chapter Eight

It wasn't a pleasant trip from Lyon to Rouen, as the driving winter rains from the northwest were still in evidence, and it was a cold, wet March. It took them much longer than expected and the mood was gloomy as they rode their dripping horses into the stables each night. Edvard was in a particularly dour mood as he watched his cloak steam and listened to a whistling Finian, dubbing his bridle by the fire.

'God's bones, how can you be so damn cheerful when we are soaked to the skin each day?'

Finian smiled. 'Normandy is pleasantly green for a reason, Edvard, as is Ireland. Over there, if it's not raining, it's about to rain. We are used to it, and we prepare everything accordingly,' he said, rubbing more grease into the leather to stop it from cracking as it dried. Edvard just grunted in response.

They had seen little of Chatillon each evening as he'd given his time to a rather shaken Isabella. 'Come, let us go down to the taproom. I can hear my men laughing and I'm in need of company,' said Finian hanging his bridle over a chair and hoping to lift Edvard's mood.

When they entered the large, warm room, which was humid from the drying cloaks on every stool and chair, they were surprised to see Chatillon holding court by the fire, a tankard of warm spiced ale in his hand. He was regaling the crowd with various adventures, including the recent Saracen attack, and they were hanging on every word. Some of his men joined in to embellish the details, which became even more terrifying in the telling—although, three of their group had been killed on the Saracen raid and two others were badly injured enough to have been left with a physician in Marseilles to join them later.

The two men smiled as they pulled up stools.

'How is Isabella?' asked Finian.

'Tired and cold after today's journey, but resilient. She regaled me, full of fury, last night, for ten minutes, about what she'd have liked to have done to her attacker if we had captured him instead of killing him!'

'A woman after my own heart,' laughed Finian. 'And the deep mark on her neck where the cord cut into her skin, is it healing?'

Chatillon frowned. 'It is fading, and she's not unduly concerned. It's a vicious method of restraining prisoners Finian.'

'I was tied in the same way, and it's common practice on the Barbary Coast. It took months for the scar to fade because it had cut so deeply into my skin. When they first captured us, they threw me into the hold and left me tied like that for three days.' Edvard and Chatillon knew Finian had been taken for a while to serve in the galleys, but there are some things a man does not want to discuss, and they had never mentioned that time. They sat and listened to the laughter and conversations around them, each man wrapped up in his thoughts.

'The men seem in good spirits despite what happened,' commented Chatillon.

Finian nodded. 'There's nothing like a brush with death to lift the spirits and make you embrace life with a smile.'

'So what of our attacker? What do we know of him?' Chatillon suddenly asked, pinning Edvard with his intense, dark-eyed stare. He knew that Edvard could extract information out of any man, given time.

'We discovered that Ishmael is a man of great wealth and power, a member of the Berber Hud family in Spain. He's also the leader of a large family tribe on the Barbary Coast. He accumulated much of his wealth through piracy and the slave trade, being one of the most feared Saracens in the Mediterranean. He no longer needs to sail as he'd handed operations over to his son, but he still takes part occasionally for the thrill of the chase. The man we questioned said that Sheikh Ishmael and his son would laugh in pure delight as a small trading vessel fled before them. The man also said that the sheikh is very tenacious. He has known him to wait days for a vessel to come out of a cove. If he has sworn vengeance against you, he will do his utmost to take it.'

Chatillon inclined his head in acceptance; it didn't surprise him. He had come across such men before.

'We will be vigilant, Piers,' said Finian.

Chatillon thanked them, smiled and stretched. 'I've led such a charmed life since Prague, let us hope it continues.'

Edvard snorted with laughter at this as he reminded them of the dangers they had faced and the times they had nearly lost their lives over the last ten years. Chatillon saw the joke and laughed with them.

'Meanwhile, let us go and see what great moves are afoot in

Rouen. My informers tell me that Robert's powerful uncles are with him there. That's significant as either of them can draw on a large amount of support from the Norman nobles, and I'm pleased that he will have them giving sage advice at his elbow. Now I'm going to enjoy my beautiful wife.' So saying, he bowed and left them.

Finian sat forward. 'I don't like this Edvard, not one bit. I don't think he's taking this threat seriously.'

'I remember the last time you said that, Finian. We were in Prague, and look what happened there. Let me put your mind at rest....things have changed since Prague, and Piers De Chatillon is the most feared assassin in Europe. Who would be mad enough to try and kill him or his family?' Edvard shook his head at Finian's doubts and made for his bed.

It was midday when they passed along the narrow crowded streets and through the gates into the imposing castle at Rouen. They rode into a melee of armed men and horses in the large bailey. Many troops sported the badge of Bishop Odo of Bayeux, and others held the flags and Gonfalon of Mortain. They pulled up at the great steps, and grooms ran to take their horses. The older large stone donjon, or keep, towered above them as they entered its portal, mounting the wide staircase to the entrance chamber and the Great Hall. They found a large group of nobles and a similar amount of bustle and urgency inside.

Robert Curthose was surrounded by a covey of Norman nobles, including both uncles, who were dressed in heavy cloaks and were either leaving or had just arrived. The crowd parted, and the Duke saw them and shouted a greeting.

'Chatillon, my old friend, you're most welcome, and you have brought your beautiful bride with you to my new capital in Rouen. I'm sorry I couldn't attend your wedding in Genoa as I had intended. As you can see, things have moved on here apace, which prevented me from leaving the Duchy at this time.'

Chatillon bowed and then clasped arms with the Duke; they had been friends since his days in the French court. Chatillon had also played a key part in facilitating Robert's successful rebellions against his father, King William. Always a charming man to the ladies, Robert stepped forward and kissed Isabella firmly on the mouth before shepherding her to a chair by the massive fireplace.

'You didn't tell me she was so stunningly beautiful,' he said in a clearly audible whisper that made everyone smile. 'There will be much lip-smacking tonight at dinner when the men see her,' he added loudly behind his hand. Isabella blushed delightfully but smiled up at the Duke while Chatillon inclined his head in thanks and bowed to Bishop Odo and Count Mortain, the two powerful men in front of him. Both of them had dealt with him in the past. Both of them had been King William's half-brothers and principal advisors.

'Tell me, does Pope Urban realise what I'm about and that my cause is just and right? Do I have the Holy Father's blessing for this venture Chatillon? After all, he gave the Papal Banner, the Gonfalon, to my father when he invaded England in 1066.'

Chatillon took his time to choose his words carefully as he didn't want to offend, or disillusion, the Duke.

'The Pope agrees that your challenge as your father's eldest son and heir is right and just. He hasn't sent his banner. Instead, he sent something far more useful.'

He waved Edvard forward with a small but heavy wooden chest, indicating that he should place it on the table and unlock it. Robert was impatient, and stepping up to the table, lifted the lid while the nobles crowded around the table, looking over each other's shoulders to see. Odo stayed by the fireplace, but looked at Chatillon, and raised an eyebrow at the size of the chest; surely, it should have been bigger, he seemed to infer. With the lid open, they could see that the chest was packed to the top with bulging red leather drawstring bags, each bearing the papal stamp. Robert, always impetuous, couldn't resist and untied the bag spilling the contents onto the table. There was an audible gasp from those who could see the table; heavy gold coins rolled out instead of the expected small silver largesse. This time, Odo, hearing the gasps and comments, nodded his approval at Chatillon; the Pope would be supporting the rightful heir to the English throne.

'God's blood, this amount of gold will buy us some more ships,' shouted Hugh De Grandesmil.

'When you next send your pigeon to the Lateran Palace in Rome, Chatillon, make sure the Pope knows how grateful we are,' said Robert.

He waved his Steward over to them. 'Please take the Lady De Chatillon to her chamber. I am sure she will wish to rest after such an arduous journey. The other ladies of the court will be gathering in the solar before dinner, Lady Isabella, and we look forward to seeing you then.'

'And a deadly journey,' added Finian, forgetting himself for a second.

'Deadly?' asked Robert turning to look at Chatillon and the warrior beside him.

'We nearly lost your gold, Sire, to Saracen pirates on the way here. They followed and attacked us outside Marseilles, and we lost several men and crew. Fortunately, with the help of Finian and my men, we managed to fight off Sheikh Ishmael and his attackers, and we limped into Marseilles.'

Robert swore long and loudly. 'They are a plague, a pestilence on our seas and your Sheikh Ishmael is one of the worst. They need wiping out!' he said while turning to regard Finian with interest. 'Another Horse Warrior, Chatillon? You do seem to collect them.'

'Sire, may I present Lord Finian Ui Neill, cousin of the recently murdered King of Meath.' Finian bowed to the Duke and the assembled nobles, and Robert acknowledged it while looking thoughtful.

'Yes, I know of the Ui Neills of Meath. My father had many links in Ireland and thought about a campaign, backed by the church, for a while. He said the Ui Neills were a fearsome and warlike family, and I have indeed heard of you,' Robert said, jabbing a finger at Finian in a way that Chatillon was not sure he liked. 'You killed the King of Leinster, I believe, and wasn't there a price on your head? I remember my father talking about it.'

Chatillon jumped in before Finian said something cutting. 'This was all many years ago, Sire, a ridiculous blood feud that got out of hand. Since then, Finian has fought and ridden alongside the Malvais brothers with the Breton Horse Warriors for several years. Now he's back at my side, and I owe him my life after what happened in Prague.' That cleverly produced an expected silence, as almost every man there knew the story of those horrendous events in the Prague fortress in 1073, which had sent shock waves across Europe.

Robert regarded the Irish lord again in a more amenable way. 'I know he's your man, Chatillon, but if you and he agree, then I may have a use for him,' he said, glancing over at Bishop Odo. Chatillon raised a questioning eyebrow at Finian, who gave an almost imperceptible nod.

'Of course, Sire, but I warn you, his services don't come cheap.'

All of the assembled nobles laughed at this comment as the campaign was already short of funds, and any reward would only come after a successful invasion, with Robert on the throne of England.

'Come Chatillon, and I'll show you our plans,' Robert said, waving them over to a large table with several maps.

'I am sending my uncles back to England to prepare men, horses and weapons for the invasion. They are planning a series of simultaneous uprisings in different places in the south and in the west at Bristol. My uncle Mortain will go to Arundel Castle with Montgomery, the Earl of Shrewsbury, and Bishop Geoffrey of Coutances. Odo goes to his castles in Kent with our dear friend De Clare at Tonbridge Wells, and the southeast is covered. All will be ready to rise when the word is given. Then, once preparations are underway, they will travel with the King, north to York for the Easter court, to allay any suspicions and to win over York, Durham and Northumberland.'

'This is an ambitious plan, Sire, and you certainly have powerful allies on your side, but can you think that the King will remain unaware of such preparations?' asked Chatillon, his head tilted to one side.

'We believe so as we have informers in his court, and we know our supporters are loyal,' stated the Duke.

Chatillon raised a quizzical eyebrow. He'd found Robert to be somewhat naive on previous occasions. 'This is why my uncles and others are travelling to the Easter court at York. Their presence there will allay any possible rumours,' added Robert seeing the doubt in the papal envoy's face.

Odo interrupted. 'We must go, Brother, if we are to catch the tide,' he said to Mortain whilst striding for the door, his retinue racing after him. Robert De Mortain clasped arms in farewell with his nephew.

'Godspeed, Uncle, and I know we will prevail,' Robert shouted after him.

Chatillon watched them go. *Surely, William Rufus has spies in this camp as well; he must know what is happening in Normandy,* he thought as he scanned the hall. *Surely, he cannot be unaware of what is afoot here.* Chatillon would make it his business to find out, and Edvard would root out any traitors here in Rouen. They all needed to be vigilant. For now, though, he'd bide his time, wait and watch while providing guidance and sage advice to Robert.

Isabella had removed her gown and reclined on the bed in her thin linen chemise. She was eating a ripe peach, and the juice was running down her chin as she smiled at her husband coming through the door.

'I hadn't expected you for hours, my Lord. There was such an array of nobles around the Duke and such discussions!'

'Ah, but some things are more important, Isabella, such as licking peach juice from your lips and breasts,' he said, laughing and lowering his head. She giggled and daringly moved her hand to his swelling manhood. He sat back and smiled; she'd come on so much, and her enjoyment of bedsport was refreshing and infectious. He pulled his tunic over his head as she untied his braies. He gasped as she took the initiative and lowered her head to use her tongue to excite him further. He closed his eyes, giving in to the pleasure until he had to pull her away.

'We don't want to waste any, Isabella; I want you to give me children as beautiful as you and, of course, as clever as me.'

She playfully slapped him as he pushed her backwards and buried himself deep inside her. She wrapped her legs around him and wove her fingers into his hair as he kissed her deeply.

Later they lay entwined and replete on the bed, and he knew the time had come to have a serious conversation with her.

'I can see that I may be here in Rouen for some time, Isabella, perhaps as long as four or five months, looking at the scope of Duke Robert's plans.'

She nodded in acceptance, so he continued....

'You, however, will only stay here another week,' he said, sitting up and swinging his legs off the bed to reach the wine. 'I am sending you to Paris to spend time in the French court. Ostensibly, you are redecorating and altering the Paris manor house to your tastes. I assure you money is no object; do what you will with it. However, you'll take long messages to King Philip and Gervais for me. You'll also spend many afternoons with a friend who will teach you what he taught me.'

'You're sending me on my own?' she asked in surprise.

'Edvard will accompany you, and he will arrange everything. You'll stay there for two weeks and then return to me here.'

Isabella was excited by the thought of going to the French court; she was already discovering the freedom of being a married woman. She enjoyed throwing off the constraints placed upon her as a young maiden. Chatillon climbed out of bed and stood naked in front of a jug and bowl of water

CHAPTER EIGHT

to wash. She lay and watched him, this fascinating man, her husband and lover. She'd also discovered he was extremely fastidious, washing most mornings or after travelling, such as today. She slipped off the bed and quietly moved to put her arms around his waist, pressed her soft body against his hard one, and gently kissed his shoulder blades. Her fingers ran lightly over the scars on his back. Most were just faint ridges apart from two bigger puckered scars, which looked like burns. Piers didn't talk about them, so she resolved to ask Edvard at some point.

'I'll miss you,' she whispered. His hands dropped to hers, and he pulled her around to face him.

'I'll also miss you, Isabella, but we will be here together for a week before you leave, and in no time, you'll be back again, in my bed and my arms.'

She nodded and raised her face to be kissed, knowing she was falling in love with him.

'You'll be very useful to me, Isabella, and I expect you to use everything I've taught you while you're in the French court. Gather every piece of useful information that you can while you're in their beds.'

She stepped back, eyes wide, and her mouth dropped open in astonishment. 'You expect me to make love to other men?' she asked in a hoarse whisper.'

Chatillon laughed. 'Of course I do. I'm training you to be the perfect courtesan and spy, Isabella. In a year or two, you'll be desired and talked about by men all over Europe, and if you do this well, they will never know that you're cleverly using them, their servants and even their friends for information. Now go to Paris and hone your lovemaking and diplomatic skills. While you're away, I shall be bedding Almodis, the new young and pretty wife of Count Robert De Mortain. She will tell me exactly what the Count thinks of Robert's plans. In no way is this love or affection, Isabella. This is pure swiving and, of course, some physical pleasure, to get crucial information. Think of yourself as an actress, as this is a role you're playing; become someone else when you do this, but no one except me gets to see the real you.'

Isabella blinked rapidly as she took all this in and ran it through her head again. She was not naïve and knew that her father and many of his friends had several mistresses, which was accepted by society. Isabella had never really thought that women might be able to enjoy the same freedoms. She said nothing, so Piers continued....

'King Philip will want you as soon as he sees you, but make sure that you keep him at arm's length for the first week. For there may be more interesting men at court with information that we need, and if you're in the King's bed, they will not dare to come near.'

Chatillon could see the confusion on her face and thought she needed time, so he dressed quickly, kissed her and returned to be with the Duke.

Isabella sat on the bed, deep in thought as she came to terms with what he'd just described. It was exciting and certainly had its attractions, but as a newly married bride, it felt strange to contemplate doing this. However, she understood the idea of being in a role, for in many ways, she'd been doing this in society since she was a young girl. It would come naturally to her.

9

Chapter Nine

When Chatillon rejoined the Duke, a group of five sat around the table. An older man he didn't know well was Lord William De Warenne, although he knew this noble had fought with King William at the Battle of Hastings. He sat with a small notebook at the end of the table and listened, contributing little, a sceptical expression on his face as a heated discussion took place about ships.

'How many ships have you assembled here in Rouen, Sire?' asked Chatillon.

'Not enough,' replied De Warenne bleakly to a glare from Robert. However, it didn't deter the older man.

'Robert, your father, King William, took five months to assemble his invasion fleet, and we waited another two months for a favourable wind and a lull in the weather to get the entire fleet across. You are impatient and itching to go off half-cocked!'

Robert ignored him. 'Your gold will help Chatillon, but it takes time to buy or build ships. I've sent men up into the low country to see if we can buy or even hire them there.'

Piers nodded; he knew that Robert had to launch this invasion in the summer months, June, July, and August, to have any chance of success, so time was of the essence in having those ships here, provisioned and ready to sail.

'Why don't you steal them?' said Finian.

This comment produced a long silence from the assembled lords while they watched the faces of Finian and then the Duke. Chatillon covered his mouth to hide the smile that had come involuntarily to his lips.

'What did you say?' asked Robert in an incredulous tone.

'The ships, steal them. It is the only way you'll get them on time. You can reimburse them afterwards if necessary. It used to happen all the time in Dublin Bay,' he added. Robert's companions looked at the Irish warrior in disbelief that he could suggest such a tactic, Chatillon smiled again as he watched them, but Robert had a gleam in his eye.

'So you're suggesting, Finian Ui Neill, that I become one of the very pirates that I said we should wipe out.'

'Yes, Sire, that's if you're serious about wanting to sail this summer!'

De Warenne looked at Robert in dismay. 'Please tell me, Sire, that you're not considering this madness?'

Robert ignored him again and stared thoughtfully at the Irishman while chewing his bottom lip.

'And would you be prepared to train my men as pirates and then go and get me those ships, Finian Ui Neill?'

The Irishman grinned and nodded whilst Chatillon snorted with laughter, which he quickly concealed with a cough. This was more like the young, daring Finian of old, and he was pleased to see it again.

Robert laughed. 'I told you I would have a use for him,

Chatillon, a very resourceful man,' he said, tossing a gold coin high in the air. All eyes were on it, spinning through the air as the warrior deftly caught it.

'Another one of these is yours if you bring me a ship,' said Robert.

'Give me twenty decent men, and I will bring you your ships, Sire.'

'You'll have them and a captain who knows how to sail them—unless that's another one of your many talents, Ui Neill.'

Finian just laughed, bowed and went on his way to assemble his crew of raiders.

The other nobles dispersed apart from De Warenne, who took himself to a table by the window with his writings. He was obviously displeased by events and Duke Robert's refusal to listen to, or heed, his advice.

Chatillon drew Robert to one side. 'The Pope's gold will be useful, but I notice, Sire, that you still need other funds.'

Robert nodded. 'The money seems to disappear, Chatillon. War is expensive.'

Chatillon stared at the Duke, who was now pacing back and forth. He needed to find the right words to make a tricky suggestion.

'What of your younger brother, Henry? I believe he was left a large amount of gold and has claims on his mother's lands in England. Where does he sit in all of this?' he asked.

'He is here in Rouen with me, but he has said little. I think he's trying to remain neutral. He's much younger than William or I. We had our own camp of friends, so we had little to do with him. Then I spent many years away from court in France and Ghent, and William was, of course, in England, so honestly, we barely know him. He spent much time with my father, I believe.'

Chatillon glanced across the hall at De Warenne, who had stopped reading and was staring intently at them, evidently trying to follow their conversation. Chatillon lowered his voice. 'I'll speak with him, Sire. He must feel the loss of prestige by having no land to call his own. How old is he now? Twenty?'

Robert nodded, intrigued by what the Papal Envoy was suggesting.

Some hours later, Chatillon managed to track Prince Henry down in the stables. He'd just returned from several days at Fecamp checking the defences, where a significant castle and Abbey overlooked the port. As he rode in, the young man raised an eyebrow when he saw that Chatillon was waiting for him.

'Well met, Piers De Chatillon. Can the famous, powerful Papal Envoy possibly be waiting for me? I had assumed I would be the smallest political pawn on the Pope's chessboard.' He grinned, but his eyes were interested as he appraised the man in front of him. He'd heard his father curse and praise this man in equal measure at times, but Henry was well aware that Chatillon was one of the most dangerous men in Europe, and an arch-manipulator.

Chatillon inclined his head respectfully and assessed the young man in front of him. Taller and slimmer than his brothers, he had more of his mother's looks. It must be at least five years since he'd seen him, and the clever, learned, studious boy had grown into a handsome, confident young man.

'I assure you, Sire, that the Pope never ignores or forgets any members of the royal families in Europe.'

Henry smiled. 'I hear that you brought my brother gold. That must have brought a smile to Robert's face.'

Chatillon inclined his head, for that sentence told him Henry had informers working in the court. He might have been away at Fecamp, but he knew exactly what plans were afoot here in Rouen.

'A moment of your time, Henry, for I believe I have a suggestion that may benefit you and your brother.'

'Which one, Chatillon? I haven't decided whose side to lend my sword to yet. Let us find some wine to take the dust from my throat,' he said, striding away to the donjon with Chatillon following.

An hour later, Chatillon emerged from the Duke's solar with a frown on his brow, as he went to summon Robert. Henry had driven a hard bargain, and he was not sure Robert would agree. One thing was clear to Chatillon: of the three brothers, Henry was definitely most like his father. He was focused, tenacious, and quick in his thoughts and arguments, with that innate stubbornness of King William. More importantly, he had been right in his judgement because Henry was ambitious.

As he approached the staircase, he noticed two figures silhouetted in the long narrow window embrasure. He stopped for a second; his soft leather boots had made little sound on the stone-flagged floor. He saw the tall man on the left hand a small roll of vellum to the other man, who cringed when he turned and noticed Chatillon. He tucked the vellum inside his tunic and departed. Chatillon noticed his pock-marked face as he hurried past him. Moving quickly forward to stop the other man from departing, he recognised De Warenne, who stepped back in alarm when he saw who was there.

Chatillon's dark eyes stared intently at De Warenne in the silence that followed. 'Are you well, my Lord? You look pale,' he said in concern but with a hint of mockery in his voice.

'Yes, Chatillon, I just jumped as you crept up on me!' he spat.

'I assure you, my Lord, I don't have to creep anywhere. Those days were over in my misspent youth. Now people bring news and information to me, often without asking. But no, I was striding down the corridor, with purpose, as I may have good news for Duke Robert,' he said, smiling and turning to leave.

Warenne stepped forward with interest. 'And may I ask what this good news is that you have?' he asked.

'I would rather the Duke heard it first,' stated Chatillon with a raised eyebrow.

'Of course, of course,' muttered De Warenne, as Chatillon descended the staircase to the Great Hall.

Once there Chatillon waved Edvard over. 'A pock-marked servant has just left. I suspect he's a messenger for a spy and will be heading for the docks. Find him, follow him and let us ascertain whom he's meeting and where he's going. Then slit his throat before he gets on a boat for England.' Edvard acknowledged the instruction and swiftly made for the doors. Chatillon went to the fire and bowed to the Duke, who waved him over to the table where they could talk privately.

'I've negotiated a deal with your brother Henry. I assure you that it was hard work; he is a shrewd negotiator, and you'll need to consider whether you'll accept it. You must see it as short-term losses for long-term gains. Henry is prepared to give you the funds you need for the invasion to succeed. In return, he wants the Cotentin peninsula and the area known as Avranchin down to Mont St. Michel. He wishes to become the Count of Cotentin and be recognised as such.'

The bullish expression on Robert's face was followed by anger and indecision, as he weighed the pros and cons. It was exactly what Chatillon expected. No Duke would want to give away part of his lands, and Robert had waited long and hard to be Duke of Normandy.

Chatillon stepped forward and put his hand on his friend's arm. 'Sire, you can always take it back on some pretext later, if necessary. This desire for land is one of the few weaknesses I see in your brother Henry. This is your chance to use that to your advantage.'

De Warenne had entered the hall and now stood and stared at them intently, but Robert turned and announced in a loud voice, 'So be it, for it is the means to an end. Let us go and clasp arms with him on this!' Chatillon grinned and slapped him on the shoulder, reminding both of them of the light-hearted friendship they once shared, before becoming players on Europe's political stage.

'You'll not regret this, Sire,' he said, leading Robert up to the solar where an ambitious Henry waited. Piers was pleased with how easily he'd united the two brothers against the third, and there was no doubt that he had increased Robert's chances of succeeding.

Chapter Ten

Finian's ship sat in the lee of a steep cliff not far from the busy fishing port of Fecamp. None of the fishing boats was big enough for the purpose the Duke had in mind, but Finian sent men into the taverns, and coins loosened a few tongues to tell them of larger prey.

He stood on the foredeck with the Captain staring north into the haze. They had been told that a large trading cog was expected today, full of supplies for the abbey and castle at Fecamp. Finian intended to capture the boat and its cargo when it appeared. Suddenly, a keen crewman shouted, and the shape of a vessel appeared. It was very large and wide, perfect for loading horses and men.

'How do we do this, Finian?' asked the Captain.

'Hide your men under the covers. We pull broadside on and shout for help for a broken steorbord,' Finian explained.

'You do realise that they will know me as I sail up and down this coast, and they will never suspect me of piracy. This attack may be good for you, but my reputation will be ruined after this,' the man said, spitting on the ground in disgust.

CHAPTER TEN

'I promise we will spread the word that you had no choice but to do this. You were threatened, and you've been well paid.'

The Captain reluctantly nodded and began shouting orders to his crew while Finian pulled his cloak tightly around himself, to hide his warrior garb.

The plan worked just as Finian had said. The large trading cog furled its sail and slowed while manoeuvring to come alongside. Finian had told his men to avoid bloodshed where possible, so many of them were armed only with small clubs. The approaching cog only had six crew, while Finian had twenty men hidden under the covers waiting for the word to attack.

The Captain of the cog threw his ropes across to the Santa Maria, a large ship, asking them to tow him. Suddenly over a dozen men appeared to the other captain's dismay, some throwing grappling irons. The stranger on the fore deck threw off his cloak and, revealed to be a warrior, shouted, 'We are commandeering this boat for Robert Duke of Normandy. We intend you no harm, but we will kill anyone who attacks us or stands in our way!' The unarmed crew backed away, although one man jumped over the side and began swimming for the distant shore, fearing capture and years in the galleys.

In what seemed like no time, it was over. Only one man, the mate, who realised he was losing his share of the cargo fee, had rushed at his men with a dagger, and he was quickly put down with one blow. The Captain was red-faced and spluttering with anger as Finian, sword drawn, mounted the stern deck beside him.

'You can be tied and bound with your crew, or you can follow my orders to sail for the mouth of the Seine,' offered Finian regarding the big burly man with a dagger at his belt. The man reluctantly agreed, realising he'd no choice, and Finian relieved him of his weapon. Finian leaned against the gunwale and raised a hand to Captain Masson to untie them and head back to port.

By the early evening, they were passing Le Havre and sailing up the Seine to tie up at the trading wharves west of Rouen. Finian was pleased but didn't believe they would all be this easy, especially as word got out and the crews would be bristling with weapons. However, as Chatillon always drummed into him, information was everything. In two days, they would sail further north and dock at Dieppe, a busy trading port, where he'd send his men into the taverns again. Laden or empty, all Finian wanted was the ship, but the cargo was a bonus for Robert, and Finian's men would get a small cut to keep them keen.

Robert was delighted at Finian's success, even though he had to deal with an angry delegation, which arrived from Fecamp two days later demanding reparation. However, they were suitably awed by the presence of Chatillon, the Papal Envoy, who assured the Abbot that they would be repaid for the seized goods. Edvard arrived and stood quietly inside the hall's doors as the delegation left. Chatillon could see that he had something of import to tell him, so they walked out into the bailey, away from any chance of being overheard.

'It was as you suspected, Sire, the pock-faced man was a messenger; he was to board a ship for England this morning with a message for King William. His body is now floating out on the morning tide.' Chatillon gave a tight smile of satisfaction.

'William De Warenne is, as I thought, passing information to the enemy, to King William Rufus or his creature Flambard.

This is useful because we can pass disinformation that way. Thank you, Edvard. Now go and help Finian celebrate his success as I don't need you tonight, and tomorrow you leave with Isabella for Paris. You know what I expect?' he asked, becoming serious for a moment. Edvard smiled and nodded.

'I will watch over her like a hawk, make sure that she comes to no harm, and I'll send any interesting information to you immediately.'

Chatillon slapped him affectionately on his shoulder. 'What would I do without you, Edvard? I have a small box for you to give her on arrival at the Chatillon house in Paris. Could you pick it up before you go? Now go and get drunk with Finian.' He grinned, sending him on his way.

Later that evening, Edvard joined Finian in a lively tavern in the city. 'Well met, Ui Neill. I believe I have to congratulate you on such an astonishing success in piracy! You're the talk of the castle.'

Finian laughed, pleased to see his friend. 'You expected me to fail, Edvard?' he asked in amused surprise.

'I just remembered how poor you were with grappling irons!' Both men roared with laughter at first, but quickly sobered, as the memory took them back to that night in Prague when they were trying to get over the high fortress walls to rescue Chatillon. This brought back memories of the horrors they found inside when they succeeded.

However, they were soon laughing again as Edvard described the outraged Abbot of Fecamp demanding the return of his cargo. Finian had sold half of it, and the other useful stores for the invasion had been placed in the Duke's warehouses. Edvard watched Finian joking with his men. He looked much better than the white-faced, sad-eyed warrior that had arrived in Genoa a month before. Finian's life had been traumatic; banished and then hunted, with a price on his head from a young age. Finally, returning home only to have his young family slaughtered would leave deep scars on any man. Now he was amongst friends, and they would do what they could to help him forget.

Chatillon made love to Isabella for hours that night, taking her to new heights of pleasure over and over. They lay entwined, perspiration damp on their bodies. She held him close.

'I love you, Piers,' she whispered, and Chatillon felt his stomach clench. Only two women had ever said that to him and meant it. The first, Gabrielle, had betrayed him and married another. The second, Bianca, he had truly loved in return, and she'd died because of the danger he'd placed her in.

Piers was not at all prepared to fall in love again yet. He kissed her gently. 'I'll miss you very much, Isabella, while you spread your wings in the French court, but you're there for a reason. The most important thing is to choose lovers who will be useful to you. They might not always be the handsome young men you're used to.'

After noticing how he sidestepped replying to her declaration, Isabella decided to pay him back. 'If, as you say, we are allowed other lovers, and it is only for physical pleasure, then surely I'm allowed some fun. I find Finian very handsome and exciting. I've always wanted a warrior to take me, and I could imagine him lying naked on my bed,' she said with a wide-eyed look of anticipation, whilst running her tongue over her lips.

Chatillon turned away and frowned in annoyance; his lips were a thin, hard line as he began to answer. Then turning, he saw her laughing eyes, and he started to laugh. 'You little witch,' he said, pulling her into his arms.

The next morning he waved Isabella off on her journey to Paris. Not only was Edvard by her side, but half a dozen of his men formed their escort. He'd listened to their concerns and assured them that he didn't take Sheikh Ishmael's threats lightly, so he ensured that Isabella was well protected.

He returned to the Great Hall, where Duke Robert was still in a buoyant mood with not only the acquisition of funds from the Pope and his brother Henry, but now Finian Ui Neill was bringing him ships. He couldn't see how the invasion could fail.

Chatillon was not as complacent. If De Warenne and others had started feeding information to the King, then he was certain William Rufus would know what was happening and was making plans to deal with it. They needed to ensure that William Rufus thought the invasion was coming from a completely different direction, and he had an idea for that.

11

Chapter Eleven

Isabella arrived at the Chatillon House in Paris and was entranced by the large fortified walled house, which sat in gardens full of fruit trees, with a meadow running down to a gate leading to a jetty on the River Seine. From here, they would take a boat down to the palace of King Philip. After looking around the house with Edvard, she decided that there was little she would change. Piers' mother had excellent taste, and the household servants were well-trained. As the Steward handed her the Chatelaine's keys, he assured her that beds had been aired and the tapestries had been gently beaten and cleaned that summer before being re-hung. There were fresh, sweet-smelling rushes on the floor of the Great Hall, and roaring fires welcomed them.

   Edvard and the Steward guided her around every room, and she insisted on touring the stables and outbuildings. For the first time, she really felt mistress of her domain, and she thought if all of his properties were this well looked after, and ran as smoothly, then her job would be easy. As she walked through the large kitchen garden, she smiled at the outdoor servants as they bowed and doffed their caps to her. There were twenty resident servants, and the Steward told her they hired more for seasonal work or events.

Edvard saw the pleasure, pride, and satisfaction on her face and he was pleased. These properties had been his responsibility in the past, and he was certainly not sorry to lose that domestic role. Here and there during the tour, he added personal information, the history of the family and even Chatillon's likes and dislikes. Isabella was amused to find that Piers hated raspberries. It made him more human somehow.

The next afternoon Isabella dressed with care as she was to be presented to the King. Edvard revealed that King Philip liked to know exactly who was in his capital and expected them to present their credentials and respects. She dressed in her favourite blue silk, adorning her hair with a wide, embroidered, blue silk band, but with her long, honey blonde hair cascading down her back. She mounted the stairs to the King's chambers in some trepidation. Gervais de la Ferte, the Seneschal of France, was waiting for her at the top. She was relieved to see him as she'd met and liked him immediately at the wedding.

'Isabella, marriage certainly suits you as you're positively glowing and looking more beautiful than ever.' He kissed her hand.

She smiled as she'd been warned that this handsome older man, although a close friend of Piers, was known to have had at least a dozen mistresses. He even had a long-term relationship with the woman Piers had been about to marry, the dark beauty Bianca Da Landriano. However, she was not worried. Due to her mother's training in Genoa, she certainly knew how to keep unwelcome advances at bay. So she smiled sweetly at his compliment and assured him it was because she was so in love with her husband. Gervais took the hint and laughed aloud, as she took his arm to go and make her bow to the King of France.

The King was entranced with Isabella; he found her stunningly beautiful, but unlike his previous conquests, he was wary of this Genoan beauty. She was the wife of Piers De Chatillon, not a man to trifle with or upset in any way. To his delight, he found her very interesting to talk to on many matters, especially with her knowledge of the political affairs of the eastern Mediterranean. Her links with the powerful families of northern Italy and Milan kept her at his side until the candles were being lit. He parted with reluctance and demanded her presence at dinner that evening. Meanwhile, the watching courtiers shared salacious gossip about her charms and laid bets about how soon she'd be in the King's bed.

One younger man, however, came in late and could not take his eyes off her. He was English but of Norman parentage, and he'd been sent by his father to ascertain what position King Philip would take in the possible conflict between the two elder sons of King William. After all, King Philip had always supported Robert Curthose, but was it in his best interests to do so now? This young man hoped to persuade him to support William Rufus.

Isabella was aware of the attention she was receiving from the young man. He was tall and blonde with blue eyes, probably slightly younger than her. He came across as confident, and quite forceful when she watched him interacting with others at his table. In her experience, this often meant money or position. She tasked Edvard to find out who he was, and Edvard returned within an hour.

Edvard rarely showed emotion, but she could see the enthusiasm on his face as he made his way to her side and whispered that he had the information, *but it was not to be spoken of here where people could overhear them.*

She made her bow to the King and returned with Edvard to the house. Once inside the solar, she waved Edvard to a seat and poured some wine for them both. It had taken no time for her to realise the importance and usefulness of Edvard. The man was invaluable as he was not only the manservant he portrayed to the world, he was Chatillon's trusted friend, who facilitated the whole system of informers and assassins that Piers had set up. She did not doubt that he'd give his life for Piers. Her husband was an enigma indeed, as so many people hated or feared him; yet his friends loved him and would die protecting him.

'Tell me what you found.'

'It couldn't be better. As you know, William De Warenne is feeding information to William Rufus in England?'

She nodded. 'Yes, Piers told me.'

'Well, this is his son, young Viscount William De Warenne, who is here as the envoy of King William Rufus, to try and garner support for his claim to the throne. He could prove to be very useful, and he's very attracted to you. Fortunately, he hasn't heard the Chatillon name; the courtiers here have dubbed you the 'Genoan Beauty'. However, it may not be long before he becomes aware of your identity, so if I may be so bold, I suggest you strike tonight while the iron is hot.'

Isabella suddenly burst into giggles, not only because she was having this conversation with a monk, albeit a defrocked one, but for his choice of words. Realising what he'd said, Edvard grinned as well. It was common parlance in some circles for a man's cock to be called a rod of iron.

Suddenly Edvard stood, and she wondered if she'd been too

lewd, or had offended him, as he crossed to the side of the room and returned with a long thin rosewood box bearing a carved lotus flower on the lid. Edvard was still smiling as he handed it to her.

'My master bade me give you this when you had found your first target,' he said, placing it on her lap.

She smiled and opened it. Her face lit up with surprise. She had expected jewellery or some such keepsake, but no, it seemed full of strips of coloured silk. She picked one out and began to giggle again at the absurdity of the situation, as she held up what was clearly some kind of penis sheath.

Edvard couldn't help smiling back as he explained. 'My master has these delivered from the east, from the land of Cathay. I believe they are double silk, and the inner one is coated in some form of bee's wax. They will protect you from pox and reduce the chance of pregnancy, if the man doesn't withdraw as you've told him to. The only child, my master, wants you to bear is his.'

Isabella's face became serious for a second as she turned the thin, soft, silken sheath in her hand. It had a drawstring cord at the top to tie and fasten it tight. 'Chatillon thought of everything, didn't he,' she said wryly to Edvard, while playfully wiggling her fingers inside it. They both laughed again.

'He is thinking of you and your well-being, my lady.'

She nodded, and Edvard rose to leave. 'Thank you, Edvard.... for everything,' she said as he left.

She contemplated the young De Warenne taking her into his bed. She sat, the box still on her knee, gazing into the distance, her mind a whirl of thoughts. How different her life had become in only a few months. Tonight she'd no doubt be in the bed of a handsome, virile young Englishman, and she'd be kneeling at his feet, tying this onto his manhood. She laughed again, but then admitted to herself that the thought quite excited her.

Viscount William De Warenne had swived at least a dozen women, over half of them serving girls, most of them willing, although some had been persuaded or forced. So he considered himself an experienced lover, giving him something of a swagger. However, nothing had prepared him for Isabella.

She'd played it well; coy and almost shy at first, she'd used all of her wiles, and those that Chatillon had taught her, to lure him in. By the end of the evening in the King's hall, he thought he'd burst if he didn't have her. They had danced twice, and she'd deliberately trailed her hand tantalisingly across his groin, while her tongue ran around her lips. He could imagine sliding himself into that red, inviting mouth.

As the entertainment finished and the King retired, he appeared at her side. 'May I have the honour of escorting you to your chamber?' he asked. Isabella's eyes blatantly raked over his body, as if assessing if he was worth it, and he felt himself colouring up until she placed her hand on his arm.

'I believe there's a nice walk through the physic garden. I would rather take the air for a while first.' William couldn't believe his luck. He'd take her in a rose bed if he had to. However, once there, although she allowed him to fondle and squeeze those beautiful round white breasts, he was prevented from going further.

'Can I trust you, William De Warenne?' she asked. In the bright moonlight, he gazed down into her large eyes.

'Of course.'

'If we go to your room as we both desire, the King must never hear of it, or he will expel you from the court, and I cannot answer for what my husband would do if he found out.'

William nodded enthusiastically, the danger adding even more to his excitement as he led her swiftly back into the palace. She smiled as he checked every corridor before leading her to his chamber.

He opened the large oak door into a commodious room, where he removed her cloak and invited her to sit by the fire. 'I would like some wine,' she said quietly. He poured them both a large goblet of red wine. 'Now, William, tell me about yourself. I have never made love to anyone except my husband, so I want to know who I'm going to bed with.'

The thought of this beautiful woman, naked in his bed, was almost too much for William, and he found his breath was coming far too fast. He described his family and his background and even some of his hopes for the future, as he expected preferment from King William Rufus. She encouraged him even more.

'Wait, was your father not a hero of the Battle of Hastings? Did he not ride beside King William?'

William was pleased and nodded enthusiastically. 'Yes, he's now in the court of the new King and hopes to be rewarded for his loyalty.'

'As he should be,' she added. She stood and turned her back to him, judging it to be time. 'Unfasten my gown, William, and kiss me just there,' she said, lifting her hair to expose the nape of her neck. He unloosened the ties and ran his lips and teeth over her neck. He pulled her against him, and she could feel his hardness, his need for her. He lifted her gown and chemise and pulled them both over her head. His hands grasped her breasts and then ran down over her body. She put up her hands, removed the pins from her hair, and let it hang long and loose. She calmly emptied her goblet and stood, unashamedly naked in the firelight. He couldn't take his eyes off her as he pulled off his tunic and moved his braies and chausses.

'Please fill up the goblets again, William. We have all night so let us take this slowly and enjoy ourselves.' With a goblet in each hand, he dropped to his knees beside her, but she stroked and caressed him, so he closed his eyes while she told him not to spill the wine. He almost lost control when she pulled him to his feet and lowered her mouth to him.

'So, William, tell me what you're doing in Paris?' He told her everything while she brought him to the brink again and again. She absorbed everything he said and pushed for more details. By the time she took the goblet from his shaking hand, she knew exactly what the De Warenne family were planning, and a pigeon would be winging its way to Rouen tomorrow.

She led him to the bed, and positioning herself over his loins, she revealed the silk sheath, which she tied expertly on his rigid manhood. He watched her in amazement and gasped as her hand smoothed it down. It didn't feel as intrusive as he expected as it slid smoothly against his skin. She gently lowered herself onto him. He closed his eyes as she began to move, but opened them as she gasped in pleasure.

Sometime later, he lay on his back, gently snoring, and Isabella lay awake. She rolled onto her side and watched him. He was a very handsome young man, and her fingers gently followed the contours of his muscled body. Isabella knew that she'd given the performance of her life, and it had been pleasurable enough. He'd never forget her and no doubt beg for more, but she didn't need him further.

He was not Chatillon. There had been no tingling excitement when he touched her. Although she'd pretended, William hadn't excited her enough to bring her to a climax, which her husband could do in minutes. However, she'd enjoyed the experience, playacting, and extraction of information and had no apprehension about doing it again.

The next time might be with King Philip, which would be a different proposition. He would be an experienced lover with jaded tastes. She decided she'd be positively virginal, innocent and naïve and laughed at the thought.

Edvard was waiting for her on the palace grounds. She chided him immediately. 'You should not have waited. You must be frozen. What if I had decided to spend the night with him?' she said, shaking her head and taking his arm.

'Chatillon would have killed me if I hadn't waited, and I would never have forgiven myself. Also, I knew you wouldn't be so foolish as to stay the night and risk being seen. If I can offer a small amount of helpful advice? Never become too familiar with them or affectionate. It can lead to further problems, as it did for Bianca, as she began to like her horse warrior almost too much.'

Isabella was in a pensive mood as she walked back to the house. Bianca, the woman Piers had loved, yet he turned her into a courtesan for his own ends, and it ended badly. She knew an assassin sent to kill Morvan De Malvais had killed her instead. She vowed that she'd be careful, in control, and not make the same mistake.

12

Chapter Twelve

Chatillon smiled as yet another pigeon arrived from Paris. Isabella had certainly been successful in her first endeavour, and what a catch she'd made. They now knew that King William was highly suspicious of his older brother in Normandy. Still, no mention of the invasion fleet had been made, which meant that the elder William De Warenne hadn't successfully sent that information across the channel. Not surprising as Chatillon had now slit the throat of two of his servants.

Duke Robert suddenly appeared beside him in the far corner of the battlements where a pigeon coop had been built. Robert watched with interest as the Papal Envoy unrolled the tiny piece of paper. He knew there was no point in reading it as it was in code.

'What news?' he asked, turning to gaze at the wide ribbon of the River Seine looping out towards the sea.

'As expected, Sire, I now have proof that William De Warenne is your spy. His eldest son is in Paris petitioning the French King for support for William Rufus.'

Robert slammed his fists down onto the stone battlements

in a fury. 'Can I trust no one?' he shouted.

Chatillon smiled, 'Quite honestly, Sire, there's only one person I trust. Myself!'

Robert gave a wry laugh. 'Wise council indeed, Chatillon, I'll have him arrested at once. He will not see the light of day or shores of England for many years.'

Chatillon put his head to one side and raised an eyebrow regarding the Duke's demeanour. He was rightly angry at the betrayal by someone who had always been loyal to his father.

'That may give you some satisfaction, but I've got a better idea. Let us make use of him. Let us feed him falsehoods to take back to William Rufus. Imagine this, if you will, you're sailing to Scotland, Sire. King Malcolm, who respects you, has offered you support, and you'll march south together to take Durham and York.

The Prince Bishop of Durham, William de St Calais, is an old friend and will come out in support of you, as will many northern lords who have pledged to you.'

Robert's face became animated. 'Chatillon, why did I not think of this instead of landing in Kent and Sussex?' Chatillon couldn't contain himself and snorted with laughter.

'No, Sire, this isn't a real plan. It's a story, a falsehood we will make up so that William Rufus sends his forces north, and we land in Kent and on the south coast unchallenged.' Chatillon watched the confusion and indecision cross the Duke's face, and he sighed as he again explained how it would work. Finally, Robert agreed, and they devised a strategy whereby De Warenne would learn of the plan.

'I will challenge him in front of the others on his son's mission to Paris, and I'll lay money that he will flee, Sire.'

Robert nodded. 'Then we will pursue him, hot on his heels

CHAPTER TWELVE

so that he escapes only by the skin of his teeth,' he said with enthusiasm.

Chatillon smiled. 'You must go and tell the nobles of your new plan, Sire, so they don't look surprised when you discuss it.'

'I will,' he said, heading for the narrow stone stairs. Then he stopped and turned. 'Your man, Ui Neill, he certainly delivers.'

Chatillon inclined his head. 'He has that reputation, Sire, and is one of the bravest fighters I've come across.'

'I need him, Chatillon. That is if you and he are agreeable. I need him to go to England with Odo and help ensure that everything goes to plan. I don't want to send another Norman lord who might be afraid of saying what he thinks to Odo.'

'Do not fear, Sire. Finian is certainly not backward in coming forward. He will certainly share his views when necessary, and I'll go and speak with him and see if he is amenable.' Robert left, and Chatillon returned to the pigeon coop and scattered some corn absentmindedly while mulling over what had just been said. He was reluctant to lose Finian, having just found him again, but it would do the Irish lord good to go to England and take his mind off the past. He'd put it to him.

They strolled down the narrow streets of Rouen to their favourite tavern that evening. 'The piracy seems to be going exceptionally well.' suggested Chatillon, with a grin, as they called for mulled ale.

'The men work well together, but the captains of the merchant ships are becoming wary on this coast. They have heard what we are doing and are avoiding the area,' said Finian taking a long draught from his tankard.

'Tell me, do you have someone amongst your men who could step up for a few months if you were elsewhere?'

Finian raised an eyebrow, then mulling Chatillon's question over for a while, he nodded.

'As you know, Lazzo came with me from Ireland. He could certainly do it, and he's a natural leader, my second in command. The men look up to him with respect because of his experience and fearlessness.'

Chatillon nodded as he tried to picture the man. 'Ah yes, I remember him, the big brute of a man that Edvard fought and defeated on the road to Prague. I thought I recognised him from somewhere on the wharves the other day.'

Finian laughed. 'Yes, Edvard certainly taught him a lesson, and they resolved their differences, although Lazzo's pride suffered for months. You must miss Edvard and Isabella,' suggested Finian. Chatillon looked across the large smoke-filled room.

'They are about my business for me in Paris, and I have you to keep me entertained for a while, Finian.' He took a draught of mulled ale from his tankard while his eyes swept the room. 'I presume you noticed that we were followed in here.'

Finian glanced fleetingly at a table on the far side of the room and saw two men: one was tall, thin and had a dark visage; the smaller one was stocky but solidly built, with a bald head and small narrow eyes. Finian looked across at Chatillon.

'Their cloaks suggest that they aren't from Normandy. The material is heavy and rich, the best wool, so they are no common robbers. I would say they are assassins in the pay of a wealthy master. Possibly from England, to stop you from aiding Robert, or possibly from your new friend Sheikh Ishmael. They are brave men indeed if they know who we are yet are prepared to take us on.'

'Yes, either brave or foolhardy, but they may be no more than on surveillance to establish our routines, for there seem to be only two of them,' suggested Chatillon. Finian casually took another sweeping glance across the room, his gaze passing for no more than a second or so on the two men.

'I would say that it is more than that, the way the taller man is constantly fingering the hilt of that dagger,' added Finian while turning to look into the flames of the nearby fire.

'There's an old archway on the left of the Rue de Bac on the way up to the cathedral; you may have seen it. It leads to a ruined chapel. We will make for that and wait to see if they follow, then we will deal with them,' responded Chatillon, draining his ale and pulling his dark cloak around him.

The tavern was down near the River Seine, so they always came well armed with both sword and dagger. It was a good venue to frequent because of the news the river and sea captains brought, but it was a dangerous area, and Chatillon never came here alone. Finian stood and threw a few coins on the table as he followed Chatillon through the tables to the door, where he halted to put his cloak on.

'They picked us up not long after we left the castle gates. The smaller one followed us down at first, at a distance. The second man joined him as we passed the cathedral. They must have been waiting for some time as you haven't left the castle for five days,' added Finian reaching to pull open the heavy door.

They left the tavern without a backward glance, but as soon as they were outside, they broke into a trot. They raced up the narrow streets, knowing there would be pursuit. They entered the Rue de Bac and ran towards the archway on the left. It was a dark night with only a quarter moon in the clear sky, but it was enough to show them the darker entrance in the carved pointed archway. They quickly entered an overgrown area surrounding a partially ruined chapel that had lost its roof. They flattened themselves against the ivy-covered crumbling stone walls, in the deep shadows, and waited.

Some time passed before they heard soft voices. The men had followed them, but being unable to find them, had backtracked. The voices were raised as they were now arguing. Finian put a hand out to grip Chatillon's arm.

'There are now more than two; they must have had others waiting near the castle. This is why they have come back to search.'

Chatillon squeezed his wrist to show that he understood and slowly and quietly drew his sword.

The walls of the enclosed gardens and ruins were built of limestone, so even in the faint moonlight, they could see the outline of their attackers silhouetted against them, as they came through the archway and spread out. Finian and Chatillon couldn't be seen amongst the dark foliage on the north-facing ivy-covered wall.

'There are five of them,' whispered Finian. 'Stay here until I shout, for it will give us an advantage if they think you've gone.' So saying, he stepped forward and loudly drew his sword. As he stepped out of the deep shadows, the rasping sound of the blade drew their attention. Moving down the chapel's side walls, he suddenly appeared in front of them.

'Are you looking for me? I'm afraid you'll be disappointed, gentlemen. The bounty on my head has been lifted. There will no longer be any gold for taking the head of Finian Ui Neill.'

One of the men gasped as he recognised the name. 'No one told us we were taking on the Irishman,' he muttered. Finian thought he was a local man from the accent.

'So who will be first?' he asked, but no one moved.

CHAPTER TWELVE

The taller man stepped forward. 'It isn't you that we want, but your master, Piers De Chatillon. Although I know you were there when Sheikh Ishmael's son was murdered, I think he would also be happy to hear of your death. He may even reward us for it,' he said, turning to grin at his men while trying to allay their fears about taking on the Irish warrior.

Finian grunted with amusement. 'His son attacked us in a sea battle, and he was trying to kidnap our women. We did what any red-blooded warrior would have done. Indeed you would have done the same yourself,' he suggested, leaning on his sword to allay their fears of a sudden attack. 'Also, Chatillon isn't here. He will be now safe in the house of his wealthy mistress on the other side of the river, and I know she has at least twenty well-trained men within her walls.' He saw the men look at each other in doubt and then at their leader, who kept his eyes on Finian and didn't speak.

'If you stay, I will kill at least three of you in the first minutes. You know my reputation.' He pointed his sword at the smaller man. 'Is that what you want?'

The leader was not convinced. 'How did he escape so quickly? We would have seen him.'

Finian laughed. 'We spotted you long before we reached the tavern. If I were you, I would think about a change of career. The tavern has an outside staircase at the side, and he ran up that and back into the tavern to watch you leave. Feel free to search here if you don't believe me, but if any man comes near me, I'll kill him.'

The tall hawk-nosed leader indicated to two of his men that they should search in, and around, the ruined chapel.

Chatillon, who had heard everything, stepped over an empty window sill and quietly dropped to the floor inside the chapel.

He saw the shape of the smaller man entering and walking up the nave, scanning from left to right. As he reached the large rectangular altar stone, he didn't see the dark crouched figure that rose behind him. Within seconds he was pulled back over, a hand clamped over his mouth while a dagger was thrust under his rib cage and into his heart. Chatillon held him tight for a few moments until he felt the struggling body slump, and he lowered it to the floor without a sound. He crossed to the other side of the chapel, leaving through a narrow stone doorway whose wooden door had long been stolen.

This placed him behind the second man searching the ruins in the dim light amongst the large stones that had fallen against the ivy-covered wall. The deep carpet of leaves would have been a problem as he crept forward, but fortunately, it had rained recently, and they were wet. Just as Chatillon reached him, his arms raised to grab his hair, pull back his head and slit his throat, the man turned.

The attacker ducked forward in shock, and Chatillon's dagger met nothing but air. The attacker let out a shout as Chatillon launched himself at him and pinned him first to a rough stone block but then managed to push him to the ground and kneel on his chest. They struggled for what seemed like an eon, as the man gripped Chatillon's wrist to prevent the dagger from descending. The sound of clashing blades now filled the air behind them, and the harsh sounds echoed off the walls of the enclosed space.

The attackers' leader had been undecided, as his men went off to search, but when the shout came from behind the long ruined chapel, he knew immediately that the Papal Envoy was still hidden.

'Kill him,' he shouted to his two men as they surged forward to take on the Irish Warrior.

Finian flicked his wrist and sent the first man's sword flying across the grass before he ran him through. The second was decapitated as Finian leapt, and whirled, taking his head off his shoulders. Finian smiled as he saw the panic on the Saracen leader's face, for he was left alone to face this formidable swordsman. At that moment, an out-of-breath Chatillon appeared at Finian's side, and without a word, the man turned and fled.

Chatillon rested a hand on Finian's shoulder 'Thank you,' he murmured, taking a deep breath.

'I have a feeling they will be back, Chatillon. You need to take care. I will do what I can, but we could do with someone to take Edvard's place at your side, until he returns. Meanwhile, I'll send all of my men out to scour the city tonight for this Saracen. If he's still here, we will find him.'

'I promise I'll be vigilant, Finian, but alas, you'll not be here either. Robert has asked that you sail to England. He needs a trusted and competent warrior at Odo's side; not only a paid sword but also a strategist to assess the plans that Odo makes. Also, we need Earl William De Warenne dealing with as soon as he has delivered his false message to William Rufus. I want his throat cut, Finian. Find an opportunity to kill this traitor for me.'

Finian was silent for a while as they emerged from the chapel and walked back towards the castle. 'Do I have a choice about going to England?' he asked in an amused voice, but Chatillon could hear the cynicism there.

'Not really, and it may well play into our hands to have you there in the heart of things. I was hoping you could establish a larger network of informers over there, so take some baskets of pigeons. I also have a message from the Pope for Archbishop Lanfranc, to be given into his hands only. The Pope wants to ensure that the clergy of England back Robert if the invasion succeeds. I'll supply you with the usual bag of silver for payments and bribes. I want you to find an intelligent but greedy man close to the King. A clerk would be best. Pay him well for information with an offer of much more if he can set up a network.'

Finian smiled. 'I know how it works, Piers. I will do as you ask. When do I sail?'

'Tomorrow! Take twenty men with you,' answered Chatillon and Finian burst into laughter, which echoed around the gatehouse and bailey, as they strode through the massive gates.

'I had better go and pack my chest!' he shouted over his shoulder while shaking his head, and Chatillon smiled, pleased to have Finian back in their lives.

Chatillon did admit to a certain amount of relief as he entered the Great Hall of the castle, which he knew was ridiculous. If they wanted him dead, then assassins could be anywhere. However, he pushed it to the back of his mind as a messenger awaited him. He took and unfolded the paper, which told him that Prince Leopold of Swabia would be arriving in Ghent this week for a short stay. Chatillon poured himself a glass of wine as he mulled over that information and its opportunities.

He'd gone out of his way to punish the people behind his torture and incarceration in Prague castle and for the murder of the Legation and Pope Alexander. He'd laid misinformation and rumours of plots and betrayal around Duke Welf, which had led to the Duke being ostracised from the court and suffering the loss of the Duchy of Bavaria. The mistress and son of Bishop Jaromir had been poisoned with figs—a clear message to say they knew how Pope Alexander was killed. Count Beno lived with a poison-induced bloody flux he'd suffered for years, weakening him and making him shake. Chatillon had let them live but ensured that they had suffered. However, now he knew he wanted the unsavoury, murderous, slippery Leopold dead, who had managed to escape the attempts on his life. Now he had the chance to bring it all to an end. He was waiting for this opportunity, and he'd send Isabella and Edvard to Ghent.

He decided that she would pose as Bianca's Italian cousin, saying she was there to close up and sell her cousin's house. Once there, she'd lure the womanising Leopold into her net, and with the newly acquired skills she'd learnt in Paris, she would kill him. Chatillon smiled at the thought.

13

Chapter Thirteen

Isabella sat in the long narrow room entranced. It was the second day she'd spent with this intriguing man. Edvard had told her a little of his history. Ahmed was an Arab physician who had arrived in Paris nearly forty years ago. He let it be known that he came from an area known as the Levant. The truth was that Ahmed had fled Aleppo due to rumours of alchemy. Al-Dawla Thimal, the powerful Governor of Aleppo, had imprisoned him to force him to demonstrate how to transmute base metals into gold. With the help of a guard whose daughter Ahmed had cured, he escaped and fled to Europe. Once there, he established a practice as a physician in Paris, which came to the attention of King Henry I, who used him as a court physician and set him up inside the grounds of the palace. A year ago, his brother Alam, who ran an apothecary's shop in the city, had died. Ahmed sought the King's permission to move back to the city's winding streets. He now ran a thriving establishment, providing lotions and potions for the middling classes, and wealthier noblemen.

However, that was a fraction of his trade. Chatillon and

various others were his main customers, as he specialised in over forty different poisons of differing strengths. He'd recently bought a pleasant house in the south of the city with his money and set up his larger workshop there.

When he received Chatillon's request, he smiled. Since those early days in Paris, he'd become firm friends with the Papal Envoy. Ahmed had two things that Chatillon required, loyalty and discretion, and he paid Ahmed a high price for both. As various reports of the deaths of counts, princes, and even a Pope filtered into the back streets of Paris, Ahmed could recognise Chatillon's stamp upon them. Most of the time, it was Ahmed who had provided the means.

Now he had Chatillon's beautiful wife in his workshop for four days. As instructed by his friend, he was teaching Isabella everything she needed to know about poisons, their uses, the symptoms and the time they took to work. She was interested, asked questions, and absorbed the information like a sponge.

Today's lesson was on plants, and he handed her a pair of leather gloves before carrying a wide trug basket to the table.

'Many of the plants I'll show you today are exceptionally poisonous. Their leaves, stems, berries, and sap often leave disfiguring burns. But often, the most poisonous part is the root which we grate and then press or squeeze out the precious drops of liquid in the plant press, which I will show you.'

Isabella pulled on the long supple leather gloves, which came almost to her elbows. Ahmed donned the same, and they both wore coarse, heavy aprons covering their clothes. Edvard sat on a stool at the end of the wide wooden bench. In front of him was a container of goat's milk, mixed with vinegar, and a sponge lay beside it. If a noxious substance accidentally splashed either at any point, he'd be at hand to immediately wipe or soak the skin.

This was the one mixture that Ahmed found to be efficacious in minimising the effect of poison splashed on the skin.

Ahmed laid the different plants out along the bench, naming them as he did so. 'We will only use the well-known and more poisonous varieties. This is Water Hemlock, also known as devil's blossom. The seeds of this plant are highly poisonous. Initially, they cause dizziness and numbness in the body, so just one or two seeds can be very useful to incapacitate someone for a short time.' Ahmed handed her a cluster of seeds and indicated the pestle and mortar beside her. 'Grind one seed and then a second to see the proportion you need.' He waited until she'd done that and then spooned it onto a small board, moving it into a pile the size of a small pea. 'Now grind three more!' She obeyed, and he added it to the rest. 'You now have enough to trigger what I call waking suffocation. It paralyses the body slowly over twenty-four hours, particularly the lungs and throat, and the victim will die trying to gasp for their last breath. A good choice if you want your enemy to suffer.'

Isabella's eyes widened, and Ahmed smiled. She was proving to be an interested and apt pupil. 'Now repeat all of that back to me,' he demanded, and Isabella did, word for word.

They moved on to deadly nightshade, which she knew as Belladonna, but Edvard admitted that he called it dwale. Then Ahmed introduced foxgloves or digitalis, which could cause disorientation and heaviness in limbs, rendering the victim almost immobile. However, a large amount of this would produce seizures and death.

He'd saved the most lethal until last. Isabella recognised the plant but couldn't name it; however, Edvard could. 'As garden plants, they are very pretty and called aconites. Most people don't realise how toxic they are to animals and humans.'

Ahmed nodded enthusiastically. 'Its common names are Monkshood or Wolfsbane, as it has put an end to several dogs who have merely brushed past it in the woods, and then licked the pollen from their fur. It will cause immediate pain in the limbs and suffocation. It is often used to poison the enemy's wells during a siege. However, it is the root that's formidable. He handed her a plant and told her to carefully separate the root and grate it. He did the same until they had a substantial pile. He waved at Edvard to bring a contraption from the laden shelves on the wall, and Isabella looked at it with interest.

'It is a miniature fruit press!' she exclaimed.

'It is indeed,' he said, unscrewing the top, and Isabella helped him place the pulp inside. He slotted a wooden slab in and, replacing the top, began turning the handle to crush the pulp. In what seemed like only moments, the first drops of the syrupy sap began to run into the container below. Isabella gazed down at the deadly liquid, as Ahmed asked Edvard to remove the press into the yard. He explained that his servant would remove the pulp, spread it out to dry and then grind it into a toxic powder that could be mixed with food.

'The tiniest drop possible would kill a sparrow in a moment, a rabbit in only slightly more time. Monkshood is known as the queen of all poisons, causing an instant erratic heartbeat and difficulty breathing, before death within an hour. Today's poisons will kill fairly instantly, and tomorrow we will look at fungi such as Fly Agaric that give a poisoner twenty-four hours to escape.'

Although disappointed that the session was ending, it was quite hot in the workshop, and there was sweat on Isabella's brow. She needed some air. She climbed off the stool and reached to wipe her brow with her wrist.

Ahmed almost screeched, 'No!' and grasped her wrist in a hard grip.

Edvard, too, let out the breath he'd been holding.

'Never, ever, touch your skin with the gloves you've used; they must be burnt immediately.'

Isabella was pale and shaken and allowed Ahmed to pull off the gloves and drop them into a sack on the floor. Edvard, shaking his head, escorted her into the garden. 'You would have been dead in minutes. Then Chatillon would have killed me!' he exclaimed.

She looked contrite. 'I did not think,' she admitted.

'Come, you'll need to make ready for tonight at the palace.' She followed meekly behind him to the horses.

She'd decided to give herself to the King tonight, so she must dress carefully. As she sat in her chemise in her chamber that afternoon, she thought through her strategy. Philip was a highly astute man, not someone to be taken in by the wiles of a woman. She needed to give him information he didn't have to get her desired response of information in return. Suddenly she smiled as one or two interesting facts sprang to mind.

Isabella looked stunning as she entered the King's hall that night. She wore a green silk overdress embroidered in gold. She'd daringly left off her chemise, and every curve was outlined as she moved. She heard audible gasps as she walked slowly down the Great Hall towards the dais to make her bow to the King. She'd also piled her thick blond hair high in a Greek style. She could see that she certainly had King Philip's attention as she swayed towards him. He sat forward in his chair to watch her approach, and she could almost feel the heat from his gaze as it travelled over her body. His tongue moistened his lips as he welcomed her, and he demanded that she sit next to him at dinner. She lowered her eyes and demurely agreed.

Young William De Warenne watched spellbound; he'd tasted her delights and wanted to again. 'Well, that's her in the King's bed and no chance for the rest of us now,' said the young French nobleman beside him.

'Why is that?' asked William naively.

'No one touches the King's mistresses if you want to keep the ballocks between your legs!'

De Warenne's eyes returned to her as the King took her arm and led her to dinner.

'Who is she?' asked another awed young man behind him. 'She's breathtaking!'

'Isabella,' answered De Warenne, almost caressing the word as he said it.

'She is Isabella De Chatillon. King Philip is certainly brave to even think of dipping his plough in that furrow. He will need food tasters for the rest of his life!' answered Ettienne de la Ferte.

De Warenne paled. 'Chatillon?' he whispered, not sure he'd heard correctly. 'The Papal Envoy? The assassin? Surely she cannot be his wife.'

'Yes indeed, they were married recently. My father is an old friend and was at the wedding in Genoa. Piers De Chatillon is a master swordsman and is rumoured to be the most highly-paid assassin in Europe. He once fought more duels in six months than most noblemen fight in a lifetime, and he won every one of them.'

De Warenne felt his mouth dry as the thoughts raced around his head. *What have I done? What did I tell her? Will she tell him?* he thought, making for the door outside. He needed air. He needed to breathe. Suddenly, he heard a noise and found Isabella's huge manservant beside him. Edvard had watched with amusement as young De Warenne had discovered Isabella's identity from Gervais's son, Ettienne. The emotions had raced across De Warenne's face, plain to see. He'd watched him dash for the door and had followed where he found him outside on a balcony, his hands gripping the stone balustrade, while gulping in air.

'I want you to leave Paris tomorrow, De Warenne. If you do, I promise Piers De Chatillon might never hear that you were his wife's lover. I watched you seduce her, pin her unwillingly against the rose arch, and I could tell him everything. If I find out tomorrow that you're still here, I'll send a missive to him immediately.'

William found that, although his mouth was open, he couldn't speak and was sweating with fear to his embarrassment.

'I will make arrangements to leave tomorrow, making my bow to the King in the morning. I'll make an excuse and head for the coast to take a ship, I swear.'

Edvard nodded in satisfaction and began to turn away, then stopped. 'Oh, and if I hear one word from you to impugn the Lady Isabella's reputation, either now or in the future, I will personally find you, and I promise I will rip your tongue out!'

William stood terrified on the balcony for some time, his hands still gripping the balustrade. His legs wouldn't move. He realised what he'd done and now had to leave, even though he hadn't received the assurances of support from King Philip that William Rufus wanted. However, he'd seen the gleam in the French King's eyes at the mention of English gold, and there were possibilities, so the trip was not a complete loss. William would describe the King's response to Ranulph Flambard. He'd certainly know what to do with that information, and his reputation might be saved.

14

Chapter Fourteen

Things didn't pan out as Isabella expected in the King's chambers....

After removing his outer surcoat, Philip dismissed the servants and poured wine for them. He then waved her over to sit by the fire.

'Pull off my boots, please, Isabella,' he said, holding up a foot. She smiled, recognising the ploy for what it was. She knelt at his feet and placed her hands on his thighs. His eyes widened as she caressed the powerful muscles in his legs and then ran her hands down to his strong calves. She unlaced the sides of the soft leather boots and peeled them off, placing them neatly beside his chair. She remained, eyes downcast, kneeling between his feet. Then he reached out a hand and pulled the pins from her hair for it to cascade down over her shoulders. She could feel her heart thumping with a mix of apprehension and anticipation. The silence seemed to go on forever as he gazed down at her.

'Chatillon is a very lucky man to have a beauty like you in his bed every night. However, I've always found that my friend

Chatillon makes his own luck.' He smiled at her and raised her to her feet between his legs. He reached down and placed the hem of the green silk gown into her hands. 'Take it off,' he whispered, which she did, dropping it onto the floor.

For the first time, Isabella felt shy. She was standing naked in front of a man she hardly knew, but this man was the King of France, who was never denied anything. She stood as a wave of panic rose in her chest while still, he gazed at her. Then he pulled her down onto his lap.

'So, Isabella De Chatillon, tell me, have you ever been in love? I mean deeply in love, not just the calf love of a young girl for a young boy.'

'Yes, Sire, I truly love my husband, Piers,' she answered.

His hands ran over her naked body, and as he caressed her, he looked at her speculatively. 'So why do I find you so willing to be here with me, sharing your very obvious charms?'

She hesitated for a moment and then gave a slow smile. 'Our dalliance is pure pleasure, Sire, and is no threat to my husband.' To her consternation, he burst out laughing.

'You're very amusing, Isabella, and I'm sure you'll become a perfect foil, and very useful consort, to my friend Chatillon. However, although I intend to enjoy our pleasure together, we both know why you're here in my chamber.'

It was her turn to laugh, and he smiled as she threw her head back and enjoyed the moment. 'I suggest, Sire, that we do something about this first,' she said, her hand dropping between his legs to his large erection. 'Then I shall share some interesting information with you, and I would be grateful if you would share your intentions about King William Rufus with me.'

He grinned in delight at her audacity and then groaned softly as her hand moved back and forth. She leaned forward and kissed him, her tongue entering his mouth, and he suddenly stood, holding a naked Isabella in his arms. He moved them both towards the bed, and she watched him through lowered lids as he removed his clothes. He was a similar age to Chatillon, but there the resemblance ended. He was still a handsome man, but was thickening around the waist, whereas Piers was all muscle from his hours of sessions with Edvard, and his men, most mornings. She tied a silk sheath to his manhood, which he admired, not having seen that type before. Then she closed her eyes and thought of Piers as the King laid her on the bed, knelt between her legs and took her.

The next day Isabella walked her horse through the gates of Ahmed's country house. It was her last session with the learned physician, and she felt a poignancy about it. She'd enjoyed his instruction and the stories from his youth and travels across North Africa. What a week it had been, bedding English lords, French courtiers and a king. Chatillon talked about 'the game'; now she knew what he meant. It was all an act, a performance that differed depending on where she was or who she was with, and she had to admit that she loved it.

Last night, after they had made love, she'd stayed with King Philip, reclining on his large bed, and they had chatted and laughed like old friends. Then he became serious, and raising her hand to his lips, he asked, 'So what do you have for me, my beautiful Isabella?'

She had told him about Robert's secret deal with his brother Henry—gold for land in Normandy. Philip had been shocked.

'Is Robert mad to give away chunks of his territory that he has waited so long for?' he asked, climbing off the bed and pacing across the room. She watched him with interest as she remembered Piers saying that gaining more land was everything to King Philip. She knew he also had designs on absorbing Normandy into France, and he was purely playing a waiting game while the brothers fought between themselves.

'It was the means to an end, Sire. Duke Robert found the invasion far more costly than he expected and was dangerously short of funds. This move allows him to continue and, hopefully, be successful. Also, if he wishes, he can always reclaim the Cotentin lands when he pleases. His brother Henry does not have the support or resources to stand against him.'

The King stopped pacing and looked thoughtful as he absorbed what she said. 'You are an astute and clever woman Isabella. You aren't just repeating what you've heard as you obviously grasp the situation.'

She inclined her head at the compliment. 'So, Sire, will you also support Robert Curthose against his brother, William Rufus? The Pope believes it is a just cause and has sent some financial support.'

At this point, Isabella had to look away and suppress the desire to laugh. The naked King of France stood across the room from her, his hands on his hips, weighing up her words and making a decision that could make or break Robert's invasion. The crux of the matter was that Duke Robert needed to know that Normandy was safe during his absence and that Philip would protect and respect his borders.

The King returned to the bed and sat down. 'I will not officially recognise the claim of William Rufus to the throne of England or provide any support for him when his brother, Robert, invades.'

Isabella thanked him and swung her long naked legs off the bed. She reached for her gown on the floor.

'Are you leaving already?' the King asked in surprise. Usually, his mistresses stayed the night with him. Isabella gave him a sweet smile, as she pulled her gown back into place.

'Sire, I've very much enjoyed your company tonight, but we both know this liaison was about more than the pleasure it gave us. If I spent the night, I worry that you and I might become more attached to each other than would be wise. We both know that neither your wife nor Piers De Chatillon would be happy with that arrangement.'

King Philip had laughed. 'You've a wise head on those delightful Italian shoulders, Isabella. I look forward to our next liaison as it is a far more pleasurable way to exchange information.'

She gave a tinkling laugh, and he walked over and kissed her on both cheeks. Then she bowed and left, leaving him looking thoughtfully after her.

The next day she was walking around the physic garden with Ahmed. He grew the poisonous plants in a small area surrounded by a wattle fence. He made Isabella identify and describe the effects of each one. He beamed with pleasure at her correct responses before leading her to a stone outbuilding, in the sun, at the end of the garden. Inside was a large array of pots and covered baskets on a wide table. The large oval pots were covered in a thin linen cloth tied tightly around the rim. Again, he handed her long, supple gloves, which she pulled on.

'So this is the last area of expertise you need, my lady, and certainly one to be handled with care.' He stepped forward and, removing a linen cloth, waved her over. She warily looked inside to see a bed of damp moss and two large toads. She audibly let out the breath she'd been holding, and Edvard smiled.

'These can be very useful for incapacitating someone for a day or two. The large poison sacs are behind the eyes.' He lifted the larger of the two toads and held it in his palm. Reaching for a small flat wooden spatula, he showed her how to press the sacks to release the poison. She was surprised at how much came out. Ahmed nodded. 'It is also odourless so that it can be dripped into wine or food. Your husband, Piers, uses it to remove someone he doesn't want at a meeting or negotiation. Is that not so, Edvard?'

The big man nodded.

Ahmed continued, 'It is only life-threatening if you use a lot of it, both sacs. I've noticed that it can severely affect the heart's beat, similar to foxgloves. It is also useful for affecting a man's ability in bed if you don't want him to perform. I know several ladies who carry a vial of this substance because they are tired of their husband's advances. A few drops will suffice,' he said, smiling while Isabella looked across at Edvard and giggled.

He opened several other baskets describing the small lizards and frogs until he finally picked up a long forked stick and asked them to stand back. He removed the woven lid of a large basket. At first, nothing happened as Edvard and Isabella watched in trepidation and anticipation. Then slowly, a large snake emerged. It was as long as she was tall, and it raised its head and regarded them with a silent, unblinking stare. Isabella stepped to one side and noticed that the snake's head moved to watch her.

'I call him Khalid, after one of the greatest undefeated Muslim warriors of all time,' said Ahmed removing the leather glove from his left hand. With one finger, he stroked the flat head of the snake, which swayed slightly with pleasure. 'The other attribute he has of the original Khalid, apart from aggression, is that he lulls you into a feeling of false security. He has been with me for seven years; I almost think of him as a pet. However, to him, I'm still the enemy. Watch,' he said, removing his finger from the snake's head.

In a flash, the snake struck, burying his fangs deeply into the back of Ahmed's hand. Isabella jumped back with a shriek, and even the imperturbable Edvard recoiled. Ahmed, however, calmly gripped the snake's mouth on either side and pulled the fangs out of his hand. Two bleeding puncture wounds could be seen.

'Now, while I have his mouth open, come here, and I'll show you the poison sacs I emptied an hour before you arrived.' They both breathed a sigh of relief and watched with interest as he demonstrated how to release the poison. He then gently placed the snake back into the basket. Opening the lid of a large wooden box, he extracted a live mouse and dropped it into the basket, replacing the heavy lid. Isabella watched wide-eyed as the snake thrashed around in the basket. 'Khalid prefers to catch and kill them himself. He likes them warm and fresh.' explained Ahmed, and Isabella could hear the affection in his voice.

Finally, he led them to a smaller basket and, putting his glove back on, he turned and smiled at Isabella. 'And these are yours!' he said.

She leaned forward and, carefully removing the lid, saw three smaller snakes. 'There are two males and one female. Like Khalid, they are from the aspis family, which can include the Egyptian cobra, the asp or smaller vipers like these. Don't be taken in by their smaller size; they are about three years old, and the female will be producing offspring anytime now. Once bitten by one of these, instant pain, confusion, convulsions, and death will follow. They do give you a warning, for when threatened, a small hood will open at the back of the head. Be warned, they are very aggressive and will attack across quite a distance, often propelling themselves through the air. Remember, no matter how fond you become of them, you can never trust them!'

Edvard stepped forward and peered into the basket, a look of concern on his face. He hadn't realised they would be taking these snakes with them. 'Is it true that one of these can kill something as huge as an elephant in only three hours?' he asked.

Ahmed nodded. 'I witnessed it myself while travelling the northern plains of Africa.'

The silence that followed this information spoke volumes as they regarded the three snakes with apprehension. 'Pick one up,' said Ahmed. Isabella's eyes flashed to Edvard for reassurance, and he reluctantly nodded.

'Do it firmly but not so you hurt or alarm them,' advised Ahmed, demonstrating with the smaller male. Isabella did as she was told, holding the larger male behind the head. Surprisingly, looking at him, she felt a sudden affinity with this snake. He had more distinctive markings on his head. 'He is a beauty, isn't he?' commented Ahmed, as the snake wrapped his tail firmly around her wrist, and she stroked his head.

'I will call those two Antony and Cleopatra, and they will

become my first breeding pair,' she announced, to Edvard's surprise.

'And what will you call him?' asked Ahmed regarding her with interest and pointing to the large male.

'Why Octavian, of course. He defeated Antony and Cleopatra and became one of the greatest Emperors of Rome as Augustus.'

Both men laughed at her wit.

'They will eat rodents, small birds, lizards and frogs but only feed them once a month, to keep them lively, and remember to empty the poison sacs, Edvard.'

The big man shook his head in amusement. Snake keeper was not in his job description, but he would find a bright young man who would relish the job.

'I believe you're now travelling to Ghent, and apparently, you'll be taking Octavian with you,' said Ahmed helping her put the snake back in its basket.

Isabella turned to Edvard. 'Is that true?' she asked with surprise.

'Yes, a message came from Piers this morning. He has business there that he wants you to deal with,' replied Edvard looking at Ahmed in surprise, as he'd just found this out himself.

They bid farewell to Ahmed and mounted their horses.

Isabella closed her eyes; she had been looking forward to returning to her husband's side. Now she was going northwest to Flanders, with more weeks of travel and further away from Piers. The next morning they bade farewell to King Philip and headed for Ghent and the court of Count Robert of Flanders.

Chapter Fifteen

The sound of the horses' hooves changed as Finian and his men rode across the old wooden bridge, from Southwark to London. It was busy as usual, with dozens of carts, wagons and riders going back and forth. They were forced to stop for some time to let a dray laden with barrels of ale pass, and Finian relaxed for a moment and glanced down the broad River Thames. Due to the river's wide loop, he couldn't see Thorney Island, where the Palace of Westminster and its Abbey had been built. It would take them another hour or two to get there, and Archbishop Lanfranc, at Canterbury, had assured him that Bishop Odo was still there.

It was almost twelve years since Finian had been in the city. Before returning to Ireland, he'd spent a few weeks here and could see the changes. Almost every available space seemed to be built on; bigger, more prosperous merchant's houses had sprung up, many with their own access to the river. The streets seemed far noisier and crowded, with more hawkers, beggars and groups of young apprentices up to mischief. He glanced back and could see the wide-eyed expression on some of the faces of his men, the ones who had never been in a teeming city before.

He waved them on, and soon they left behind the narrow, stinking streets. They followed the busy rutted road for a while, with its clusters of hovels and houses, but then happily cantered along the open meadows on the riverbanks. The imposing buildings of Westminster came into sight, and they were challenged as they reached the well-guarded gates. Finian explained their purpose, and they were shown into the large bailey, under guard, while a message was sent to Bishop Odo.

Finian glanced around; the buildings were an impressive sight. He knew that the palace and Westminster Abbey had been built by King Edward the Confessor on the site of an older, smaller palace, but he'd never seen it before. Now, Westminster Hall towered ahead of them, and Finian noticed that the high stone encircling walls went right down to the river, where dozens of boats plied back and forth delivering goods and passengers. He knew the River Thames would be a far quicker and safer route than the roads.

After some time, two manservant's in Bishop Odo's livery appeared, one being his Steward, who recognised Finian.

'Lord Ui Neill, we were not expecting you. We are shortly to leave the palace.'

Finian sighed. 'Well, my men and horses need food and rest for several hours first. Where is the Bishop heading?'

'We go to York with the King and the Royal Council. I'll take you to Bishop Odo.'

'Good, as I have several missives for him.' Finian dismounted and indicated to his men to do the same. Then he took a large leather pouch from his saddlebag and followed

CHAPTER FIFTEEN

the Steward towards the impressive entrance. Odo was sitting with the Prince Bishop of Durham, William St Calais, in his chambers when Finian was shown into the richly furnished room. He greeted the Irish warrior warmly, waving him to a seat, as Finian handed him the folded vellum sheets.

The Bishop read in silence the message from his nephew, Duke Robert, explaining why he was placing Finian by his side. The second message was from Chatillon, forewarning him of De Warenne's betrayal and the false plans he'd been fed. Odo regarded Finian with interest; he knew of his reputation, and he would certainly be useful.

'As far as I know, Earl William De Warenne hasn't arrived in Westminster to warn the King.'

'No, Chatillon ensured that he boarded the wrong ship. The Captain was paid to sail to Ghent first and then to London, so he should be a full week behind us.'

William de St Calais sat forward in concern. 'Does that mean we have to strike earlier?'

Finian gave the Prince Bishop a sharp glance. He knew that the man had been a firm supporter of King William I and had been amply rewarded with the Prince-Bishopric of Durham, but Finian didn't like the nervous stammer in his voice. However, Odo seemed unconcerned.

'No. We will proceed as expected. De Warenne may catch up with William Rufus at the end of our weeks in York. Then we will let Rufus muster his troops and travel north to meet what he thinks will be an invading force coming from Scotland. This gives us more time to prepare and more time for Robert's ships, full of men and weapons, to land on the south coast and take London and then Winchester.'

William de St Calais nodded but didn't look convinced;

he rubbed his hands together nervously, and Finian sent a questioning glance to Odo, who reassured the Prince Bishop.

'Calm yourself, William. We will be with the King in York, so he will not think for a second that we are involved in this plot. You're one of his main advisors on the council. He will never suspect you. Now go and pack, for I believe we leave in an hour.'

As soon as the door closed behind him, Finian turned to Odo. 'Are you sure he's with you in this rebellion? For he looked very uncertain to me.'

Odo waited until a servant had brought food and wine before answering. 'I know for certain that William de St Calais believes it is wrong that the Anglo-Norman lands were divided between the two brothers. He believes it weakens us, and he is, therefore, willing to publicly offer his support to Duke Robert Curthose as the eldest son, but he will not provide troops to fight against William Rufus.'

Finian shook his head in disbelief. 'So one of the most powerful men in the north, and we've his stamp of approval and nothing more.'

'Yes, but the support of the chief member of the Royal Council is worth its weight in gold when it comes to influencing others, who may be sitting on the fence.'

Finian didn't look convinced, but he applied himself to the food and wine while Odo called for his Steward, to give further orders for their journey north.

'Chatillon mentions that De Warenne's son is trying to garner support in Paris. Do we know the intentions of King Philip?'

'Yes, he will support the claim of Duke Robert,' said Finian, through a mouthful of roast fowl.

CHAPTER FIFTEEN

'That's a relief and adds further credence to Robert's claim. I believe that Count Robert of Flanders and Duke Alan of Brittany have also pledged support; is that correct?' asked Odo

Still applying himself to his food, Finian inclined his head before adding, 'If the weather holds fair and his armies arrive, I cannot see how Robert can fail with the support he has.'

'I assure you that I pray daily for a fair breeze. Rest your men and horses, Finian Ui Neill and follow us to York at your own pace. The King intends this as a 'Progress' through his country, so I imagine we will be travelling excruciatingly slowly.' So saying, he bade the Irish Warrior farewell, leaving him to finish his meal.

Four days later, they rode into York. Odo quietly told him that William Malet was now Sheriff here and supported Duke Robert and the rebellion. The castle at York had been built between the River Ouse and the River Foss but had been destroyed in 1069, after a joint attack on the Norman forces by the Vikings and northern rebels. However, King William had always recognised the importance of York. He had the castle rebuilt with a much larger bailey, including a large hall with chambers, a chapel, barracks, stores and blacksmiths. As they approached, Finian saw that a large moat and a lake now surrounded it. There were well-appointed chambers within the keep, and Odo stayed there while Finian and his men found accommodation in the bailey.

On that first night, there was a great feast for the new King and the Royal Council. It was a splendid affair, and Finian watched his men relax and enjoy the food, wine and entertainment. Finian watched the new King with interest. William Rufus was not attractive and seemed to have few social graces. He was nicknamed Rufus for his ruddy complexion. He was stocky with a protruding belly and lank hair, parted in the middle. Odo had also told him that he was not popular with the church either, as he'd little morality or religious piety. What did surprise Finian, who was used to the warrior kings and princes of Europe, was that William dressed in flamboyant, almost foppish clothes.

On the King's right sat Odo, his Uncle, but on the King's left was Ranulph Flambard, one of the King's advisors and a close friend, if stories of wild parties and excessive drinking were to be believed. Finian had heard much about this ambitious, rapacious man. Odo had previously employed him as a clerk, but he soon came to the King's attention and rapidly rose through the ranks. Odo believed that William Rufus was held in sway to Flambard, whom he seemed to almost caress, an arm often thrown around his shoulders. There was no doubt, however, that he was effective. The man was financially ruthless, constantly increasing taxes and stealing land, to raise funds for the King.

William de St Calais sat on the other side of Odo, and to Finian's eyes, the man didn't look at ease. He was drinking too much and throwing nervous glances at the King. Fortunately, William Rufus was too fully occupied with Flambard, and the Sheriff, to notice. Finian sat back and finally began to relax. He filled his goblet, drained it and asked for more just as a commotion began near the large doors. His hand went to his sword, and he stood to have a better view, as he was tasked to both protect Odo and facilitate the invasion. To his dismay, he saw Earl William De Warenne striding up the hall, looking exhausted. Finian's eyes widened in surprise. He could only think that instead of going to London as expected, he must have persuaded, or bribed, the Captain to sail directly from

Ghent to the northeast coast, probably up the Humber Estuary. He was here almost two weeks earlier than expected.

Knowing that De Warenne would recognise him as Chatillon's man, Finian sat down again to watch developments. Odo sat narrow-eyed, watching him approach, while William de St Calais was wide-eyed and gripping the table in alarm.

As De Warenne neared the King, he shouted, 'Treachery Sire! Treachery is afoot!' William Rufus had partaken of a great deal of wine and sunk in his chair; he simply regarded him with a smile and a raised hand, taking little notice of what De Warenne was saying in his high strained voice.

'We are delighted that the Earl of Surrey can join us. We thought you were in Normandy,' he slurred.

Ranulph Flambard, who hadn't imbibed half of the amount of wine, now stood. 'De Warenne, what is this? Explain yourself to the King!'

The older man stopped and drew several breaths. 'I've been with your brother, the Duke, Sire, and I've uncovered his plot to steal your throne!'

Finian could see the King trying to focus on what was being said.

'What do you mean?' he spluttered, pulling himself up in his chair.

'Robert Curthose has allied himself with King Malcolm of Scotland, and they will be marching over the border to seize the throne of England, which he thinks is rightfully his, as the eldest son. I heard them say that most of the nobles in England and Normandy supported this rebellion.'

'Rubbish!' shouted Odo, standing up. 'Where did you get such lies? I don't believe Robert would ever ally with the Scottish King. He fought and defeated him at Falkirk. You're confused, or someone has been feeding you jests.'

'I tell you what I heard is true and ask yourself, who is missing here tonight? Which members of the Royal Council and court are absent?' he asked, his eyes sweeping the hall and top tables. 'Where is your Uncle, Robert Mortain? Where is the Earl of Shrewsbury and his sons or Hugh Grandesmil? I tell you they are coming to depose you!' he shouted, spittle dripping from his chin with the emotion of it all.

Flambard glanced around the faces in the hall, which was packed. This was not a conversation to have here. 'Come, De Warenne, join us in the solar above, with the council members here, and you can tell us calmly what you know.'

They headed for the stairs, but William de St Calais stayed in his seat and grasped Odo's arm. 'We must stop this madness. We can never succeed, and if Flambard finds out we are involved in treason, he will kill us!'

Odo glanced around and took his hand. 'Come, nothing like that will happen. You need to listen to De Warenne and say very little. You're on the outside of this plot. You aren't actively fighting against William Rufus, but when Duke Robert lands here shortly, he will need you by his side in triumph.' Instead of calming William de St Calais, this seemed to agitate him further until Odo, who never suffered fools, had to speak to him sharply and threaten him.

Finian watched this with concern, but Odo met his eyes and shook his head. Neither of them saw De Warenne's youngest son, Raynold, who had watched this interplay with interest. He was a rising young star in the court of William Rufus and could see an opportunity here, as William de St Calais was obviously rattled by something. He decided to go and share this with his father.

16

Chapter Sixteen

It would take them three days to reach Ghent, and Isabella didn't mind at all. She'd been provided with a spirited little palfrey that was a joy to ride, and she was enjoying the early summer sunshine. As she rode behind Edvard, she reflected on what she'd achieved in her week in Paris. Edvard had told her that Chatillon was delighted at the information she sent, giving her a flush of pride. She wanted to please her dark, enigmatic husband. She'd been told they would spend a week or so in Ghent and then take a ship to return to Caen, and she longed to be back with him. Her reverie was spoilt for a moment as she thought of him with the pretty, dark wife of Robert Mortain. She knew this was to be expected, but her stomach clenched at the thought of his hands on another woman's body.

Edvard rode back to her at that point, and she smiled up at him. 'How much further to the Abbaye?' she asked.

'I believe the Abbaye Sainte Marie is only about another three leagues. I'm told they make a famous cheese there, which is delicious.'

Isabella laughed at the expression on her bodyguard's face.

'I, too, am ravenous, Edvard.'

He grinned back. She really was a joy to be with; Chatillon was a very lucky man. How she'd changed from the petulant, demanding young woman who made her parents' life miserable. While others had seen a spoilt and disobedient daughter, he'd recognised a streak of rebellion and a thirst for adventure, away from her cloying life in Genoa. She'd blossomed in Chatillon's hands and was now spreading her wings. He prayed that this next assignment went well, for Chatillon was sending her to kill a man, not any man but a German prince. She might not return if it went badly, but he refused to contemplate that. At that moment, two of his outriders trotted up beside them.

'There are three men behind taking the same road as us, we've watched them, but they seem to be merchants by the baggage on the mules.'

Edvard stood in his stirrups and squinted into the distance across the flat Flanders countryside. 'Ride back occasionally and watch them. Check that there are always three men there.' They saluted Edvard and cantered off. He turned to find Isabella looking at him quizzically. 'Do not fear. I'm not concerned, as we've a dozen men with us. Come, let us make haste,' he said as he trotted on.

They reached the Abbaye Sainte Marie at dusk. Edvard had sent men ahead, so the Prioress was there to greet them. She was delighted to be hosting Isabella De Chatillon, the wife of the influential Papal Envoy, and a sumptuous meal was offered. A handful of other travellers were around the table, so there was good company and conversation. She knew some of them might be making for Ghent, so she asked the Prioress to keep her name quiet. The Prioress understood. She knew Chatillon's name could instill fear and apprehension.

They had just become seated when another traveller arrived, a wealthy merchant from far off Castile. He was a darkly handsome man with a distinct accent. These were undoubtedly the merchants that they had spied in the distance behind them. He seemed amiable and happy to talk about his home in Burgos and the goods he was trading.

'Chests of rare spices from the far east came from Muslim Spain. Aromatic oils from the middle east that last on a beautiful woman's skin for days,' he said, holding his audience rapt as he pulled out a cobalt blue, stoppered, glass vial and handed it around the table. Even the Prioress herself was not immune and dabbed a small amount on her wrist, to Isabella's delight. Isabella re-stoppered the bottle and passed it back to the merchant, who waved his hands in refusal.

'No, Lady Isabella, please keep it. Perfume such as this was made for a woman such as you!' Isabella blushed slightly and thanked him.

Edvard had watched the man and his two Castilian servants like a hawk. However, he seemed genuine enough, and his two men enjoyed the food and wine. Before long, one was asleep with his head on the table, and the other muttered he was off to find his bed in the stables, drunkenly making his way to the door. As the evening drew to a close, Edvard escorted Isabella up the narrow stone stairs to her room. It was commodious with a large shuttered window. It had certainly never been a penitent nun's cell.

She bade Edvard goodnight, placing her candle on the table, along with the small blue bottle of perfumed oil. She held the bottle up to the flame. It was an old design, and she'd never seen one of its like before. It was thin at the neck with a pretty blue ribbon, but it bellied out at the bottom, and when she held it up, she could see a distinctive mark; a triangle with a line through it. It was almost like the masons' marks she saw on the dressed stones of the cathedral. She cradled the bottle in her hand; it could be hundreds of years old. In her mind's eye, she could see the craftsman in the east carefully moulding the bottle, in the burning heat of a brazier, and then etching his mark onto the cooling glass.

The merchant had told them they came from Egypt, where a cache of them had been found. He'd bought them all and now kept them as perfume bottles, for women of noble birth. She took off her jewellery and silk scarf and placed them on the table, where she rubbed a small amount of the oil into the scarf. Blowing out the candle, she opened the large wooden shutters. It was a warm night, so she breathed in the cool night air for a while. Her room looked down onto the stables below, but it was a bright moonlit night, and she could see the mist-covered fields in the distance. She closed one of the shutters but left the other ajar to let in the slight breeze. In the shadows of the stable block, two men stood as statues and watched her.

Only one more day and they would be in Ghent, where she'd present herself as a cousin to Bianca Da Landriano. This had a grain of truth, as Bianca had been a distant cousin of her mother's family in Milan. She climbed into bed and pulled the cover up to her chin; it had been a long day in the saddle, and before long, she drifted into a deep sleep.

Isabella was unsure what woke her; at first, she thought she was too hot. However, for a few seconds, she opened her eyes, and the moonlight shone on the side of the bed. She blinked and realised that both shutters were wide open. Her first thought was that a gust of wind had blown them open, but

CHAPTER SIXTEEN

then she saw a dark figure outlined against the opening. She stifled a gasp and reached for the dagger that Edvard insisted she keep under her pillow. As her fingers closed on the hilt, she slowly and imperceptibly raised her knees towards her chest, so she could kick or strike out when he approached the bed. She heard him moving around the room, and from the distinct clink, she knew he was handling her jewellery on the table. He was a thief!

Then to her surprise and relief, she saw him swing a leg over the sill to leave. He sat for a few moments and surveyed the stables below so she could see his profile, before stepping out onto the roof below. She climbed out of bed. Dagger in hand, she went to the window. Using the shutter to shield herself, she watched him make his way along the stable roof before he dropped, lithely, to the courtyard below. Clinging to the walls of the building, he made his way swiftly to the corner before sprinting through the arch, leading to the trees beyond.

Isabella let out the breath she'd been holding. She scrabbled around on the table and, finding the tinderbox, lit the candle. Some of her jewellery was on the floor, but the rare pearl necklace from her mother was missing. So he was a thief, an opportunist; she realised that she'd recognised his profile. The high cheekbones, the jutting chin; it was Ferdinand, the Castilian merchant, but she was perplexed. Why would he give her such an expensive gift and then risk everything to steal a silver and pearl necklace? It made no sense. She closed and barred the shutters and stood pondering whether to wake Edvard. There was no doubt that the man would be long gone, so she decided to leave it until the morning. However, once in bed, unsurprisingly, sleep wouldn't come.

Isabella had just finished dressing when a knock came on

the door. He stood in the doorway and gave a half-apologetic smile. 'I know it is early, but we've a full day's ride to Ghent. I've sent two men ahead to inform the Steward of our arrival.' She nodded absentmindedly; she looked tired. 'Did you not sleep well?' he asked in concern.

'I had a visitor,' she said.

Edvard froze. 'Who?' he demanded.

'I was not sure at first. I thought it was just a thief until I saw him silhouetted in the window, and now I'm sure it was the Castilian merchant.'

Anger bubbled up inside Edvard. 'Did he touch you?' he whispered.

'No. But he stole my necklace, which my mother gave me on my wedding day.'

'May I?' he asked and walked into her room. Going to the shuttered window, he glanced down, and swore softly, as he saw how close the stable rooves were to her window. He blamed himself, as even though it was dusk when they arrived, he should have checked that.

'I watched him. He was like a cat in the way he softly crept across the rooves and dropped almost soundlessly onto the yard below before running for the trees. He made it look so easy.'

Edvard stood thoughtfully; Isabella said that she'd moved nothing, her small jewellery box was still open on the table, the scarf and cobalt blue bottle beside it.

'He took nothing else?' He looked at her soft leather saddle bags containing silver bags.

'No, I checked; they are untouched.'

'And you say he did not approach the bed?'

'I was asleep at first, but I'm sure I would have known had

he come near me.'

'Go down and break your fast with the Prioress. I'll go to the stables and ascertain exactly when our merchant left. Neither he nor his servants are in evidence this morning.'

She agreed and left him standing there, a frown on his face. After she'd gone, he searched the room thoroughly for any clue, but there was nothing. He didn't like it, not one bit, as it didn't make any sense.

When Isabella entered the refectory, many people were partaking of the Abbaye's hospitality. Platters of freshly baked bread and chunks of golden butter were side by side with trenchers of cold viands and cheeses. Jugs of fresh buttermilk and jugs of the weaker morning ale stood side by side. She took her place beside the Prioress and asked about the Castilian merchant.

'I've been told that he was suddenly called away last night. The gatekeeper tells me they woke him in the early hours, but fortunately, they left very quietly.'

Edvard stood in the stable yard; he'd just received the same information, but he was unsettled as nothing about this felt right. Why would a man like that risk everything to climb into a young noblewoman's room to steal a necklace? An expensive one, to be sure, but the man was obviously wealthy. So was it purely for the thrill of getting in and out undetected? He admitted that he'd watched Chatillon do the same with a gleam in his eye.

He strode back and forth in the courtyard. His men, waiting for orders, watched him uneasily. One of the braver men, a young tow-headed one, finally asked, 'Is there something amiss?' The unfortunate man got the full force of Edvard's anger in return.

'Amiss? Amiss? A thief steals into Lady Isabella's room in the middle of the night and steals her jewellery, yet not one of the twelve of us managed to see or hear him, despite some being on duty!' He glared at them. To give them their due, the men looked shocked. They would protect Isabella with their lives. Edvard, seeing their faces, relented slightly. He turned to the window and pointed as, on cue, Isabella flung the shutters wide before moving away to pack.

'He climbed onto the stable roof, stole her jewellery and crept out again like a cat,' he said.

'Or like an assassin,' said the tow-headed young man.

They all obediently followed the route with their eyes while Edvard repeated to himself, 'Or like an assassin...' Then he yelled, 'No! No!' and shouted Isabella's name up to the window. 'Isabella, get out, get out of that room!'

She appeared briefly at the window and then turned and ran, not knowing what she was running from in there. Edvard, with two of his men, appeared in the narrow stone corridor. Telling her to wait out there, the three of them entered the room.

'Pull on your gloves as there may be poison. We will search everywhere and every inch of the bedding and chests for scorpions or snakes.' They systematically searched it twice before Edvard reluctantly called a halt. They had found nothing.

'Have you found something? Was it a snake?' she asked, reappearing in the doorway.

Edvard shook his head. 'I have my suspicions that this man was here for something else, and yes, I imagined scorpions or snakes,' he said, his eyes still darting to every corner, as if waiting for them to scuttle out. He sent his two men out to ready the horses.

CHAPTER SIXTEEN

'Are you almost ready?' he asked. Isabella smiled at the big man.

'Yes, and perhaps we are wrong. He may not have been an assassin, and perhaps he just wanted the necklace for his own woman. It was unusual.' Edvard shrugged and watched as she folded her clothes. She picked up the blue bottle of perfumed oil and carried it to the light.

'Have you seen this, Edvard? It is possibly the mark of an ancient Egyptian craftsman. It is a triangle, but I think it is a pyramid.'

He moved to see what she meant but heard her whisper, 'No, it can't be! It is gone! It was there, I know it was, but now there's just a circle.'

Edvard took the bottle and held it to the light. He removed the stopper and got a faint sweet sickly smell of lavender and something else.

'I think I know why our friend was in your room,' he said, waving her away.

Instead of moving, she stepped forward and sniffed. 'Aconite or monk's hood; he has switched the bottles. If I hadn't decided to show you the Egyptian mark, I would have used some before I packed it away.'

'You would have been dead within the hour,' he said, holding the bottle at arm's length.

'It was the Sheikh, was it not?'

Edvard nodded. 'I suspect so; he seems relentless.'

She was quiet for a while. 'We need to kill him, Edvard. We need to lure him in and kill him.'

Edvard smiled at the ferocity in her voice. 'We will, Isabella, I promise you. Chatillon's rage will be something to behold when I tell him what happened here.' Suddenly Edvard raised the heel of his hand and hit his temple. 'Of course!' he shouted. 'That's it!' She looked at him in amazement. 'You are dead, Isabella. They succeeded! Get back into the bed under the covers. I am sending for the Abbaye's apothecary and the priest. As far as the Sheikh is concerned, you're dead, for if they think you're dead, they will not try again. I'm going to the kitchen for some flour. I want you white as a corpse,' he laughed.

Isabella knew what he was doing but was not completely convinced it would work, especially with an apothecary or physician coming to see her. However, she reckoned without the power of silver.

He returned with a small brush, a bowl of water and the Prioress, who had reluctantly been brought into the plot, although it had taken the promise of a yearly stipend to the Abbaye. By the time the priest arrived, he'd found a beautiful corpse on the bed, the apothecary was shaking his head, and the Prioress was on her knees, beginning the service for the dead. She greeted him with relief and sobbed that Piers De Chatillon's wife had been murdered, poisoned by foreigners, here in her Abbaye.

The priest leant forward, but the apothecary quickly waved him back as the poison they had used was virulent and might leak through the skin.

There was a cluster of servants around the door whom Edvard left for a while before finally shooing them away. By midday, it spread like wildfire throughout the local community—a noble lady poisoned by foreigners. Edvard was satisfied, and a bundle of covers was buried later that day. A man watched in the trees at the edge of the churchyard, before mounting his horse and galloping after his master. Ferdinand would be pleased that his plan had succeeded, and they would all be richly rewarded by Sheikh Ishmael.

Meanwhile, Isabella was dressed as a young man; her hair bound and tied in a cap and dark soot smeared on her cheeks to resemble stubble, from a distance. She rode off on the road to Ghent, amazed at how well the deception had worked. However, she was also astute.

'Did it cost us very much?' she asked.

Edvard smiled ruefully. 'I'll ensure you're there when I tell him exactly how much! I'll stand near the door when we tell him what we've promised the Prioress.'

Her laughter echoed around the tree-lined track as she kicked her horse into a canter.

She couldn't believe the freedom she felt dressed as a boy. She remembered the stories that Chatillon had told her about Ette, the wife of Morvan De Malvais. At the time, she was shocked to hear that this young woman had ridden into battle, but now she understood. They stopped at an inn for food, and it was as if she almost disappeared as a young stripling left holding the horses. Unfortunately, it would be short-lived, for they would soon be in Ghent, and she'd assume a completely different identity. Edvard could no longer be by her side, as he was known as Chatillon's servant.

Unfortunately for Edvard and Isabella, the priest who had attended was not local. He was staying at the Abbaye on his way to Paris. He stopped at Lille for a night and imparted the sad news about the poisoning of the Papal Envoy's wife to the bishop. He, in turn, sent commiserations to the Pope in Rome, asking him to send his condolences to Chatillon.

The Papal Envoy in question had just dispatched another informer, one of Count Mortain's young men. He'd followed him, as the man dared to make his way to his pigeon coop, on the roof with a message. As one of Mortain's squires, he'd know how to use the birds. Once on the battlements, Chatillon crept up behind him and garrotted him silently for his betrayal and let his body drop with a satisfying thump to the steps below. He'd taken the message from the man's fist. He saw it was to be sent to London, intended for De Warenne. So the Earl had infiltrated other households. He needed to pay for his treason; hopefully, Finian would make him do just that.

He now made his way to the bed of the lovely Almodis De Mortain, who was proving very useful. She was one of those rare women who listened to her husband's conversations and had a firm grip and understanding of European politics. He was to continue to enjoy her favours for several more nights, oblivious of the impending tragic news that was to arrive.

Chapter Seventeen

It was crowded in the solar as King William Rufus seated himself and Flambard waved the Norman nobility to sit if they could find a space. William de Warenne was still on his feet, but looking much shaken. He realised the magnitude of what he'd announced but hadn't expected disbelief from some senior figures in England.

'Bring a stool or chair for De Warenne before he falls down,' muttered William, who was still somewhat the worse for wear. Flambard always drank sparingly on these occasions, as he liked to watch and listen to others who may become indiscreet. A chair was brought, and Flambard took charge.

'Now, my Lord, tell us calmly about what you've seen and heard. You talk of treachery, but the court hasn't heard a whisper of it here. As far as we know, Duke Robert is in Caen, and he is stabilising his borders in Normandy against our old enemy, Fulk of Anjou.'

William De Warenne took a grateful gulp of wine. 'No, my Lord, you are behind the news. Duke Robert has just moved his capital to Rouen, but he's gathering a great army over there and over here. He intends to invade and seize the throne, which he believes is rightfully his. He has assembled a fleet, and even now, Irish mercenaries are stealing ships for him.'

He paused, and there was utter disbelief and silence as they all looked at the King, who slumped in the chair and had closed his eyes. He now opened them wide and gave a snort of laughter.

'I think the Earl of Surrey may have lost his wits, Flambard, or this is some moon madness. We've heard nothing of armies from Scotland, and surely messengers would have arrived to warn us?' He looked up at his friend, who usually had his finger on the nation's pulse, but Ranulph Flambard shrugged and shook his head.

'Then you tell us my brother has become a pirate and is stealing ships!' Seeing the King's obvious amusement, the assembled nobles laughed as well. The king turned to his uncle, 'Odo, you returned from Normandy a few weeks ago. Do you know anything of pirates?' Odo shook his head.

'It makes no sense, Sire. When I left Robert, yes, he was planning to move to Rouen, but he was full of his plans to widen and deepen the River Seine, build more wharves and warehouses, and not steal ships!'

De Warenne pulled himself to his feet and glared at Bishop Odo. 'You were there, you heard it. You greeted the Papal Envoy, Piers De Chatillon, when he brought gold from the Pope!'

Flambard suddenly sat up at the mention of Chatillon, and narrowed his eyes at Odo.

'I tell you that the Pope is supporting this invasion of Duke Robert!' he yelled, his voice rising and breaking, as he tried to make them understand.

Odo also jumped to his feet. 'The King is right. You are moon-touched, De Warenne. Chatillon brought welcome funds for the campaign against Count Fulk, who Pope Urban despises for his brutal and immoral behaviour.'

However, De Warenne was persistent. 'I saw it! I saw the red leather bags of gold. Gold I tell you—not silver—from the Pope.'

'If this dream, this fantasy of yours, is true, De Warenne, did you see the papal banner? The banner of support for Robert that the Pope would have sent?' hissed Odo turning away with a sneer of disbelief.

De Warenne faltered and dropped back into his chair, shaking his head. 'No, there was no banner, but I know what I heard.'

Again, silence reigned until Flambard spoke. 'Where is the Count De Mortain?' he asked, scanning the room. Odo shifted in his chair as he knew several powerful nobles were missing.

'He has gone to his estates in the west, my Lord, for there is, as you know, trouble on the Welsh borders. He has gone to take charge. He is about the King's business, and this man is accusing loyal nobles of treason because they are not here!' he spat in disgust.

Flambard nodded. He knew this was true. 'Is there anyone here who can confirm these ramblings, De Warenne?' he asked.

The Earl of Surrey's eyes raced around the packed room, but there was no one here who had been in Normandy, and his gaze dropped from Flambard to his clenched hands, as he wearily shook his head. At that moment, De Warenne's youngest son Raynold, who had helped his father up the stairs, and had no right to be in the council, whispered into his father's ear.

'William de St Calais, the Prince Bishop of Durham, may

know something of this!' he shouted.

Odo clenched his hands on the arms of the chair until his knuckles went white. Odo had realised immediately that William de St Calais was missing from this council tonight. Flambard, glancing around, also realised that the Prince Bishop was not there. Thinking quickly, Odo interjected, 'He was taken ill before the end of the meal, Sire, with the gripping sickness, and given the rumours of the sweating sickness and plague in the city, I believe he summoned a physician. Is that not correct?' he said, indicating their host Sheriff Malet of York, who nodded vigorously.

There were nervous glances around the room, and shifting of feet, at the mention of the word plague. However, William Rufus had heard enough.

'This is all a waste of time, rumour and conjecture. Flambard, question the Bishop of Durham on the morrow if we must, although he hasn't been to Normandy for over a year, I believe. Now, let us return to the hall and the music.' So saying, he stood and swayed towards the door while the council stood and bowed. Odo pointedly walked to Warenne and placed a hand on his shoulder.

'You have this very wrong, my friend, as you've obviously misheard snatches of conversations. I suggest you go to your estates and rest.'

De Warenne blinked in confusion. 'I know what I saw and heard, your grace. I may be advanced in years, but I'm not in my dotage yet!'

Odo shook his head and made for the stairs. Flambard stood, his hands resting on the back of a solid oak chair while his eyes followed Bishop Odo. He pulled the chair forward in front of De Warenne. 'Tell me it all again from the beginning,' he said, filling the Earl's goblet and waving his son Raynold to sit.

Odo returned to his seat in the hall and waved Finian over to join him. 'It didn't go well then?' asked the Irish warrior, sliding into the chair beside him, while watching the Bishop's face. Odo shook his head, and Finian's eyes swept the hall, wondering if they would have to fight their way out.

'Tell your men we leave before dawn. We are undone. The King doesn't realise it yet, but Flambard is suspicious, and he will dig and dig like a terrier after a rat. We must send messages to all involved, especially my brother Mortain in Bristol, and Roger, the Earl of Shrewsbury, in Arundel. I need you to send a bird to Chatillon; Robert's fleet must sail immediately for the south coast. We will go to Rochester and then meet Mortain at our castle at Pevensey. We will ride out from there.'

Finian nodded. 'So what of the false plans with the invasion from Scotland?'

'They are all in disarray; I'm sure that Flambard will question William de St Calais tomorrow, and you saw the state of him. He is terrified, and he will probably spill all to them. We've been betrayed by not only De Warenne and his family but by one of our own!'

Finian sighed, his mouth in a grim line. This was not good news. Would Robert's supporters in England be ready several months before they expected? A lot would be left to chance, and much depended on the weather in the channel as to whether the fleet could sail. Finian felt a foreboding about all this that he could not shake.

Two pigeons arrived for Chatillon on that Friday morning in Rouen. Both messages were removed from the birds and brought to his room. However, the first was of such import that the second lay unread until much later.

Chatillon read the first message with dismay and annoyance. It was from Finian describing what had happened at York. De Warenne had arrived far too early and denounced them. He swore softly and then went to find Robert, who had gone hunting. Chatillon cursed again as he didn't have the authority here to order the ships to make ready. He paced back and forth in frustration as he awaited the return of the Duke.

Finally, they returned, and Robert found an angry and agitated Chatillon waiting for him. 'Sire, there are more serious things afoot than hunting when a throne is at stake! I sent two messengers after you!'

Robert was taken aback. Like most, he respected but was wary of the powerful Papal Envoy, but he'd never seen him this angry.

'God's blood, Chatillon! What is it?' he asked while peeling off the thick leather hauberk he used for hunting boar.

'Your brother knows of your plans, Sire. We've been betrayed. Even now, William Rufus may be moving against your supporters in England. You must sail immediately. The captains tell me the weather is fair for the next two days.'

There was no doubt that Robert was shocked. He ordered all of his nobles to the hall immediately. An hour later, Chatillon was satisfied to see them running in every direction to gather their men and supplies to board the ships. They planned to sail on the morning tide and land on the beaches of Pevensey Bay just like his father before him. However, it was to be two full days before all the men and weapons were loaded. Only to be all unloaded again as a storm swept in from the Atlantic, bringing the wind onshore.

Two days later, Chatillon returned to his room. It was late, and he was wet and cold but still burning with anger at the incompetence in loading the ships, which meant they couldn't sail. He prayed that Bishop Odo and his brother, Mortain, had coordinated things over the Channel. Robert had significant support in England, even if he wasn't there to lead them immediately. He peeled off his wet clothes and hung them in front of the fire. It was at times like this that Piers missed Edvard. He'd been so preoccupied that he guiltily admitted he hadn't thought of them in days. They must be in Ghent by now.

He climbed under the heavy fur cover and stretched out naked in bed. Closing his eyes, he thought about his wife, the lovely Isabella. Edvard had sent a message saying they were leaving Paris and all was well. They would no doubt be sailing into Rouen in a few weeks, and her warm, soft body would be entwined with his again. He began to drift off when he suddenly jerked awake. There had been a second message. He'd forgotten all about it. He swung his legs out of bed and padded lightly, in the firelight, over to the table against the wall. The message was nowhere to be seen. He moved the items on the table; goblets, wine, and several vellum scrolls, but still no sign of the message.

He lit the candle and checked the floor and surrounding area. There it was, a long thin waxed piece of vellum lying in the dust and rushes against the wall. Picking it up, he carried it over to the firelight. He hadn't even noticed whom it was from, but now he recognised the small red cross at one end. It was from his Uncle, Pope Urban II, in Rome. Piers straightened it out and read the contents. Then he read it a second and third time before dropping into the chair. The message made no sense.

I was devastated to hear of Isabella's death. My thoughts and prayers are with you at this sad time, Piers. Your loving uncle.

Piers sat and stared into the flames for some time, as if in a trance. Then he leapt for the box containing the long strips of vellum he kept and quickly wrote a message. Pulling on his braies, he raced barefoot and bare-chested up the narrow stone steps to the pigeon coop. The weather hit him as he battled his way across the roof, but he got some respite once inside He tied the message securely to the leg of a large pigeon and, carrying it to the walls, launched it on its way to Ghent. He stood for a while, battered by the wind and the lashing rain which ran in rivulets down, his face and chest, and he prayed that the bird would make it in this weather. For he refused to believe the message. There was no way that Isabella could be dead. She had Edvard by her side and their men. He found he wasn't capable of coherent thought and even reasoned that he'd surely know somehow. Surely, Edvard would have been in touch... unless.... Was Edvard dead? Had they been attacked? He held his hands to his soaking face, his wet hair whipping around his face as he yelled the word, 'No!' over and over to the wild sky above him.

18

Chapter Eighteen

It was still dark when the door to his room flew open. By the light of the glowing embers of his fire, a shocked William could just make out the figures of three burly members of the King's guard. His heart leapt into his mouth, and his stomach clenched as he sat up.

'Prince Bishop, William de St Calais, you've been summoned immediately, Sire.'

His worst fears had been realised. He suddenly found that his mouth was so dry that he could not answer them. He slowly swung his legs out of bed and, retaining some control, bade them wait outside while he dressed.

A little time later, he was ushered into the solar to find Ranulph Flambard standing with his back to the fire, but there was no sign of the King. Ranulph was a clever, cunning man who knew there were more ways to kill a dog than choking it with butter, or pudding. Flambard dismissed the guards and waved William to a chair.

He would try the softer way first. 'Apologies, your Grace, for disturbing your slumbers in the early hours, when we hear that you aren't well, but the King and I need your help.'

The bishop was astute and knew when he was being played. 'Fortunately, it was a touch of the flux, my Lord Treasurer, nothing more serious.'

Ranulph nodded. 'It has come to our attention that certain noble lords seem to have transferred their allegiance, from the King to Duke Robert of Normandy. They seem to have foolishly decided to support his claim to the throne of England. As you're aware, this is a treasonable offence, punishable by a brutal death.' He smiled at the Prince Bishop.

William de St Calais knew a threat when he heard one, no matter how nicely it was phrased. He also knew he'd have to throw Flambard a sop or two if he was to save his own skin.

'As you know, my Lord Treasurer, as Prince Bishop of Durham, an estimable position of great power in the north of England awarded to me by the King's father, I would never risk becoming involved in a plot against the new king.'

Flambard finally moved from the fire and sat down opposite William de St Calais, steepling his fingers, so they rested on his lips, as he regarded the Prince Bishop for some time. He now knew without a doubt that William had some knowledge of the plot, but was he involved? He doubted it, but to get more information, he needed handling with care.

'So, did these plotters approach you as well?' he asked.

William considered his answer carefully; he didn't want to condemn himself from his own lips. 'I was not approached directly, my Lord, but men who said they were representatives from Bishop Odo and Count Mortain came to sound me out, several months ago, and I refused to give them consideration or let them have troops.' This was a clever answer and not strictly untrue.

CHAPTER EIGHTEEN

Flambard sat forward in alarm. 'Both of the King's uncles are involved?' he asked in a strained voice.

Again William dissembled. 'I was led to believe so, but it was not definite. They were vague when I pursued this. Perhaps they were hoping to recruit them, and seeing Odo here at York, supporting King William Rufus, I believe it is highly unlikely.' William's voice faded slightly towards the end as he found Flambard's intense gaze unsettling.

Flambard stood again and paced the room before turning on the Prince Bishop. 'We will face Bishop Odo in the morning, and you'll be a witness to confront him. We will see if there's any truth to this and if so, we will act!' he announced before telling William to return to bed.

As William walked along the dark stone, dimly lit corridors to his room, he found that he was shaking. He was like Homer's Odysseus, caught between Scylla, the six-headed monster, and Charybdis' huge, deadly whirlpool. He could see no way out. William lay down on his bed, knowing that sleep wouldn't come, for he only had one option.

Flambard arose early the next morning and went directly to the King's chambers. There were several young men in the chamber, who Flambard dismissed, holding the door open as they left. William Rufus was partaking of breakfast, looking paler than ever, after a late night of carousing.

'Sire, I have news of import.' The King looked up in interest at his friend's tone, and his eyes widened as he heard of the admissions of William de St Calais.

'Bring them before me immediately,' he demanded. 'Let us hear the truth of this!'

However, neither men were to be found. Odo had left for Sussex before dawn, and William de St Calais had left barely an hour later, heading for his fortress and stronghold in Durham. They would have to dig him out of there if they wanted him. William de St Calais prayed that Odo's plan to put Duke Robert on the throne worked, or he would probably lose everything; position, power, and life.

King William Rufus gathered his supporters around him in York, including the powerful Robert de Beaumont, Count of Meulan. The latter had led a company for William I in the Battle of Hastings. William De Warenne, his sons, and Gerard Baron de Gournay were there. Flambard had sent messages and scouts north to see if there was any truth of a Scots army, and to find out the scale of the rebellion. According to the Prince Bishop, it seemed that Robert had some of the most powerful English and Norman lords on his side.

'What of Mowbray? Is he with us?' the King asked Flambard, who, grim-faced, shook his head.

'God's blood, that means that my brother, with the support of Durham and the Earl of Northumberland, now holds the north against us!'

Robert de Beaumont listened to this in growing anger. 'Sire, I believe that speed is of the essence here. The north, we must leave, for now. Instead, we take our forces south. With Odo and his brother Mortain in Kent and Sussex, we can beard them in their lairs down there. It may discourage the others if we can lay siege and defeat them.'

William Rufus turned to Flambard. 'Can we do this?' he asked.

'Sire, you've several things that your brother does not. You have money, land, and, more importantly, you have the fyrd. Every manor has an obligation to raise troops for you. However, we must ensure that the treasury is secure in Winchester. I suggest we make for London at first, assembling the fyrd on the way. Make the proclamation now, place yourself as the 'Defender of England' and call on the loyalty of your citizens.'

The Baron de Gournay was more sceptical. 'Forgive me, Sire, but hearing the names you mentioned, as supporting Duke Robert, I don't think that a few hundred farmers with pitchforks will stand against the private armed forces of Bishop Odo and Mortain. They have had time to prepare for this. They hold the north, the west, Arundel and the south, and we are sandwiched in between. They can attack us from front and rear.'

There was silence, as they considered his words until William De Warenne spoke.

'I believe, Sire, the rebel forces were not quite ready. From what I heard, they planned for this rebellion to happen in mid to late summer. They are undone, exposed, and fled like foxes back to their dens. I believe that Beaumont is right. We must take the war to them, to Rochester in Kent and Pevensey in Sussex.'

King William nodded in agreement. 'Set things in motion, Ranulph. We leave immediately. We also send a summons to all those missing lords and ask for their loyalty. As you say, I'm wealthy in land, and what noble would turn down the offer of more land? We bribe them, Ranulph, and if that doesn't work, then we threaten them.'

Ranulph bowed and left to send out messengers to raise middle England in support of the King.

'What of my brother Robert, De Warenne? Did he seem ready to sail?'

'I did send you a messenger, Sire, near a month ago, detailing the ships, but apparently, he didn't arrive in England. When I left, Robert bought and stole more ships; his warehouses were full of supplies and weapons. I fear he'll sail shortly, and if he lands on the south coast with his army, as your father did in sixty-six, then I suspect it will not go well for us, Sire. Duke Robert has a good reputation in battle.'

William Rufus ran his hands through his hair. Privately he agreed with Warenne. Robert was battle-hardened and even defeated his father at Gerberoi, while he, as a younger brother, knew little of warfare or strategy. It seemed likely that he would lose his throne, but he must never admit that in public. He stood and addressed the crowded room.

'Do not fear De Warenne. We will defend our country, defeat and punish these treacherous rebels!'

Robert de Beaumont nodded his approval, the nobles cheered, and young Raynold de Warenne glowed with pride at the thought of fighting for his king.

19

Chapter Nineteen

Isabella loved Ghent; the colourful tall wooden houses, the swarming busy streets that seemed cleaner than any city she'd been in before. Ghent was prosperous; a trading centre full of rich and influential merchants. This, in turn, meant the streets were teeming with vendors, and market stalls, selling everything from lace strips to amber jewellery from the north. They had camped in the birch forests to the east the night before, and Isabella had changed from her boy's clothes into a dress and cloak suitable for riding.

Edvard had booked them a room at the large inn in the marketplace, and he made sure that the innkeeper and his wife knew that this was Isabella de Embriaco, the wealthy cousin of Bianca Da Landriano. The city had been rocked eight years ago by the murder of the beautiful Italian Contessa, and no one had forgotten the incident. Edvard knew it would go around the city like wildfire that another Italian beauty was residing in Bianca's house on the city's outskirts. He visited the house to ensure everything was ready and gathered all the servants together. Most of them were the original ones who had been retained. He explained that he wanted them to go into the city waxing lyrical about her beauty, but also expressing concerns for their jobs, as they believed she was here to wind up the estate and sell it.

Edvard moved into Chatillon's smaller, but elegant, house in the city but kept a low profile, putting his hood up when outside and trying to only go about their business when it was dark. He was far too easily recognisable in Ghent as Chatillon's Vavasseur and ensured he was never seen with Isabella. However, he organised everything from there. Edvard sent six of his men with Isabella, two to patrol the walls and gates, and two remained as guards inside the house. Two younger men, of smarter appearance, accompanied Isabella everywhere. They were dressed in the Embriaco livery, which Isabella had made in Paris, when she learned of the deception in Ghent.

Isabella liked Bianca's house very much and was now determined that they should keep it and, instead, sell the smaller townhouse. The house was an old fortified manor that had been extended quite recently. The lower floor was double-walled with tiny windows, but the large upper floor had been fitted with large, modern windows that gave a sweeping view of the coast. It was on the city's outskirts, and its gardens ran down to a gate in the wall that opened out onto the estuary with a path leading to the beach. The gardens were large and well-tended, with espalier fruit trees sheltered from the cold, winter, western winds by high stone south-facing walls. She felt comfortable here. It had a warm, welcoming feel to it.

Bianca had spent a lot of money on new fashionable items of furniture; long padded divans that looked to be from the east with their carved mahogany legs, velvet cushions and covers in bright hues. The walls were all covered in large, expensive silk and velvet tapestries. She had a knack for turning the bleakest fortress into a comfortable home. The high-backed wooden settles had gone to the servant's quarters, and now, instead, there were several wide wooden armchairs, with cushions and leather padded footstools, in front of the fire. Edvard had explained that Bianca's first older husband had been a collector of Roman and Byzantine artefacts, which were now scattered around her houses. But it was the preserved books and drawings that had interested Bianca. She'd spent hours poring over them. She made sketches and had furniture made; most of them were beautiful, although Chatillon had ordered her to burn one chair because it was so uncomfortable.

In the bedroom, there was a small but life-like portrait of Bianca. Isabella stood in front of it for some time. At one point, she'd resented Bianca, for even though she was gone, it had felt, at first, as if there were three of them in their marriage. He'd obviously loved her deeply, but she'd come to terms with that. She even had a moment of sadness, knowing that this was where Bianca spent her last night in the arms of Chatillon, the man she truly loved, before riding out the next day, on his instructions, to meet her horse warrior on the beach.

Edvard had ordered her to stay out of sight for three days, although she'd sent Count Robert and Countess Gertrude of Flanders a missive announcing her arrival and asking for their permission to attend court. However, Edvard returned with news that evening after dark.

'Count Robert isn't in residence. He has gone on a pilgrimage to Jerusalem. His absence is good for us because not only did he know Bianca well, he's a very astute and clever man, who is always watchful of people in his court. I also believe that this might explain the sudden visit of Prince Leopold of Swabia, for the Count was not fond of him. Leopold will be hoping that the Count doesn't survive such a dangerous journey, while he ingratiates himself with Countess Gertrude and young Robert, who is acting as a Regent in his father's absence. That may well be in name only as the Countess is, apparently, still firmly holding the reins of Flanders.'

Isabella absorbed all of this and sat in silence, looking thoughtful. 'Stay for dinner this evening, Edvard, for I have many questions about what you've related, and I wish to know more about this man I am to kill.'

Edvard stared for a second. Was she having second thoughts? he wondered. He hoped not, for Leopold was a devious, slippery character, who had survived three assassination attempts already, and went everywhere with an armed guard and food tasters. This was their chance to get him and make him pay for what he'd done. He smiled at Isabella.

'Of course, my Lady, now shall we go and visit your pets?'

She gave a tinkling laugh as he held up a hessian sack, which was visibly moving with mice or something similar.

A few moments later, accompanied by their young keeper, they entered a room on the attic floor. Inside were two baskets. She took the lid carefully off the first basket, which held two snakes.

'My mating pair.' she announced as the young man lifted the larger male, which coiled around the y-shaped stick.

'Ah yes, Antony and Cleopatra, I believe,' Edvard said with a mock bow as she laughed.

'We always separate them at feeding, as Cleopatra can get very territorial and aggressive with her mate if food is involved. She always recognises the biggest mouse and will attack him to get it.'

'Like most women,' murmured Edvard, receiving a mock-horrified look from Isabella.

She moved to the much larger basket and, pulling on long gloves, removed the lid. Edvard took a step back as the much larger asp was lifted out. He knew this family of snakes had a history of striking out. Undoubtedly, he was a beauty, a large male with distinctive markings.

'I'll be so sorry to lose him, I talk to him almost every day,' sighed Isabella. 'I've wracked my brain for a strategy whereby he kills Leopold, but somehow we manage to rescue him afterwards.'

Edvard looked at her in surprise. He'd never thought for a moment that she'd become attached to them. He stood and watched her for a moment as she expertly held her snake just behind its head while it coiled itself around her forearm.

'Remember Ahmed's words, Isabella; never trust them, no matter how long you may have them.'

She smiled and nodded, assuring him that she was always careful while, with one finger, she stroked the snake's head, and it closed its eyes in pleasure.

At dinner that evening, he thought she'd never looked more beautiful. She positively glowed. A sudden thought occurred to him, but he stored it away until later. They had work to do in Ghent and now was not the time to over-complicate things.

'So Edvard, tell me about Prince Leopold of Swabia and explain why it is so important that he dies?' She sat back and waited.

'When Piers was a Papal Secretary and envoy for Pope Alexander, he made two major enemies, Cardinal Beno, a German, and Duke Welf of Bavaria. They both tried and nearly succeeded in killing Piers. Prince Leopold was the third person in this unholy triumvirate, and they went on to poison Pope Alexander. The Pope was an honest and decent man whose only mistake was reforming the Catholic Church, as he tried to do away with corruption. Leopold's idea was to coat the Pope's favourite figs in poisoned honey. Within a week, Alexander was gone.

'Meanwhile, they had lured Piers to Prague on a mission doomed to fail. They set him up to be captured by Bishop Jaromir, along with his whole legation. He was tortured and beaten, and he almost died. You will have seen the scars on his body from the red hot irons.'

Isabella nodded. 'He still flinches when I touch them, but he refuses to talk about it.'

Edvard sighed. 'It was Duke Welf, with the help of Beno and Leopold, who trapped him in Prague, but they tortured and slaughtered the whole legation of young, innocent priests. Piers can never forgive them for that, and thirsts for revenge. He has punished the others, but Leopold always escapes. Cardinal Beno has a never-ending bloody flux that's wearing him down. He has employed food tasters, but they can find no evidence that he is being poisoned. Piers was clever. The poison is in the first goblet of communion wine and only once a week when the Cardinal celebrates mass. Duke Welf is still visited once a year, close to the anniversary of what happened, in the blood-stained octagon chamber. His men, or his horses, or his dogs all die with their throats cut, and a drawing of an octagon is pinned to their bodies. So we take our revenge and leave him alive, in fear. He has never caught our men yet. So this is our chance to finally get Leopold, Isabella, after years of trying.'

CHAPTER NINETEEN

She sat, quite shaken by what she'd heard and, staring at him wide-eyed, nodded.

'I understand, Edvard, so tell me how I should do this.'

For the next hour or so, they ran over various scenarios. The Prince had a reputation as a lecher. No serving girl was safe. He assured Isabella this reputation was well deserved and well known, so she'd have to handle him carefully. In public, she must be seen to treat him politely but with a barely hidden contempt. But occasionally, she'd give him encouragement with a shy smile. No one in the court would believe that she'd any interest there. Instead, she'd flirt openly with the good-looking young gallants of the court and one in particular, who might have useful information, she should bed. If this worked, the Prince would become fascinated by her. Because of his wealth, and title, he was not used to women giving him the cold shoulder. She'd make herself aloof and unobtainable. He would become increasingly frustrated. After several days of this, Edvard would ensure that her servants would let drop that she went riding on the beach very early each morning.

She needed, somehow, to drug Leopold's wine and then release the snake from its leather bag into the room with him. In a drugged state, he'd probably drop into a deep sleep. Once released, Octavian would be attracted both by the sound of him breathing heavily, or snoring, and his bodily warmth and when Leopold stirred or woke, Octavian would feel threatened and was bound to strike. This could be worked out. Isabella thought the plan sounded plausible, but Edvard was not sure. She seemed to have a lot of confidence in an unknown quantity; the snake.

'I need two things, Edvard. Firstly, send the boy, at dusk, to the ponds we rode past on the way into Ghent. I need a large toad.'

Edvard laughed, realising what this was for; the mind might be willing, but the body would be weak.

'Secondly, we need a servant in the house who can place Octavian in the room we will use and remove him after he strikes,' she said earnestly.

Edvard smiled. 'We've two informers in his house already. I'll see what I can do.'

Early next evening, Isabella dressed for her appearance at the Flanders Court. She would first visit Countess Gertrude in her chambers and then join them for dinner in the Great Hall. Although Edvard had forewarned her, nothing had prepared her for the opulence or wealth of the court in Ghent. She was shown into the solar; every inch of the walls was covered in rich tapestries. She could see where Bianca got her inspiration. Isabella made her bow, and the Countess made her welcome. A blonde-haired handsome young man sat beside her. He had the same piercing blue eyes, so she knew it was one of her sons.

'May I introduce you to my youngest son, Viscount Philip van Loo, who has obviously lost his tongue or has been struck dumb by your beauty!' Philip laughed aloud at his mother, sending her a reproving but playful glance.

'She's not far wrong. I was too young, a mere stripling, when your cousin graced the court, but they still speak of her today. I see the same stunning beauty running in all of your family.' he said, raising her hand and kissing it. His mother snorted with contempt.

'See what I have done, Isabella. We wanted another warrior son at last, and we get a courtier and flatterer instead.'

Isabella smiled; she liked them immediately. She could see the love and affection there, and she felt a small amount of

CHAPTER NINETEEN

guilt at the deception she was playing on them.

'Come, let us go into dinner. The wolves out there will no doubt want to get a look at her.'

Philip gave Isabella his arm. 'Do not fear, Isabella de Embriaco. I'll protect you from them. I am a diplomat, a soldier and a good swordsman, for all of my mother's jokes.'

For the first time, Isabella felt apprehension about walking into a hall packed with nobles. In Paris, it was different. She was acting out a role, but she was the wife of Piers De Chatillon. Now she was pretending to be single again to trick a German prince. In doing so, she had to hide her marriage. Fortunately, it had only been three months since the wedding ceremony in Genoa, and the news hadn't spread. None of the servants at Chatillon's house knew that he'd married, and Edvard assured her that servants were usually the first to learn of these things. She took a deep breath as the Steward announced the entrance of Countess Gertrude and her party. The assembled crowd bowed deeply until she finally waved them to take their seats. Then a babble of conversation broke out as they speculated on the identity of the beauty on Philip's arm. Some knew, and before long, it had spread that this was the cousin of Bianca Da Landriano.

Once the extensive dishes and covers were cleared, musicians struck up on a gallery above, and Philip took her arm again.

'Come, my Lady, let us promenade around the room as many are desperate to make your acquaintance. Can you not see that their tongues are hanging out, and some are even panting with anticipation when they hear the words Genoa and Embriaco and think of your family's wealth.'

Isabella found herself giggling at his audacious comments.

She was enjoying the wit of this young man. He may be a few years younger than her, but it was obvious that he'd been brought up in the cut and thrust of an exciting court, with new people arriving almost daily. His father, Count Robert, was a very powerful and influential man, and many came to seek his favour and support.

Isabella wondered if Prince Leopold was here. She didn't have long to wait. He pushed himself to the front of the group surrounding her and bowed. She immediately noticed that Philip's attitude had changed.

'Isabella de Embriaco, may I introduce Prince Leopold of Swabia,' he said formally. Isabella remained aloof but offered her hand while examining the man she was expected to kill.

He was tall and had probably been good-looking in his youth, but age hadn't been kind to the Prince, and he had a slight stoop and a protruding stomach. He had lived a dissolute life, and it showed in his face. He was a similar age to Chatillon but looked at least ten years older, with drooping eyelids, harsh deep lines down the sides of his mouth, and broken veins across his cheeks. He'd also developed the jowls and turkey neck of an older man. Apparently, neither of his two wives had survived more than a few years with him. He licked his lips while his eyes raked her body. He was not a pleasant man, and she withdrew her hand quickly.

'May I ask why such an Italian beauty is gracing the court of Flanders? Is this a visit to family, or do more important matters bring you here?' he said with a thin smile.

Isabella raised her eyebrows at such impertinent questions. Philip was also affronted and answered for her.

'The Lady De Embriaca is here to wind up her cousin's house and affairs, and what is that to you, Sire?'

CHAPTER NINETEEN

The Prince shrugged but narrowed his eyes at Philip.

'I believe you're already betrothed to a Danish princess, Philip Van Loo. Should you not be at her side?' he suggested in a languid tone.

Isabella could feel Philip bristling beside her, so she put a hand on his arm.

'She is a very lucky young woman,' she said, smiling up at him, which smoothed his ruffled feathers.

Prince Leopold watched this interplay with interest. He'd found recently that his tastes had become jaded with the women he took. However, this one was different. She obviously had no interest in him or his title, and he was not used to that. It sparked his curiosity and desire.

'Can I ask what brings a German Prince over to Ghent, while Count Robert is so obviously away?' she asked daringly.

Philip tried unsuccessfully to hide a snort of laughter, while the Prince narrowed his eyes. So the Italian beauty was politically astute and fancied herself as a wit.

'I am looking for a wife; my last wife died in childbirth, taking my son with her, and I need an heir.' She saw a flicker of emotion on his face, for a second, and put a hand on his arm.

'I am sorry to hear that; you must have been devastated.'

He was taken aback by her response, but Isabella was now in role and following her instructions. Blow hot and cold. Keep him guessing.

At that moment, Philip intervened. 'We've lingered here long enough. Let us move on to other guests.'

They bowed and continued their promenade around the Great Hall, but whenever she glanced back, she could see Prince Leopold's eyes following her, and she smiled.

Chapter Twenty

Edvard was surprised that there were no messages from Chatillon, but he supposed that the Papal Envoy was fully involved in planning the invasion with Duke Robert. However, he sent a bird to tell him that they had arrived in Ghent, and all was going to plan. Isabella had gone riding on the beach, and he hoped that Leopold had taken the bait.

Accompanied by her guards, Isabella rode to the top of one of the many dunes and surveyed the long beach in front of her. It was the first time she'd seen a sandy beach with dunes, and it was an impressive sight. She watched the waves crashing onto the beach for a while. There was a stiff breeze coming off the sea. Then her eyes were drawn to the vista of dune after dune rolling away to the north. So this was where Bianca had died. She'd made love to her horse warrior in the dunes, but his enemies had attacked them, and she'd paid with her life.

One of her guards rode forward. 'A horseman is approaching, my lady.'

She shaded her eyes against the bright rising sun, and as he came closer, she recognised Prince Leopold. He was riding a very showy, bright, chestnut gelding with several men behind him. Isabella smiled as she remembered he never went anywhere without his guards.

'This is a fortunate coincidence,' he said as he reined his horse in beside hers.

'Good morrow to you, Sire. I'm here for only a short time, so I'm enjoying the vista.'

He moved his gaze reluctantly away from her and stared at the dunes.

'Very pretty, but it cannot compete with the mountains and lakes around my home. You would be more impressed. The Black Forest nestles around the foothills at my home in Augsburg. It would take your breath away when you first beheld it.'

Isabella didn't reply, so he continued. 'Augsburg, my capital in Swabia, is an ancient town going back to Roman times. My family have had their home there for generations. They say it was named after Emperor Augustus.'

It was no good; as the situation's absurdity hit her, she began to laugh but quickly turned it into a coughing fit. She was about to kill this man using a poisonous snake named after the Roman Emperor Augustus. He was taken aback and looked at her in concern,

'Are you ill?' he asked. She laughed again. Isabella knew that he feared all illnesses, and she watched him nudge his horse away.

'No, Sire, I had a small morning pastille in my mouth to sweeten my breath, and it went the wrong way.' The relief on his face was comical.

'Your home sounds like a beautiful place indeed. When do you return there?'

'It was to be a sennight, but I feel there's more to keep me here now,' he said, looking at her pointedly. She nodded in appreciation and gathered her reins. That was enough for now, she was firmly in charge of this situation and intended to be so in future. She would always try to leave him wanting more.

'I must go, Sire. I've business to attend to.'

He bowed his head as she turned and cantered down the beach, back to the city. He was pleased with the progress he'd made with her. He was now determined to have her one way or another.

The next few days were a whirlwind of events as she was invited to several gatherings in the houses of the Ghent nobility or at the court of the Countess. Wherever she went, there were a group of admirers around her, chief of whom were Prince Leopold, who always seemed to know where she'd be, and Philip Van Loo. The latter caused some comments in the court, but the flirtation amused his mother, who encouraged it. At the same time, Isabella remained aloof and distant to Leopold in public, which drove him to distraction, as she was a different person on their morning rides. He was also infuriated by the light caresses and smiles she bestowed on Philip Van Loo. Leopold hated everything about the handsome, confident young man who treated him with thinly veiled amusement and contempt. Watching them dance together, he swore he'd see his day with this upstart Flemish nobody. He was Leopold of Swabia, a prince of the blood. This Philip was not fit to be one of his squires.

Isabella watched all this with interest. The jealousy and frustration on Leopold's face were plain to see. Philip took advantage of their growing friendship and began to whisper outrageous things in her ear that made her laugh aloud. This drew more eyes to them, which was what she wanted. She showed no inclination, or liking, for Prince Leopold, making his behaviour more boorish and arrogant.

Things came to a head at the end of the week. The Count's heir, Robert, returned from Burgundy having secured a great match with Clementia, the daughter of the Duke, and a grand dinner was planned. The Great Hall was packed with the great and good, and many visitors who, watching the players, jugglers and musicians, were entranced by their performances. No expense was spared in the wealthy Flanders court.

Isabella danced several times with Philip, whose hands became bolder with each dance. He even purposefully trailed his fingers across her breasts at each turn, and she had to admit she encouraged him. She'd discovered that he was indeed the diplomat of the family and worked with his father to formalise policy and alliances. She probed a few times and found his knowledge of the European courts immense. She'd take him as a lover and extract useful information, but she'd also keep him as a friend and future contact. She placed a hand on his arm as they finished the dance.

'It is so hot and stuffy in here, almost overpowering. Can you take me for some air?'

Philip smiled. 'Of course, let us walk in the gardens for a while.'

Leopold, who had been rebuffed for a dance with her, watched in growing fury as Philip retrieved their cloaks and led her outside. He gave it a few moments and then followed them. Philip was delighted to get the beautiful Isabella on her own. He'd been pleased by her encouragement and surprised when he saw the desire as her eyes swept over his body.

'Come, a door leads directly into my mother's rose garden.'

She smiled up at him and followed him out. It was a bright clear night, and she could see the bowers and paths ahead. Within seconds, he'd pulled her into his arms and kissed her deeply. To his delight, she responded and wrapped her arms around his waist, pulling him closer. Her hands moved up his back and gripped his shoulders. She pressed her body against his. It immediately occurred to him that she was no virgin.

'I want you, Isabella da Embriaco,' he whispered hoarsely while nuzzling her ear.

'I know,' she said, dropping her hand to his manhood and making him gasp. 'But not here. Let us go somewhere there's no danger we will be seen, which would damage both you and me. Somewhere, such as my house, where you can give me a night of pleasure, Philip Van Loo.'

He laughed aloud and, taking her by the hand, led her through the gardens to a door in the wall, which he unbolted. She recognised the long meadow beyond. It abutted the grounds of her house.

'Perfect,' she whispered.

In the shadows of the rose bowers, a figure stood with fists clenched and watched this interplay amid the herbs and flowers. His teeth were gritted. He hadn't felt anger like this for many years. He knew it was a foolish and dangerous thing to do, but he couldn't help himself. He wanted to kill Philip Van Loo, so he followed them.

Piers De Chatillon had just experienced some of the worst days of his life.

The invasion plan was in tatters. Messages suggested that Finian and Bishop Odo were holed up in Pevensey Castle, and unless the forces regrouped and ventured out, they would soon be under siege. He just hoped Finian had cut the throat of that devious, treacherous Warenne, who had fooled them all by arriving weeks earlier than planned in York. Now, Robert's fleet was still trapped in the harbour, and the weather was so bad that even the smaller supply ships couldn't get over to the south coast of England. His mind was racing to find other possibilities, but he couldn't think because bleakness kept descending every time he thought of Isabella. He found he couldn't sleep. He was pacing his room at night. The food he ate seemed tasteless and unappetising. Even the attractions of the lovely Countess of Mortain had paled.

He raced up the steep stone stairs twice daily to the pigeon coop, but the only messages came from England. The worst thing was not knowing. *Was she dead? If so, was it quick, or was it slow and painful? Was she murdered, or was it some terrible accident?* His fingers raked through his hair as he paced. He couldn't understand Edvard's silence and the complete lack of communication. It now seemed likely that he'd died defending her. He dropped into the chair by the fire, his head in his hands.

Piers was shaken. 'Have I truly lost them both?' he whispered. He'd only felt this heart-rending loss twice in his life - when his parents died of the plague and when Bianca was slain. Now he may have lost the two people in his life that he loved, for Piers had come to realise he was falling in love with Isabella.

Chapter Twenty-one

William Rufus and his forces surrounded Bishop Odo's castle at Pevensey. As Flambard had advised, they moved swiftly, and arrived in Kent and Sussex long before anyone expected them. The King had forced young Gilbert De Clare to surrender at Tonbridge, in only two days. He had then moved directly to attack his two uncles at Pevensey.

Finian stood on the walls of the gatehouse and gazed out at the forces arrayed in front of them. Count Robert Mortain stood beside him.

'What are your thoughts, Ui Neill? Will my nephew attack?' he asked. It was a few moments before the Irish warrior answered him.

'I think, my Lord, that we either sit here and starve while we await supplies and reinforcements from Duke Robert, or we take our chances and ride out and attack them now, when they least expect it.'

Mortain shook his head in a resigned way. 'It looks to me as if we are sorely outnumbered.'

'Not really, Sire, for if you look closely, you'll see that he has raised the Fyrd, which means that half of his force will be peasants and farmers. We can cut our way through them with ease. Remember that we have Eustace of Boulogne and his Flemish mercenaries with us now. All trained men.'

'Odo will never agree. He believes that Robert will arrive any day, and then we will have the numbers to drive William Rufus away and defeat him.'

Finian raised a sceptical eyebrow, and Mortain sighed.

'I read the last message from Chatillon. I know that storms have kept him trapped in port, but I know my nephew Robert, and he's no shirker or coward. He'll be full of frustration and impatience to be here.'

Finian shrugged. 'And meanwhile, we sit cooped up in here, rationing our food supplies, while more forces arrive to bolster the King and surround us,' he said, pointing to a large troop of men galloping towards the camp of William Rufus.

'That's De Gournay's banner. There must be close to sixty men with him, all soldiers by the look of it,' spat Finian, turning away in disgust to stride along the walls. Mortain watched him go. Finian was right; they should have attacked the King two days ago when they first arrived. Now he just prayed that Duke Robert would arrive.

Finian felt a cold anger building inside him. He hated sieges. He was a warrior who needed to be charging on the back of a horse, not holed up like a rat in a barrel. He approached the north tower where several men were watching the enemy and two or three archers were encouraging the enemy to stay back from the walls. One young hooded archer was the best he'd ever seen. His arrows seemed to find their targets unerringly. The speed with which he drew and fired was twice that of his compatriots. Finian leaned against the stone door frame of the tower and watched him for a while. A slight figure, he ignored the banter and praise of the other men.

He noticed they wore a different livery from Odo's men. They had dark green tunics, a feather badge, and good quality grey woollen hooded cloaks. They also all wore soft leather masks covering their noses and lower faces.

Finian waved the Serjeant over. 'They are exceptionally good,' he commented.

'They are the best archers I've ever seen, Sire, and that livery merges into stone walls, or trees, so that they aren't too much of a target. They are the Castellan's own band of about twenty archers. He was a famous archer himself in his time. His heirs follow in his footsteps and insist on making and fletching their own arrows.'

This was the way forward, thought Finian, specialist groups of fighters with specific skills, like the famous Genoan crossbowmen. It made sense to have similar groups over here. He stepped over to congratulate the archers, and they bowed in acknowledgement; however, the young hooded archer bowed briefly and, making for the door, descended the stairs and strode across the bailey towards the keep. Finian followed the young man with his eyes. He'd noticed that the other archers deferred to him, so this must be the Castellan's son. Well, he was obviously embarrassed by praise. Then he gave it no more thought as he turned his attention back to the besieging army.

That afternoon a bedraggled group of men were allowed into the castle and escorted across to the keep. Finian watched them arrive, ran lightly down the steps, and made for the hall. The men were in front of Odo and Robert Mortain, in front of the dais.

'My Lord, I tell you we are the only survivors. The whole ship went down, taking all of your supplies with it. It was packed to the gunwale and not so much sailing as wallowing in the sea. It was calm for the first few hours as we sailed down the coast, but as we sailed across the Channel, we were hit by a squall. We fought it for several hours and managed to get nearer the coast, but the ship was overwhelmed by high winds and water, and then the mast snapped. We clung to the barrels and debris and were washed ashore, but everything else was lost.'

Odo slammed his fist down on the table in anger and frustration. His brother put a hand on his shoulder. 'That was only one ship, Brother. Robert will send more. Soon, he'll be here himself, and we will ride out of those gates behind him. Until then, we've a good water supply and can reduce the rations slightly.'

Finian shook his head. 'More mouths to feed and not even fighting men. Sire, I suggest that we start slaughtering some of the spare animals. There are goats and a few milk cows in the bailey. Milk and cheese we can do without, but strips of dried meat keep the gnawing pangs of hunger at bay. We also need to preserve the grass and fodder for the horses.'

Odo nodded in agreement, and Finian went to order it done. He'd lived through several sieges; almost every part of the animals could be used for soups and stews. However, he was gloomy as he made his way across the grass. With the turbulent weather the way it was, Finian couldn't see any help arriving soon. Another week and they would have to risk sending small raiding parties over the walls for food.

Three days later, Finian was drawn to the walls again by loud jeers and shouts from the enemy camp.

'What is it?' shouted Odo as he hurried to join them.

'A large group of men are trying to fight their way through

from the west, but they are having a hard time of it.' Finian gripped the wall as he watched the horsemen try to push through against large odds.

'We need to ride out now, Sire!' he said, turning to Mortain. 'I recognise those banners. It's Montgomery.'

Odo, flustered, turned to his brother. 'Montgomery? What is he doing here? I thought he was holding Arundel and the south.'

Mortain narrowed his eyes at the mail-clad warrior slashing left and right at the enemy.

'No, that's a younger man. Yes, Finian, take your troop out and attack the enemy from behind.' Then he turned and yelled, 'Archers here on the walls now!'

Finian jumped back to let the leader of the archers pass, on the narrow stone staircase, as he raced down to the stables.

'Try not to hit us!' he shouted as he went past him to rally his men.

The archer stopped, narrowing his eyes. He watched him, before turning to run to the walls to take up position.

Finian's men gave whoops of joy as they clambered to tack up horses and arm themselves. Stymied by inactivity, and lack of action, several other knights rushed to join them, so at least forty men galloped out of the gates after him towards the enemy camp. Having ridden with the horse warriors for years, he knew exactly what to do to bring enemy horsemen down. Hitting them at speed while they were sideways on, the rider and horse often ended up on the ground. They may not have the huge war destriers of the horse warriors, but they had surprise on their side.

The attack from the castle disconcerted the enemy, who thought they had easy pickings with Montgomery and his men.

CHAPTER TWENTY-ONE

The sight of Finian and his troop spurred on the men, riding under the Montgomery banner, while the deadly archers on the castle walls picked off the enemy.

Soon it was all over, and they were riding into Pevensey Castle to the cheers of the forces on the walls. The huge gates slammed shut behind them, and Finian trotted into the bailey, a grin on his face. He dismounted and strode over to the leader of Montgomery's men, who was pulling off his helmet.

'Well met, Ui Neill. I'm pleased that Chatillon sent you with Odo. Your help was most welcome.'

Finian stopped and bowed, but his smile was frozen, for this was Roger Montgomery's son, Robert De Belleme, a particularly unpleasant individual. He'd heard all the stories about this cruel and arrogant man. Ette, the wife of Morvan De Malvais, had stabbed him through the thigh with a long dagger, pinning him to the ground in her pavilion when he tried to rape her.

'I'm pleased you managed to make it through, Sire. We've received little news from other parts of England for the past four weeks, and the weather in Rouen still holds Robert back.'

Belleme grimaced. 'I have news, but it may not be the kind that Odo and Mortain wish to hear.' he said, as he made his way to the keep. Belleme was a clever, astute man and a good fighter for all of his shortcomings. Finian followed to see him clasping arms with the rebel nobles.

Mortain crossed and slapped Finian on the shoulder. 'Well done, Ui Neill! So tell us what is happening, Belleme. Where is your father? Are they marching to join us?'

Belleme downed the tankard of ale he'd been given, and wiped his mouth with the back of his hand.

'I'm afraid my father will not be riding to your aid. He is still at Arundel Castle, but William Rufus, through his mouthpiece, Flambard, has persuaded my father to change sides. He was shown, by a series of bribes and threats, that it was in his best interests to support the King, if he wanted to keep his title and lands in England.'

The assembled nobles listened in disbelief. The rebellion had lost one of the most powerful nobles in England, Roger Montgomery, the Earl of Shrewsbury.

'Will he then march against us?' spluttered Odo.

'No, he has taken the King's gold to stay at Arundel, and deny Duke Robert's claim to the throne.'

There was absolute silence in the room for what seemed a long time.

'As a long-time friend and supporter of Robert, I had no choice but to ride out. My father understood that and agreed that my brother, Hugh De Montgomery, could ride with me.' Hugh stepped forward and bowed. Belleme had his mother's dark, narrow-eyed features, but Hugh had the pleasant open face of his father.

'Do you know what is happening elsewhere?' asked Mortain in a dispirited voice.

Belleme nodded. 'The rebels in the southwest are attacking the lands around and holding their own. The north still holds, although William Rufus, with Flambard advising, offers land and money to any who change sides.'

Odo growled. 'So he's offering bribes and then using threats to take their land. These underhand methods are the work of Flambard,' he spat.

'You may already know that Tonbridge has fallen, and De Clare was taken prisoner. Rochester Castle is now under siege. William Rufus expected you to be there, my Lord Bishop. He left a small, holding force there, and the Royal Army has decamped here to Sussex. He is aware that Robert could be arriving any day, and supplying the castles, so he has set up a naval blockade of Rochester, on the Medway, and off the coast of Pevensey. They have already attacked and sunk one of Robert's ships full of horses and men.'

'God's blood, I hope Robert was not on it!' exclaimed Mortain.

'No, my father had a bird from Chatillon. Robert is still in Rouen, citing weather, but reading between the lines, my father picked up reluctance in Robert to set sail. I think perhaps it was that which persuaded him to move his allegiance to the King.'

Again, there was silence, except for the shuffling of feet, as everyone absorbed this unpalatable news.

Finian turned and quietly made for the door muttering to himself, 'Rats in a barrel!' The Castellan of Pevensey, Sir Hugh, stood at the back, his masked archer son beside him. They obviously heard him and the young man's eyes seemed to narrow at Finian's disrespect. Smiling, Finian went down to check on his men and horses. They had lost no one, but a few flesh wounds needed stitching.

As he crossed the bailey, his smile faded, thinking of the predicament they were in now. They had food stores for only another week at the most, and then negotiations would begin for surrender if they were not rescued or resupplied. Finian knew that, as an Irish mercenary, guilty of stealing ships for Duke Robert, they would hang him.

Chapter Twenty-two

Isabella and Philip had stopped to embrace on the sandy path leading to Bianca's house several times. Behind them came Prince Leopold, carelessly venturing forth without his armed guard. However, following stealthily behind him were Isabella's two guards. It was a clear night; they could see their mistress and, in front of them, the man who followed them. They were ready to step in at any point.

Finally, the couple reached the house and went inside, leaving Prince Leopold standing in the shadows opposite the gates. He knew he should leave, but it was a warm night, and the shutters of the second floor were open. He watched, waited, and was rewarded for his patience. He saw the flickering light as candles were lit in the middle room. Before long, two figures were silhouetted against that light. Leopold found he couldn't drag his eyes away as he watched Philip Van Loo pull Isabella's gown over her head, his hands caressing her body. Then he lifted her and carried her out of sight.

Leopold let out the breath he'd been holding. He was fully aroused, which was odd, as he was consumed by jealousy and

CHAPTER TWENTY-TWO

anger. He turned away and walked briskly back to his room. He would send one of his men to keep watch. He wanted to know exactly when Philip left. He was sure Philip's mother, Countess Gertrude, would want to know. She wouldn't want her son's engagement to a Danish princess to be threatened by bedsport with an Italian beauty. He had to close his eyes again to prevent the images of Philip swiving her coming to mind. What surprised him was that he still wanted her for his wife. He knew now that she was not the innocent, aloof virgin she pretended to be, and he wanted her even more. He lay on his bed, his imagination vivid, as he pictured what he would do to her, once he had her locked in his rooms in Augsburg.

Isabella was enjoying herself with Philip; he was handsome with a hard-muscled body, and he was a willing pupil, as she taught him how to please her as well. She loved how irreverent and light-hearted he was. They lay naked on his bed, and she unashamedly pumped him for information on matters in the courts of Europe, and on Robert's claim to the English throne. He was a clever and astute young man, who understood European families' history and power struggles. More importantly, he gave willingly of the information.

As the dawn light began to filter into the room, he whispered, 'You aren't what you seem, are you, Isabella de Embriaco?' His head tilted to one side, his fingers still caressing her body. 'What game are you playing, my Italian beauty, for you're certainly not here to sell a house?'

Isabella laughed and then moved her hand between his legs to gently stroke and arouse him again.

'I knew I wouldn't get an answer,' he said, as his lips descended onto her breasts, and she squirmed with pleasure beneath him. She threw her head back and smiled; after all, Chatillon did say she was allowed fun while extracting information, and she knew that she'd never bed Philip Van Loo again.

Isabella saw little of Prince Leopold for the next few days. He seemed to keep his distance and be involved with several richer merchant families in Ghent. She noticed that he was also paying attention to the very pretty daughter of one of the Ghent nobles. However, now that Robert, the heir, was back, the court went hunting each morning.

Isabella revelled in the exertion, whilst galloping and jumping in the birch forests that harboured boar and fallow deer. After a particularly hard chase, she found herself with a small group, in a clearing, while their horses caught their breath. Suddenly the Prince brought his horse alongside hers, so close that their knees touched.

'Good morrow, Sire. We haven't seen a lot of you this week.' The truth was that Leopold hadn't trusted himself to be anywhere near her. His man told him that Philip Van Loo hadn't left her bed until after dawn had risen. Therefore, he could only think that the young nobleman had taken her repeatedly. The thought of it, the images that rose unbidden in his mind, tormented him.

'Good morrow, my Lady; that's a very swift horse you're riding. I could see you galloping into the distance but couldn't keep up!'

She patted the mare's neck. 'She's part Arab and runs like the wind. A very dear friend gave her to me.'

He watched her intently, for several moments, and then put his hand firmly on her thigh. 'I would like to be a dear friend as well, Isabella. My business is now concluded, and I leave in two days. Is there any chance we could meet?' His eyes never left hers, his hand caressing her thigh.

Isabella wracked her brain; she had to move swiftly, or he'd be gone. 'Sire, I have to be extremely circumspect in the court, as my father has received two offers for my hand, which he's considering.' Leopold's eyes widened as this explained much.

'Well, now he has three offers, Isabella, for I want you as my wife, and I cannot believe that he has an offer from a prince of the blood of the Holy Roman Empire,' he stated, with a proud lift of his head.

'No, Sire, although they are two very wealthy and influential nobles in Milan and Venice.'

'As am I, Isabella. As am I. You know, of course, that I'm a personal friend, and cousin, of the Holy Roman Emperor, Henry IV. He holds sway over nearly all of those territories.'

She nodded and looked thoughtful. 'I think we need to discuss this further on our own, Sire, away from prying eyes and listening ears,' she said, glancing around at the other riders. His heart leapt at the thought of getting her somewhere on his own.

'I could come to your house?' he suggested.

'No, I don't trust my maid as she's my father's creature.'

In his mind's eye, he could see Philip Van Loo undressing Isabella. *Where was this maid then?* he wondered with a cynical smirk on his lips. However, she answered that for him.

'She has been ill for the past few days and took to her bed, but she's fully recovered.'

'I have it. I'll invite you to dinner with other guests, and we can talk afterwards. I have a housekeeper, in the residence, that would suit the proprieties,' he beamed.

Isabella purposefully looked doubtful while he continued to persuade her. She finally agreed, and he couldn't believe his good fortune. She bade him farewell, certain that she'd convinced him of her reluctance.

She sent for Edvard as soon as she reached home. 'He has taken the bait. I'm going to his house this evening. I need to ensure that our bag with Octavian is in place....'

Edvard sat down opposite her, concern in his eyes. 'Are you sure about this? Chatillon would never forgive me if you were hurt in any way.'

She smiled. 'It will be fine, Edvard. He assures me he has a housekeeper, and I'll take my usual two men in livery, who can sit in his kitchen, within call. I'm relying on his lust. He will want me in his bedroom. I need the leather sack out of sight but somewhere accessible. I'll be sure to pull the cord before I depart, leaving Octavian to do his worst.'

'I don't like it. That means you have to be with Leopold on your own in that bedroom. What happens if he prevents you from leaving when the snake is loose?' he muttered.

'I promise you, Edvard, I'll time it perfectly. I'll be able to keep Leopold at bay, I have kept him at arm's length already, and I hope you've acquired the toad venom for me. A few drops of that in his wine, and he will be incapable of swiving anyone.'

Edvard nodded, while still looking sceptical. It sounded straightforward in principle, but so many things could go wrong.

'You have one problem when you deny him what he obviously wants. He knows that Philip Van Loo spent the entire night with you. My men tell me he followed you both along the beach path back to the house. He stood and watched you take Philip to your room. He then sent a man to watch the house to see when Philip left. And as we know, it was after dawn had risen, that was careless of you.'

Isabella paled. This was a complication she'd created; she was new to this and had been careless. She looked at Edvard. She detected a hint of disapproval in his voice that Philip had stayed all night?

'I'll work around this, and I extracted a great deal of information from Philip Van Loo in that time,' she said, holding her head high and meeting his eyes.

However, Edvard just shrugged before continuing. 'There will be our men outside the house, your two men inside, and two of our informers are also inside. One is the housekeeper. If you shout, they will hear you and come running.'

She thanked him, and he went on his way with her snake in a leather bag. She experienced the first shivers of apprehension, for she was about to make her first kill; not just any man, but a Prince of Swabia. She shivered at the thought. Edvard told her that Piers had personally killed several dozen, and ordered the deaths of over a hundred more. Was Chatillon ever like this before he killed his intended victims? Did he ever lay awake at night, sweat upon his brow, contemplating what he was about to do? she wondered.

Several hours later, she was escorted to the house of the Prince. Like Bianca's house, it was set back from the bustling town, and birch forests surrounded it to the west. It was gated with high walls; another fortified manor that the spreading town had engulfed. The Prince was waiting in the hall, and he greeted her effusively.

'I thought we would be more comfortable in the smaller solar, so I have arranged that we will dine in there,' he said, handing her cloak to the housekeeper, who bowed to Isabella. 'The housekeeper will take your men to the kitchens and make sure they are fed.' He continued guiding her towards the stairs, his hand on the small of her back.

'Are the other guests here?' she asked, trying to keep the concern from her voice. She prayed they wouldn't be alone together for the whole night.

'Yes, one has arrived,' he answered evasively, leading her to the solar where a much older man sat huddled by the fire. He pushed himself to his feet to greet her.

'Lady Isabella, may I introduce the Master Burgher of Ghent. No ships would load or unload without his say in the port.'

Isabella was surprised at such a guest. Coming from the bustling port of Genoa, she knew the value of such men, who had sat at her father's table. However, the little she'd seen of Prince Leopold's arrogance, she was surprised he'd sit at a table with a merchant, albeit a rich one.

It turned out to be a lively and interesting meal with many topics of conversation. Both men were pleasantly surprised, and impressed, by Isabella's grasp and knowledge of events in Europe. She knew things about Duke Robert's plans that surprised the Prince. At that point, she realised that she'd said too much, and admitted that she'd heard the Countess relating this to her heir, Robert. Almost an hour later, Master Burgher pushed his chair back.

'Unfortunately, as you're aware, my Lord Prince, I have to meet with the Burghers of Ghent. I cannot stress how delighted I am to have been here and enjoyed your company, my Lady.' As he bowed and kissed her hand, Isabella now realised why he'd been invited. Leopold wanted as much time alone with her as possible.

She sat alone in the solar, as the Prince showed his guest out. For a moment, she felt a slight wave of panic, but quickly pushed it away, and retained control. In the next hour, she

CHAPTER TWENTY-TWO

must kill this man and get clean away. She reached into the hidden pocket in her gown and took out a small, stoppered vial. She leaned over and put several drops into his glass, which still held about a third of the deep red wine he'd poured. It was a mixture of toad venom and a small amount of belladonna, to make him sleep. She knew it would take only a short time to work, but would possibly dampen his ardour, and make him doze. However, as the door opened, marking his return, she still felt apprehension. Leopold was a dangerous, ruthless man, complicit in the murder of a Pope and a legation of innocent priests, and she couldn't let her guard down for a second.

Chatillon's fingers were shaking so much in Rouen that he could hardly open the long strip of vellum. Finally, a bird had arrived from Ghent. He walked from the coop into the light and read the tiny coded message.

We have arrived in Ghent, and everything is going to plan. An attempt was made to poison Isabella, but we foiled it. Unfortunately, they escaped. She is well and following your instructions to the letter.

Piers closed his eyes and held the message, gripped tightly in his fist, as if he didn't want to let it go. She was alive! They were both alive! And all was well. He retraced his steps down to the Great Hall, feeling euphoric, even though the message in his other hand for Duke Robert didn't bring good news.

'God's blood. Roger Montgomery, the Earl of Shrewsbury, has gone over to the King; the man who has spent the last ten years at my father's side. Why? Why would he do that?' yelled Robert, scanning the faces of Chatillon and the nobles around him for an answer.

Chatillon sighed. 'The problem lies in the fact that you aren't there, Sire. The figurehead of the rebellion is missing. Your uncles are powerful, but now, they are holed up in Pevensey Castle under siege, surrounded by the army of William Rufus. Finian tells me they have little food, and it is unlikely they will last more than a week, without surrendering. You need to sail, Sire. You need to take your fleet and risk the weather. If you truly want the throne of England, then you need to get your troops on the ground in Kent or Sussex. As soon as word goes out that you're there, men will flock to your banner. It will put heart into any lords that are wavering.'

Robert chewed his bottom lip and gazed at the floor, the indecision writ clearly on his face.

Chatillon tried again. 'Meanwhile, William Rufus and Flambard are bribing and threatening the nobles who support you. Robert, you need to sail.'

'Yes, Chatillon. Yes, I know, but everything is against me. His navy has attacked the supply and troop ships, and they are blockading the ports. How can I break through that?'

'My Lord Duke, the south coast of England has two dozen places where you could land your men. You could even go north, land in Suffolk or Essex, and then march south.' Chatillon moved closer to the Duke and whispered softly, 'I have always admired your courage and determination, Robert. God's blood! You defeated your father at Gerberoi, and he was the greatest warrior Europe has seen. Don't run away from this fight, or you'll lose a great deal more than the throne of England. Your very reputation is at stake here.'

CHAPTER TWENTY-TWO

Robert took a step back from the Papal Envoy. Chatillon had supported him for years. He was his friend, but Robert found that he couldn't hold that cold, dark gaze, and he moved away.

'I will sail Chatillon, I promise you, but at the right time.'

Chatillon shook his head as he watched Robert walk to the window. He just prayed that Odo and Finian could hold out, for the future would be bleak for any captured mercenaries. The Lombards had a history of flaying mercenaries alive and hanging them from the castle walls. He'd never forget that sight as a young man.

Chapter Twenty-three

Finian stood watching as more banners joined the King's forces. He recognised the latest ones. It was the traitor De Warenne and his sons—the man Finian had sworn to kill on Chatillon's orders. He couldn't stand to watch anymore and decided to find Count Robert Mortain and his brother Odo; they had to do something.

'We are now out of fodder for the horses and need to ride out and attack. With Belleme's troops, we've enough to make a difference and will possibly do them serious harm.' The two men looked at each other, and Belleme, walking in on the end of this conversation with his brother Hugh, surprisingly agreed with Finian.

'At this stage, it can do us no harm, showing them we still have a lot of fighting spirit left. We will attack just before dusk. They will be sitting around their campfires and settling down for the night. I'll organise two raiding parties to ride with us. They will break through and get us more supplies, while we occupy the King's army.'

Odo looked at Finian, who waited for a response, and with a

nod from his brother, Mortain, he agreed to let them try. Finian turned and left, followed by Belleme, who slapped Finian on the shoulder, in admiration. A rare gesture from the Count of Belleme.

'At last, we are doing something. I swear, Ui Neill, we would have gone mad if we had to sit here for much longer.'

Odo watched them go. 'As I said before, a very useful young man, Brother.'

Mortain didn't reply at first. 'You know they will hang him and all his mercenaries if they catch him, or if we are forced to surrender. The paid mercenaries always bear the brunt of the revenge.'

Odo grimaced and stood up. 'Always the crow of doom, Mortain. I'll try and arrange to get him out before we come to that. No matter what happens tonight, or how successful Finian is, we cannot possibly win here at Pevensey without Robert and his reinforcements. I'll try to send Finian to Rochester. After the charge, he can keep riding north with his men. He has a better chance of escaping from Rochester. Let us go and find him.'

They found Finian, along with most of his men, already in the saddle, keen to ride out. He listened to the Bishop's request, with a sense of relief, but also sadness at leaving others behind.

'I'll do this and take ten of my men. However, you must promise me you'll give the rest of my men some livery, either yours or Mortain's, so they are clearly in your paid service when Pevensey falls.' The two men agreed, and Finian drew his horse alongside Belleme, in front of his men. He looked up at the towers ahead of them and saw the Castellan's son, and his archers, crouched ready on the walls.

'Unleash the arrows as soon as we get out of the gates. They will be easy targets as they run for their horses.' The young man raised a hand in reply and shouted an order to the twenty archers on the walls, and they notched their arrows and drew their bows, ready to stand up and shoot down on the enemy. Finian then stood in his stirrups, his sword rose in his hand, and he turned to the men spread across the bailey.

'Let us give them hell, for the Pope and God are on our side. Open the gates. We ride for Duke Robert, the rightful king.'

Over a hundred and fifty men cantered out of the castle and down the hill, breaking into a gallop when they reached the flatter ground. 'Keep in line,' shouted Finian, as he watched the chaos and panic unfold in the enemy camp ahead. As good as their word, the archers behind them were dropping the men in front of them. The charge hit the enemy with a crash, driving forward into the camp, flattening men and tents, and knocking pots flying over fires. Sparks and flames leapt high, as burning embers hit the tents and the blankets on the ground, and men ran from the carnage.

Finian could see the bigger pavilions of the nobles on the right. He was unsure if William Rufus was there, but he was looking for Earl William De Warenne. He had to pay for betraying Robert.

As they had arrived later than the other troops, the large striped pavilion was one of the last on the eastern side; the De Warenne banners flying above it. 'To me!' he shouted to the group of ten men that he'd selected to take to Rochester. They pulled their horses around to follow him, while still slashing and cutting down the enemy, some of whom had finally managed to mount.

Finian still rode at a gallop through the camp. His reins knotted and dropped on his horse's neck as, using his legs to steer his horse, he cut a swathe through the camp towards the striped pavilion, slashing left and right.

The Earl of Surrey, William De Warenne, had just mounted his horse and drawn his sword, when he looked up to see the hellish sight of the charge heading straight at him. He recognised the Irish warrior immediately and paled, for he knew of Ui Neill's reputation. Finian, tugging the reins, pulled his horse up into a rear directly in front of De Warenne, causing the Earl's alarmed horse to leap sideways in fright to avoid the plunging hooves. While Finian's men attacked his household guards, the Earl tried to raise his sword to defend himself, to no avail, as it was smashed out of his hand. Finian was alongside him in seconds, pinning his panicking horse against the side of the pavilion. The Earl raised both hands in supplication, which Finian ignored as, reaching over, he plunged his sword through the Earl De Warenne's throat.

'That's for betraying us, you treacherous dog!' he yelled. Finian heard the high-pitched scream of, 'No!' from Raynold De Warenne behind him, watching his father die, but glancing around, Finian saw that King William's army was recovering, and he didn't have time to deal with the rest of the De Warenne sons. They would wait for another day.

'On me!' he shouted loudly to his men, to be heard above the screams, shouts and clash of blades around them. His men seemed unscathed apart from minor cuts and scratches as, leaving the melee at Pevensey, they galloped through the trees to the north to find the road to Rochester.

Meanwhile, Belleme and his brother Hugh, who were very satisfied with the damage they had inflicted, called the retreat in the deepening dusk and smoke and led their men back to Pevensey Castle. They were followed by the raiders laden with sacks of foodstuffs they had taken from the enemy's stores.

Three days later, a herald appeared on the causeway leading to the gates, announcing that King William Rufus wanted a parley, but would only speak to his uncle, Count Robert Mortain. An hour later, Mortain rode out with several of his retainers and talked to the King for some time. Bishop Odo and Belleme watched from the ramparts. The Castellan's son was close beside them, bow in hand.

'I could put an arrow through his throat at this distance, and it would all be over. Just say the word, my Lord Bishop,' he said in a loud whisper.

Odo didn't reply at first, and Belleme, who had a reputation for being the cruellest of men, wondered in astonishment if he was actually considering killing the King. Instead, the Bishop put a hand on the young man's shoulder.

'It would seem a solution and an attractive one, but we never break a parley under any circumstances. What price would honour have then? We would be no better than savages.' The young archer snorted in disgust, and Robert De Belleme released a breath he did not realise he'd been holding. A few moments later, Robert, the Count of Mortain, and Uncle to the King, rode back through Pevensey Castle's gates. They were all waiting for him as he strode into the hall, peeling off his gauntlets and calling for wine.

'Well? Don't keep us waiting, Mortain!' snapped his brother, Odo.

'The King is offering us terms and safe passage, if we surrender. We all know we cannot stay cooped up here for much longer. The extra food taken in the raid will only last a few days longer, a week at the most. I say let us accept his terms.'

CHAPTER TWENTY-THREE

Odo noticed that his brother could not meet his eyes, and suspected that he had come to an understanding with William Rufus.

'And what of me?' he asked.

'Unfortunately, William Rufus sees you as the architect of this rebellion, and he thinks you persuaded Duke Robert into this. He says that Robert would never have attempted this on his own. He has decided you can keep your life, but you'll lose all your lands in England.' There was a shocked silence in the packed hall at this pronouncement.

'Brother, we don't have much choice,' added Mortain.

Odo looked at the faces of all the nobles gathered around them. Many of them were nodding in agreement with Mortain. His shoulders slumped in defeat. They were right; the reinforcements had never arrived to support them. Duke Robert hadn't sailed to lead them, and now the rebels would have to pay the price for the rising against the King. So he reluctantly agreed, nodding his head and dropping into a chair. The Castellan, Sir Hugh and his son stood at the back of the hall, watching and listening. He was Odo's man through and through. He had come with him in 1066 and brought his family over shortly afterwards, so he'd likely lose his post and home, but he thought he'd keep his life. He put his hand on his son's shoulder.

'We will all have to leave the castle. We will no doubt ride or march out tomorrow, but the enemy will be waiting for us, and you know what they sometimes do to archers.' The young man nodded, and his father put an arm around him and pulled him close. 'There are other reasons why you must not get caught, Dion. You must go, escape tonight, and ride to Rochester, as they will hold out much longer there.'

His son reluctantly nodded in agreement. He didn't want to leave his father, but they had no choice, and he had a duty to save his men.

That night there was no moon, and the company of archers led their horses quietly out of the castle along the edge of the causeway. Their hooves had been padded to make no noise, and each man had his hand on his horse's nose to calm them and prevent a whinny. When they reached the meadow, an enemy sentry spotted them. He shouted a warning, but he was on foot, and by now, Dion and his archers had mounted, and they knew the lands well enough around their home, to gallop to the north and lose any pursuit.

The next day, King William Rufus rode triumphantly through the open gates of Pevensey Castle. The rebellion in Sussex was over, and the word would spread like wildfire across the south of England. Before he was taken, Bishop Odo sent a bird with a short message to Chatillon.

My brother Mortain has gone over to the King; the rest of us are prisoners. We are to be marched to Rochester. If Robert is ever to sail, now is the moment to sail up the Medway and support the rebels in Rochester before we get there.

Chapter Twenty-four

Prince Leopold closed the door behind him and leant against it, as he regarded her sitting before the fire. He was an unprepossessing sight, she thought, as she fixed a smile on her face—the thinning blonde hair, the thick lips, his cheeks red-veined from too much wine. He walked over to join her and, taking her long pale fingers, raised them to his lips.

'Have you thought about the offer I made you, Isabella?' he asked, still retaining her hand and stroking it and his eyes never leaving hers. Isabella dropped her eyes.

'I have given it much thought, Sire, and I'm truly flattered by your attentions, but as I mentioned, the decision is one my father must take.' She leaned forward, reaching for her goblet to take a sip of wine, when suddenly he picked up both goblets and flung the contents of the goblets on the fire, where it hissed and spat amongst the logs. He walked to the long high table against the wall, lit by a large candle in the centre. Isabella felt a moment of panic as he poured them wine from a different container. Her plan to make him impotent and drowsy had just failed, and she was now defenceless. A large bowl of fruit was at the far end of the table, and he reached over and selected an orange. As she watched him, she suddenly noticed leather cords hung down a finger's length below the table. They were in the shadows beyond the large fruit bowl. The leather sack with Octavian was on the table behind the bowl. The servant hadn't hidden it as well as she expected. Isabella felt herself go cold as she watched and prayed that the Prince did not notice the sack.

Leopold had taken the dagger from his belt, and he thinly sliced the fruit. She rose and walked to his left side, feigning interest in his actions. Isabella placed a hand on his left shoulder, which pleasantly surprised him, then positioned herself with her back to the fruit bowl, keeping it from sight. With her left hand, she reached behind her, felt along the edge of the table and gently tugged at one of the leather cords, which stubbornly refused to budge. These had been designed to pull straight out unless the stupid servant had tied them. Again, a wave of panic rose in her breast, but she took a deep breath and found the other cord.

'What are you doing, Sire?' she asked, to keep him there and shield her actions. As she tugged again, the cord finally came free and dropped to the floor, opening the neck of the bag and freeing the snake.

'I'm making a special drink for you from my own country. It is a mixture of a very heady sweet wine sprinkled with spices and decorated with citrus fruits. Then we plunge the hot poker into it, until it bubbles. It is a celebration drink, and I feel we've something to celebrate. Our growing friendship and hopefully our growing intimacy,' he said, turning. He pulled Isabella hard against his body and held her there. She cursed herself for getting this close to him so soon. However, she had no choice as she had to do something to release her snake. Now she was held, her back to the fruit bowl, and Octavian could be free. Edvard was right, for her plan had been clumsy. So much could go wrong and already had, as Leopold had thrown the drugged wine away. Her snake might not even emerge from the dark, comfortable warmth of the bag, but she knew she had to move away from the table, just in case.

'And I look forward to that intimacy with you, my beautiful Isabella,' he said, grasping her buttocks and pressing his hard manhood against her. She put her hands on his chest and tried to push him away, to no avail.

'Sire, we hardly know each other yet. Can we sit and talk first,' she whispered. The word 'first' brought a smile to Leopold's face, and letting her go, he took the goblets to the fire to be mulled. He lifted the steaming goblets from the hearth and, bringing them to her, raised a toast to their future. She took the warm goblet and, taking a sip, smiled to disarm him as they seated themselves.

He pulled his chair over to hers so that their knees were touching. 'You do want your father to say yes, Isabella, do you not?' he asked, leaning forward and putting his hand on her knee. Isabella sat further back in the chair away from him and smiled.

'Indeed I do, Sire. I find the life you've described to me, our position in the court of the Holy Roman Emperor, very attractive,' she answered glibly and took another large mouthful of wine. It was delicious, the aroma of the spices, but there was another smell, slightly sweet, that she recognised but couldn't quite place. She reasoned that it must be the heady sweet wine.

'And what of me, Isabella? I'm aware I'm older than you, but can you see yourself by my side, in my bed, bearing my sons? I promise you that you'll not be disappointed with the bedsport. I know how to make a woman squeal in pleasure,' he said, moving his hand further up her thigh and squeezing. She put her goblet down and raised both hands to her face. It suddenly seemed hot in there, and she knew she had to keep him at bay.

'Of course, Sire, I would be proud of my position as your wife, and any woman would be pleased to be bedded by a prince of the blood,' she said coyly as she fanned her face. He picked up her goblet and held it over to her lips.

'Let us both drink to that. I will enjoy bedding you every night, Isabella.' She took the goblet but found her grasp was loose. He folded her fingers around it, and she emptied it. She suddenly felt her eyelids becoming heavy. She felt tired and knew she had to get out of there soon, as it had become unbearably hot, and her snake could be loose in the room. She shook her head and placed the empty goblet on the table as Leopold's hand moved higher. She glanced over at the table, in desperation, and could see movement. Octavian had emerged from the soft leather bag and was now curling himself tightly around the base of the fruit bowl, as he surveyed his surroundings.

Isabella clamped her hand down on Leopold's fingers. His nails were digging into the softness of her inner thigh. 'Can you get us another of those delicious drinks, Sire, as I wish to make another toast,' she said, surprised that her words were beginning to slur.

To her surprise, ignoring her, he dropped to his knees in front of her, raising the hem of her dress over her knees to the top of her thighs. He began running his hands up her legs. As he pushed her knees apart, and she seemed unable to stop him, it suddenly came to her. The sweet smell was digitalis, and she'd been drugged. He'd played her at her own game. Oh, the irony of it was almost too much. She knew exactly what a small amount of digitalis would do. It would immobilise her, and her limbs would become leaden. A fog would descend to stop her from thinking coherent thoughts. He'd have her at his mercy to do as he wished to her body.

Suddenly the absurdity of the situation made her laugh out loud, which stopped the Prince for a moment. He'd expected shock, tears, and anger but not laughter. He sat back on his heels and narrowed his eyes at her, as Isabella fought for the right words.

'Another of those drinks, I beg of you, and then we will remove all of these,' she said, fingering her crumpled gown. Leopold was nonplussed, but he decided to do as she said. He wanted her naked and bent over his bed. The dissolute Prince liked to take his women roughly from behind, his hands on their breasts, and Isabella had large beautiful breasts. The thought of what he wanted to do to her was almost too much for him, and he hesitated, goblet in each hand, looking down at her long, bare legs and soft white thighs. But she waved him away, and he reluctantly carried them over to the table. He'd just filled them and reached for another orange when he leapt backwards with a cry, knocking the goblets flying.

Something had launched at his face, and he felt a hard blow to his left cheek. Leopold was never to know what hit him. Octavian had watched him, unblinking for a few moments, until he reached for more fruit, moving his hand into the snake's space. He'd slowly uncoiled, with the small hood spreading out in warning behind his head as he rose and launched himself at his attacker, burying his fangs deeply into

Leopold's left cheek. Leopold fell backwards, his head hit the floor, and the snake was knocked free by a flailing arm.

The Prince lay on the floor in shock as the snake, having dropped, rapidly slid into the shade under the table. Something had attacked him. It was large—a rat? It must have been a rat; the city was infested with them, and they were becoming bold and more aggressive daily in the houses. Leopold raised a hand to his face, and it came away covered in streaks of blood. He was still stunned by the fall, but he turned to raise a hand to Isabella for help, but her head was back, and her eyes were closed. She'd seen nothing, for the drug had worked; she was his now. Leopold struggled to his feet, the blood dripping down his face and onto his chin. He picked up a cloth from the table and held it to his cheek. The Prince gingerly felt his way around the wound; had the rat torn his cheek open? he wondered. But no, there seemed to be two holes from its teeth, and he could feel the wetness where they were still bleeding. He staggered back to the chair, the cloth tightly against the puncture wounds. Leopold knew it would clot and stop soon. He didn't want to cover her body in blood as he swived her.

Isabella slowly opened her eyes. She lifted her head, and realising that Octavian had struck, she now regarded the prince with mock alarm. 'What happened?' she whispered.

'A rat, a large rat, it bit me!' he answered. She opened her eyes wide, in horror, whilst scanning the room for her snake. Isabella knew he'd be hiding somewhere; his poison sacs would be empty, and she prayed the servant would find him.

'You need a physician now, Leopold. Rat bites can be very poisonous,' she mumbled at him as she forced her hands to obey her, pushing her gown down to her knees. The prince saw the panic on her face; he stood up, swaying, and made for the door. He was now sweating, dizzy, and suddenly had difficulty getting to the end of a breath. He pulled the door open and shouted for a servant.

'Send for a physician. A large rat has attacked me,' he announced to the servant, who appeared, looking in horror at his master's blood-covered face and hand. He backed away, nodding, then raced to shout for more help along the corridor. Leopold made his way unsteadily back across the room to the chair. Isabella watched him with satisfaction. The blood was still trickling down his cheek and pooling on the bottom of his chin, before it dripped onto his clothes. She knew the highly toxic venom of asps prevents the blood from clotting.

At that moment, more servants alarmed by the shouting arrived at the door, including her men. Leopold's eyes were now closed, and he gasped for breath. His blood-covered face was beginning to pale with a bluish tinge. She pushed herself to her feet, took a few unsteady steps and then placed her hands on the arms of his chair, to hold herself up. She leaned forward, barely a finger's length away from his face. He opened his eyes, feeling her breath on his face; she could see the fear in them as he fought for every breath, and she smiled as she whispered, 'Chatillon tells me you'll go straight to hell for what you did to Pope Alexander, and I have now made sure you'll be dead so he gets his revenge.'

Leopold's eyes opened wide in realisation for a moment, and then he let out a strangled choking sound and slumped in the chair. She straightened up and assumed a shocked expression.

'I tried to help him, but I think the physician will be too late,' she said, as she crumpled to the floor in what looked like a dead faint, her legs unable to hold her any longer. Before drifting into oblivion, Isabella's last thoughts were of Octavian, hidden in the unfamiliar room with empty poison sacs. She prayed they'd find him.

By midday the next day, the story had spread around the port of Ghent like wildfire. Prince Leopold, a visiting cousin of the Holy Roman Emperor, had been attacked by a rat that increased in size with the telling. It had attacked him in his own home, and he died from the poisoned wounds. No mention was made of Isabella, as her men had picked her up and whisked her out of there before the physician arrived. Edvard's first thought was that she'd been bitten, but her maid told him she'd checked everywhere, and Isabella had no puncture wounds. It looked like she was almost in a coma, and he realised that she'd been drugged. She slept all of the next day until the digitalis worked its way through her system.

The first thing she saw when she opened her eyes was Edvard's concerned face, as he sat by the bed.

'Praise the Lord,' he said as she opened her eyes, which were still hooded and heavy. She gave him a weak smile, and he helped her to sit up, propping the bolster behind her. 'I thought you were dead when they carried you in. I presumed you had also been bitten, but that seemed impossible as the snake attacked Leopold. The Prince is dead, by the way.'

She nodded in satisfaction. 'He deserved it, Edvard, not only for his previous heinous crimes but he drugged me with digitalis. I wonder how many poor women and boys he has done the same with in the past,' she whispered. Seeing the concern on Edvard's face, she placed her hand on his. 'Do not fear he did not touch me; Octavian came to my rescue. Oh, Edvard, is it wrong that I feel a deep satisfaction at his death?'

To her surprise, Edvard laughed. 'Not at all. Chatillon would be pleased and proud to know you feel that way.'

CHAPTER TWENTY-FOUR

'So tell me what happened, Edvard. I remember Leopold summoning a physician but nothing else after that.'

'Yes, he did, but the man took some time and arrived well after Leopold's death. Our servants got you out of there, telling Leopold's Steward that you had fainted in shock, and several coins exchanged hands to ensure that you were never there, as far as the servants were concerned. The story of the rat attack was masterful, and of course, it was believed because it came from Leopold's lips to his servants. I presume you told him that.'

Isabel laughed. 'Edvard, the story didn't come from me. He truly believed it was a large rat because of the force of the blow. It was frightening how hard the snake struck; it knocked him off his feet backwards, and he's not a small man.' They sat mulling over what had happened for a few minutes.

'Our young man, Jean, crept into the darkened room later and reluctantly attracted Octavian out with a half-dead mouse. He was still shaking when he handed me the leather sack. I paid him well.'

She smiled, but Edvard took her hand and became serious.

'So that was your first time, but you must see there was far too much risk in your planning. Particularly with the risks you took. I admit there are always some factors we cannot control. Chatillon's continued success lies in using his skills to mitigate, or identify, and remove those factors. He's as good as he is because he is never caught, and suspicion rarely leads back to him.'

She mulled over his words. 'You're right, of course; looking back now, so much more could have gone wrong, especially if the snake hadn't struck him. I was at his mercy at that point. I should have left when Octavian was released, if he'd let me.'

He stood. 'Get some rest. I'll send a missive to Chatillon to tell him of your success. It would be best if you appeared at the court tomorrow for the last time. I suggest you take Countess Gertrude into your confidence about your marriage. They will not be pleased to know they have been hoodwinked.'

It proved far easier than she'd imagined. Countess Gertrude had her reliable avenues of information, and it turned out that she'd known for some time that Isabella was married to Chatillon. Her son Philip however, had not, and a wave of shock went through him that he'd spent a night making love to the wife of the most dangerous assassin in Europe. The two women watched as he paled, took a step backwards, stuttered and excused himself as he left.

The Countess laughed. 'He's young and somewhat naive when it comes to women. He will learn, which may be a good lesson for him, that not everything is as it seems. I'll reinforce the importance and art of information gathering.'

Isabella liked the Countess immensely and promised to return to Ghent with her husband. 'We will be delighted as always to see Piers. He always has such amusing titbits and stories, all scandalously true. Always a man to keep on your side. Bring your children with you. There are never enough children in the court.'

'We don't have any children yet,' said Isabella with an amused smile.

'No, but you're with child, are you not, and God willing, it will be a healthy boy. If you're lucky, it may be one of each. You do know that twins run in the Chatillon family!' The Countess laughed at the shocked expression on Isabella's face, as she'd only just suspected herself that she might be with child. Isabella stood to take her leave and had almost reached the door when the Countess waved her back.

'I presume you've heard the news about Prince Leopold. I believe he circled you like a shark for a while, but you brushed him off. Do you know he came and tried to bribe me!' she laughed. 'He told me Philip had swived you all night at your house, and he'd tell his betrothed, in Denmark, if I didn't instruct you to marry him. I spat in his face and dared him to do his worst. Oh, how I laughed when he'd gone, knowing you were married to his biggest enemy.' She raised her eyebrow in a question, but Isabella, open-mouthed at what she heard, didn't rise to the bait.

'Yes, he pursued me, and I drove him away. I believe it was shocking how he died. They say a large rat attacked him.'

'Yes, filthy, stinking, pox-ridden rat, just like him, so I laughed at that as well when I heard. However, I cannot have giant rats running around my city, so I demanded to see the body.'

'How brave,' whispered Isabella, her fingers clasped tightly.

'It was as if all the blood had drained from his body; he was so white. I expected some terrible wound, but no, there were two holes in his face where it had bitten him. No rat attacked him—I would lay money on that.'

Isabella had gone cold, but she had to ask because anyone would.

'Was it something more dangerous or sinister that attacked him?'

'It was a snake. I have seen snake bites several times, having visited the hotter countries where these creatures live. The gap between the holes in his face was wide, so I would wager it was a snake of some size. However, I'm not looking for it, as it did everyone a great service in removing a loathsome man, and hopefully, it will slither away to keep the rat population down.'

Isabella shuddered, as she thought the Countess would expect that, at the least. Was there nothing this woman did not know? she wondered, as she hurried back to the house.

They were leaving that afternoon. A message had come from Piers; they were not to go to Rouen. Instead, they were to go directly to the large Chatillon estate south of Paris and stay there. Isabella was pleased; she'd heard so much about his childhood home and longed to see it. More significantly, she wanted their child to be born there.

Piers would join them in a few weeks, and she'd tell him the good news then.

Chapter Twenty-five

Finian watched the Sheriff of Leicester, Sir Hugh Grandesmil, striding up and down the large hall at Rochester Castle. Hugh had fought with King William's side at the battle of Hastings, and Finian could now see from his movements that he was feeling his age. Two of his five sons were here in Rochester. Yves and Aubrey had always fought on the side of Duke Robert Curthose. They now watched their father with concern.

Finian had arrived at the castle a week earlier, followed swiftly by the news that Pevensey had fallen. Odo had been taken prisoner while his brother Robert had been allowed to return to his estates. King William Rufus was now marching his army to attack Rochester. Hugh stopped pacing suddenly and turned on Finian.

'You are Chatillon's man. In God's name, what is happening in Rouen? What does Chatillon say?'

Finian sighed. He'd heard little since he arrived. 'The ships are there and all provisioned, my Lord. I supplied several of them myself. I was told that poor weather had held them back. I assure you that Chatillon is just as frustrated as you are. The

Pope has given support and funds for this invasion which has still not happened.'

Hugh grunted and spat on the floor in disgust.

'This is all the fault of that spineless Prince Bishop William de St Calais, who should have kept his mouth shut. He's now safe, holed up in his fortress in Durham, while we are here, awaiting the same fate as those at Pevensey if we don't get any reinforcements.'

Finian inclined his head in agreement, as there was nothing he could say. He knew he should leave Rochester; the attempt to take the throne from William Rufus was turning into an abject failure, but he'd never run away from a fight in his life. He decided he needed air, so bowing to the nobles in the hall, he walked out into the bailey.

His men had been out with Hugh's troops raiding the local villages for food and driving sheep and goats into the great castle, as they knew they could be here for some time. He ran up the steps onto the walls and surveyed the surrounding countryside. He looked north and eastwards. There was the vast expanse of the River Medway ahead of him; a perfect bay for Duke Robert to sail his fleet into and land his troops. Finian squinted into the distance, but all he could see were the two large ships of William Rufus blocking the harbour. There were no other sails in the distance, yet the weather was calm and would have been ideal for a crossing from Normandy.

'They aren't coming, are they?' asked a quiet voice beside him. He looked down into the face of the young archer. He still wore the trademark mask, as did all the archers, but his dark green eyes were narrowed in concern.

'I like to hope that they are. I cannot understand Robert's reluctance to sail. The crown was here for the taking. Now I fear that it is too late. Ranulph Flambard is a cunning and clever man. He's buying off, or threatening, the nobles in England who support Robert. Are you afraid for your father?'

The young man nodded, and Finian could see him blinking away a tear. He decided to reassure him. 'Your father never raised a sword against the King; he was just the Castellan of Pevensey castle. I'm sure he will be spared.' The young man nodded and turned away.

'Come, let us ride out for an hour or so while we still can, as I have an idea I want to test.'

The archer looked at him in surprise and, taking a step back, ran his eyes over the Irish warrior appraising him. Finian laughed at his audacity and made a formal introduction.

'I'm Finian Ui Neill, disgraced Irish lord and mercenary,' he said, sweeping into a deep bow.

'My name is Dion de Chartelle, Leader of the Company of Pevensey Archers in the pay of Bishop Odo, but not for much longer, I think.' Finian heard the bitterness in his voice and sighed.

'Yes, war alters our lives for better or worse depending on which side is winning.'

He waved to his men, and they mounted up. Heading north, they rode to the shores of the Medway. For a while, they raced each other along the beaches, weaving in and out of the rocks. Two fishermen were docking at a small wooden jetty. They had a goodly catch of fish. Finian pulled out his purse and, to their surprise, bought it all.

'Take it to the castle, and we will have fresh fish tonight. The rest can be smoked and dried; I fear we will need it.' Dion expected him to return, but he stood talking to the fishermen for some time. The young archer saw more coin exchange hands and wondered what he was arranging.

Finian threw his reins to one of his men on their return and raced up the steps to Sir Hugh Grandesmil, who was in no better mood.

'Sire, I have an idea; hear me out, and then you can say yay or nay.'

Hugh listened to what he had to say and then burst into laughter.

'If you want to risk your necks, it is a daring plan, but I have no objections. Take both of my sons with you. I'm sick of the sight of them kicking their heels around here.' His sons Yves and Aubrey grinned and came over to listen to Finian's plan. He then went to find Dion.

'Can you spare me a dozen archers, preferably any who can swim and don't get seasick?'

At first, the young man smiled, thinking he was joking, but then saw he was deadly serious. Dion's eyes widened realising why coin had exchanged hands with the fishermen. 'You're going to attack the blockaders!' he exclaimed.

Finian nodded.

'Then I'm coming with you, and I'll bring my men. You need strips of cloth soaked in pitch to wrap around the arrows if you're going to bombard them with fire. I will bring them,' he said, grinning as he ran towards the door.

Finian felt buoyant to be out and doing something against the enemy. He just prayed his plan would work. The fishermen turned up with their boats as they promised—four in total—and all had oars. Fortunately, it was a dark night with no moon—it would be hard rowing all the way out to the mouth of the Medway, but they did not dare risk a sail. They were told to be silent as sounds carried a long distance across the water.

CHAPTER TWENTY-FIVE

The archers had their instructions as they were split between the boats. The only sound that could be heard was the dip of the oars, and suddenly, Finian was reminded of the Saracens coming at them in the night. It was a similar sound—the sound of death approaching stealthily.

The two ships were easy to see as they had mast lanterns lit fore and aft. They were a reasonable distance apart on either side of the estuary, although the larger one seemed closer to the mouth of the River Thames. Finian quietly told the men to ship all oars but two, and they crept slowly in the dark towards the smaller ship. Two boats, including Dion's smaller fishing boat, went around the far side. All of them had all brought bows, although many were not up to the standard of the archers. A man in each boat was responsible for lighting the flaming torch, which he'd carefully touch to the pitch-dipped arrows. Dion's first flaming arrow would be the signal to begin.

The ship towered above them, as they waited, and all was quiet save for the water lapping against the ship's side. There was no sound from the ship itself.

Dion's arrow soared through the dark sky, hitting the sail square in the middle and within a few moments, had set it alight. Then they all fired, and dozens of flaming arrows sliced through the air, into the ship, and into the sail, which began to burn furiously. There were shouts of alarm and panic on the decks above, which now had a dozen fires from bow to stern that the crew scrambled to extinguish, pulling up buckets of seawater on ropes which made little difference as others tried to stamp or beat the flames out on the deck.

Finian shouted the order to fire again and then began to pull away, as some of the crew began to fire back. One man had a crossbow, which put a bolt through the throat of one of Finian's men. He was dying as he went over the side and hit the water. Suddenly, there were sounds of fighting and screams on the far side of the ship. Finian listened in alarm. What was happening? Surely, his men were not boarding the ship. They had orders to leave as soon as their arrows were gone. He told his crew to man the oars, pulling them around the bow. As they reached the other side, he could see little in the dark, but the flaming torch from one fishing boat cast a lurid light. Above them, crewmen were throwing missiles and barrels at the boats below.

As they pulled closer, he could see one fishing boat sinking and the men on board jumping into the water. Then, it was gone, leaving just the men's cries and the sound of splashing. Several were swimming out to try to board the second boat. Some of them were already clinging to the gunwale; too many. The boat was tipping; if they were not careful, it would capsize. All he could hear were shouts and splashes, and as his boat pulled closer, he began shouting orders to his men to swim to his boat. He helped his crew to pull men from the water, one of whom was a spluttering, angry Dion, his heavy, sodden cloak almost pulling him back into the water.

'They threw ballast rocks down on us, and one went straight through the hull. It was an old boat and went down so quickly, the fisherman with it.'

Finian looked up. The blockade ship of William Rufus was completely ablaze at one end. He could see with satisfaction that their job here was finished as he yelled across at all the crews. 'Man the oars, men! Pull us away at speed!'

He stood in the stern and looked back at the mouth of the Medway; the whole bay was now lit by the blazing ship. The second blockader was making way to try and rescue any survivors, but there was hardly any breeze to fill their sails.

Finian's other two boats followed, and soon they were pulling onto the beach where they had left their hobbled horses.

He gathered them all together on the beach and lauded their bravery. He'd lost two men, Dion had lost an archer, and a fisherman had drowned. He paid the three other fishermen, and assured them he'd personally see that the lost man's family were compensated.

They rode back through the gates, and he joined Sir Hugh de Grandesmil with the other nobles standing on the castle walls, watching the flaming wreck in the distance. They were elated by the attack and slapped him on the back in congratulation. Finian hated losing men, but it was a small price to pay for the raid's success, and may give the King pause for thought. It might also make it easier for Robert's fleet to break through and come to their rescue.

The next day the King arrived with his army. They set up a large camp, half a league away from the castle, and put a separate siege force around Rochester castle, for they had learned their lesson last time at Pevensey. Their scouts told them that he had a far large number with him—even more supporters had joined him since Pevensey. Finian stood on the walls and watched, as he set his force in a wide semi-circle facing the castle. Sir Hugh's eldest son, Yves de Grandesmil, slammed his fist down onto the stone wall.

'I don't understand it! I have fought beside Duke Robert Curthose for years, and he's one of the bravest men in battle I have known. So why is he not here, Ui Neill? You are Chatillon's friend. Do you know what is happening? Bishop Odo asked us to rise for Duke Robert, and we did, but he should be with us, and the people of England would flock to his banner.'

No one disagreed with him.

' I know little more than you, Yves, or about what is happening elsewhere in England. Except now, Bishop Odo is a prisoner of William Rufus, and the rebellion here has no one to lead it. The only things we can do are to sit and wait and pray Duke Robert comes. If he doesn't, then we will have to negotiate terms,' stated Finian, always the realist.

It was to be two days before the King's herald approached the gates of Rochester Castle, requesting the presence of Sir Hugh Grandesmil to meet with Bishop Odo, at the end of the causeway.

'What do you think William Rufus is trying to do?' asked Finian.

Hugh gave a harsh laugh. 'This will be Flambard's idea, for it has his hand all over it. I imagine he will use Odo to persuade us to surrender.'

Finian thoughtfully gazed out at the causeway for some time. 'Do nothing yet, Sire. Don't respond; I have a plan.' Hugh Grandesmil raised a bushy eyebrow in surprise and nodded. His two sons followed Finian as he strode away.

'What are you thinking?' asked Yves.

'I'll tell you shortly, but I promise you'll be part of it,' he said, striding off along the walls to find Dion the archer. Grandesmil and his sons watched with interest as Finian and half a dozen archers lined the walls.

'What is he doing?' asked Aubrey, the younger brother.

'Some Irish devilment, no doubt, but Piers de Chatillon values him, so it will be worthwhile. Look what he did to the blockade ship,' answered his father.

Shortly afterwards, Finian returned. 'I believe you're fluent in Greek, Sir Hugh?' he asked.

'Yes, but God's blood, what has that to do with anything in this situation?' he snapped.

'Bishop Odo is also fluent in spoken Greek; he read the Greek poets and philosophers aloud to us, riding down from York, when most of us had no idea what he was saying.'

'Yes, I know! He's renowned for it, thrusting his learning upon us whether we want it or nay,' answered Sir Hugh in an exasperated voice.

Finian grinned. 'This Sire is what we will do....'

He explained his plan to the crowd of assembled nobles, who looked at him in disbelief.

'They will cut us down before we get back through the gates,' muttered Sir Hugh. Finian shook his head and pointed at the archers.

'They are some of the best I have ever seen—one of them took a rooster's eye out for a bet the other day. They will drop anyone who tries to pursue you.' There was silence for a while, and then Sir Hugh reluctantly agreed.

'It may just work, Ui Neill.'

'Good, then let us prepare,' he said, waving the Grandesmil cadet sons to follow him.

An hour later, Sir Hugh answered the King's request, saying he'd meet and negotiate on the causeway an hour before dusk.

Then they waited....

Piers De Chatillon walked along the crowded wharves at Rouen. Robert's fleet stretched on both sides of the river. As he walked, he stopped and talked to one of two Captains. Most were unhappy at the wait, but Duke Robert had promised them recompense for their time, loss of earnings and ships. The crews were in the local hostelries or dicing on the decks in the late afternoon sun. However, the boredom began to tell even with them, and more arguments and fights ensued. He stood with one grizzled, older Captain gazing down the river. The sky was clear, with not a cloud in sight.

'So, why ain't we sailing, Sire?' he asked, frowning at the Papal Envoy who walked down here most days.

Chatillon struggled for a diplomatic answer. 'The best way that I can put this is that we are held up by a combination of politics, weather and a small amount of apprehension,' he finally said.

The old mariner grunted. 'But our Duke is no coward. We all know he took on and defeated his own father.'

'No one is suggesting that, but sometimes there are circumstances beyond a leader's control; the weather being one of them. The fleet must all sail at once, it cannot land piecemeal, or they will be defeated as they leave the beaches. Therefore, as you can understand, we need several days of clear weather for the fleet to stand off the coast of Kent and land in a coordinated way. The planning for that is very tricky.'

Suddenly, a figure caught his attention. Tall and thin in the robe of a Benedictine monk, Chatillon recognised him immediately. Bidding farewell to the Captain, while assuring him they would sail soon, he strode towards his visitor. They greeted each other like the old friends they were. Father Dominic had been one of the first friends he'd made in his early training at Monte Cassino; a young monk who believed that Chatillon's pigeon messengers would work and eagerly helped him set it up. They had always kept in touch, and Dominic, now a junior envoy for the Holy See, regularly supplied Piers with valuable information from the courts of Europe.

'Well met, my friend. You're a sight for sore eyes and just what I need to stop me from tearing out my hair in frustration and boredom,' he said, throwing an arm around his friend's shoulders. They headed for a better-class hostelry near the castle. Realising he was hungry, Chatillon ordered platters of fresh warm bread, soft cheese, thick slices of ham and fresh, crisp apples. While they ate, Piers brought him up to date on Duke Robert's situation and Pevensey's fall earlier in the month. Dominic listened in disbelief and shook his head.

'Has he missed his chance?' he asked.

'If Robert sails within the next week and relieves the siege of Rochester, then he can still be successful, although there will be some hard battles to fight,' said Chatillon taking a long draught of ale.

'The problem is he's frightened of sending all his forces to England and leaving his back unprotected from attacks by Count Fulk of Anjou, or even Philip of France despite his assurances to the contrary.'

'Robert has never shied away from warfare,' suggested the monk.

Chatillon shrugged. 'Enough of that. What do you have for me?' he asked, narrowing his eyes.

'I have done as you asked and used my contacts in Marseilles, Sicily and down in Moorish Spain. The man you seek information about is a complex and interesting character. He seems to lead a double life and keeps them as separate as possible. His respectable persona is that he's a high-ranking member of the Banu Hudid dynasty, who came originally from the Berber tribes that swept north through Spain. The family now rule over the Taifa of Zaragoza in Aragon. As you know, a Taifa is an independent state. His half-brother is the current ruler, Abu J'far, who lives in the breathtaking Aljaferia Palace that sits on the plain above the city. Your man uses his family name of Yusuf ibn Hud, and he resides with his family for half of each year. His wives and concubines are there. He has his own complex within the Palace and is much loved by his brother.'

They sat in thought for several moments, finishing their food as Chatillon mulled over the information. 'So, with so much prestige and wealth, why is he a pirate?' he asked.

'This is the second part of his life, for when he sails out of his port at Tarragona to pick up his ships in what we knew as Palma, he becomes Sheikh Ishmael, one of the most feared Saracen pirates on the Mediterranean. Cruel, cunning, ruthless and brutal to any prisoner. I have heard that he does it purely for exhilaration and excitement. He has bases and homes in Tripoli and Tunis as well.'

Father Dominic paused to scoop up the last of the soft Normandy cheese, while Chatillon stared across the room without really seeing it.

'May I ask if he's your next assignment, or is this more personal?'

Chatillon looked into the shrewd eyes of his friend. 'I think you've probably worked that out already, Dominic. He attacked our ship as we sailed from Genoa to Marseilles; played with us like a cat with a mouse, and then struck. He got more than he bargained for; a ship with over twenty armed mercenaries and an Irish warlord that few would take on.'

Dominic smiled and waved for more ale.

'So is this revenge for that attack? I presume if that's so, he will soon be a dead man!'

Chatillon laughed. He'd missed the irreverence and light-hearted banter of his friend. 'It is more complicated than that; my wife was on board. The Sheikh's son tried to snatch her, and I killed him. Sheikh Ishmael has now started a blood feud. Recently he sent men to follow my wife, and they attempted to poison her.' Dominic looked at him long and hard before speaking.

'Firstly, congratulations on your marriage. I heard that you stole away the beauty of Genoa. Secondly, you have a problem. The Banu Hudid dynasty is like a nest of rats. You take a cover off their hole, and at first, they run in every direction. You flatten as many as possible with a spade, but many escape and return repeatedly. Your Irish friend will tell you that a feud with the Berber tribes will continue until every family member is wiped out. If you succeed in killing Ishmael, then a dozen, maybe two dozen others may come after you and yours.'

Chatillon sighed. 'I didn't start this, Dominic. He attacked us, killed several men, and tried to take my wife. What did he expect?'

Dominic nodded in sympathy. 'Yes, but you killed his eldest son, his heir, his favourite. Also, he has at least half a dozen other sons who may carry this forward.'

'I'll have to find a way to end this. I will not spend my life in fear for my family because of this man!'

Dominic stared for a moment and then gave a bark of laughter. 'That's ironic, coming from you with your profession and reputation. I have seen men on the verge of pissing themselves with fear when your gaze descends on them for any length of time. I suggest approaching his brother might work, but it must be handled carefully. His brother will not want a feud with the Holy See, and that's whom you represent. I think our friend Sheikh Ishmael may not have realised that.'

Chatillon smiled; only Dominic could say things like this to him, but he did talk sense.

'Come, let us get drunk and talk of other things.'

He called for a sack of good wine, the best in the house. While watching him, his friend Dominic was not deceived; he'd never seen Chatillon this concerned. He was always fearless for himself, but now had a wife he obviously loved. The game had changed and not to Chatillon's liking.

Chapter Twenty-six

The tension was palpable as Sir Hugh Grandesmil and his party rode out of the gates of Rochester Castle, and down to the end of the short causeway, where a group of about twenty mounted men awaited them. His two sons, Yves and Aubrey, were with Sir Hugh at the front; a hooded Finian and half a dozen armed men behind. Hugh saw at a glance that the King was not there. Instead, Bishop Odo sat on his white mare alone at the front. Behind him on either side were several other captured Norman nobles, Eustace of Boulogne, Robert de Belleme and Duke Robert's friend, De Clare, who had been captured at Tonbridge. They had been instructed to add weight to Odo's pleas for Rochester to surrender, that a continuing siege was pointless and would only cause more suffering. Behind them were both of the sons of De Warenne, Raynold and William, with a dozen mounted soldiers in the King's livery.

Sir Hugh stopped a few horses' lengths away from Odo. 'Well met my Lord Bishop. Seeing that you're still in good health despite your capture is pleasing. May I welcome you home to your castle in Rochester?'

Odo smiled at the words. 'Unfortunately, Sir Hugh, I'm not here to return; instead, I'm here at the request of William Rufus. I still refuse to give him the title of king.' At that point, various oaths and insults were shouted by the King's men behind. Odo raised a hand for silence. 'I have been ordered to tell you to surrender at once to avoid bloodshed, and if you do so peacefully, you may retain some of the lands you hold in England.'

Hugh De Grandesmil put his head on one side and looked puzzled. 'I am sorry, Lord Bishop, you're too far away, and I cannot hear you.' Odo rode his mare forward a few paces.

'No Further!' shouted the eldest De Warenne. Odo raised a hand to show that he'd heard while he repeated the King's message in a louder voice. Hugh nodded and leaned forward. In a much lower voice, he spoke several sentences in Greek. Odo's eyes opened wide in surprise, and he surreptitiously began to gather the reins hanging on his horse's neck. He nodded enthusiastically, to show that he understood, and to fool the escort into thinking that the rebels were about to surrender.

Two of the four nobles behind also knew a little Greek, and realising what was happening, they tightened their reins and whispered to the others. De Warenne and his younger brother Raynold couldn't hear a word and demanded to know what was happening. Odo turned in his saddle and shouted back, 'I am giving Sir Hugh assurances from William Rufus. Sir Hugh is concerned with the phrase that he 'may' retain some of his lands. Will he?'

'That's for the King to decide, but he has made the offer in good faith if it is acted on immediately,' shouted Raynold De Warenne, as they sat back and waited impatiently.

Suddenly Finian threw back his hood and shouted, 'Now!'

CHAPTER TWENTY-SIX

Odo kicked his mare into a gallop and was followed by the other rebel noblemen as they made for the castle gates. Finian, Sir Hugh and his sons had drawn their swords, but purposefully waited, and didn't move forward, for to do so would be to break parley. Raynold De Warenne screamed with rage as he recognised Finian.

'Murderer! It's him, Brother, the Irish mercenary who killed our father before he'd even drawn his sword.' They surged forward to attack, thereby breaking parley by attacking first. Just then, a wave of arrows hit the King's men from either side of the gatehouse walls. Horses and men were hit; the horses screaming and rearing in pain and unseating their riders. Sir Hugh watched in astonishment as Finian and his sons rode at the King's men. That was not the plan! He decided to leave them to it, and he galloped back to the gate after Odo and the others.

The rebels had the satisfaction of killing several of the King's men, but Finian was aware that they were risking their lives needlessly and preventing the archers from firing at the enemy, so he shouted the retreat and made for the gates as more arrows came from above them. It was a satisfying sound as the huge gates slammed behind them.

There was much relief, backslapping and celebration for them as they returned to the bailey where Odo was waiting for the Irish lord.

'It was a blessed day indeed when Piers De Chatillon sent you to be at my side, Finian Ui Neill. That was a daring and ingenious plan. Greek indeed! I would love to be there when the De Warenne boys tell it to William Rufus and Flambard,' he laughed.

The celebrations were short-lived as they, yet again, settled into a long siege for several weeks. Tempers grew short, scuffles broke out as their supplies dwindled, and there was still no sign of Robert and a relieving force. At the end of June, more bad news arrived. William and Flambard hadn't been idle after the burnt ship, and they had doubled the blockaders in the channel. They were waiting for part of Robert's fleet, which they spotted, intercepted and destroyed. This was a huge loss in men, horses, weapons and supplies, which had been bound for the Medway and Rochester.

After hearing the news, Finian found Sir Hugh in a grim mood, as he stood on the walls, looking down on the huge army that William Rufus had assembled around them. 'Well, we tried Ui Neill, but we will have no choice but to surrender by the end of the week.'

Finian put a hand on the older knight's shoulder. 'You did your best, Sire, and no one could fault you. Circumstances were against us. Duke Robert Curthose and Bishop Odo would say the same about you.'

Hugh shrugged. 'Robert was not in the fleet that sank, God be praised, but it means that he never left Rouen, and now I wonder if he ever intended to leave?' He turned, eyebrows raised at Finian as if the Irish warrior would know the answer.

'When I left Rouen, Duke Robert was determined to sail with the fleet and seize the throne, but we don't know what has occurred since.'

Hugh looked sceptical, but he'd never make any disloyal comments. His family had always supported Robert Curthose and would probably always do so if they lived on after this debacle.

Bishop Odo, who had remained optimistic throughout, was now also becoming disillusioned and sent bird after bird to

CHAPTER TWENTY-SIX

Chatillon, who seemed unable to give him any answers. Yes, Robert would sail, but he didn't know when. Yes, they knew about the siege at Rochester but had no idea where Robert would land his forces. All of which was frustrating to hundreds of rebels with dwindling food stocks.

A week later, in July, with no news or supplies from Normandy, Bishop Odo, Sir Hugh and the other rebel lords decided to surrender and opened the castle gates.

Odo told Finian to go to the back of the group and to try to stay inconspicuous and quiet. Always a difficult task for a warrior of his height and breadth with shoulder-length hair. It was a hot day, so a cloak and hood were not an option, and he plaited his hair into one warrior braid as they prepared to march out. King William's supporters and their men had lined the route to the pavilion of the King, who stood with his favourite, Flambard, and his loyal nobles. This group even included the King's uncle, Count Robert Mortain, who had the shame to look abashed as the jeers, abuse and insults were thrown at his brother, Odo, and the surrendering rebel lords who had been his friends.

Finian looked straight ahead and tried to ignore the angry spitting men who lined the road, some even pissing on them. The cries of 'Hang them, traitorous dogs!' were growing in volume. As they approached the King's pavilion on a slight rise, the clamouring died as the column halted. The King regarded them in silence as the noise died, and people strained to hear what was said.

'Is that what I should do with you? Hang you all?' he asked, head on one side, a slight smile on his lips. 'It certainly seems a popular choice with the people of England!'

No one in the rebel ranks spoke as the silence descended again. They all knew that if it had been his father, the conqueror, they would all have been blinded and maimed, leaving them alive to suffer.

The King looked up at Flambard, who seemed to nod to permit him to go on.

'I have decided to be a merciful king and let you keep your lives, but you'll all be put on ships to Normandy. You will be banished from England, and all your land, possessions and wealth will come to the crown, which we will redistribute to loyal subjects. Take them out of my sight, chain them and put them on ships tomorrow.'

He turned to go into his pavilion when a voice stopped him.

'My Lord King, a boon, pray grant our family a boon. We want the Irish mercenary Ui Neill to hang and be gutted. He killed my father, your loyal supporter, in murderous cold blood, and broke the laws of parley at the gates by attacking us. He's no Englishman, no Norman. We should use him as an example of what happens to foreign mercenaries who come to our shores to rebel against us.'

William Rufus looked at young Raynold De Warenne. It was true that his father, William, had risked his life to get the information to York about the invasion. He nodded at De Warenne, whose men laid hands on Finian and dragged him out of the group. They punched him and threw him to the floor, four or five of them still beating and kicking him viciously. Suddenly, they were attacked from behind by an angry young man who laid into them with fists, boots and teeth. Raynold De Warenne dragged the young rebel backwards, ripping off the cloak and hood.

'God's blood! It's a woman!' said Flambard. As his attackers paused, Finian struggled to his knees, blood running from the corner of his mouth, to see Dion held by two men, and the young archer he'd befriended was indeed a woman with long dark hair; her green eyes flashing in fury as they tried to pin her down. Finian seeing this and not quite believing it, laughed in surprise, to the annoyance of De Warenne, who strode forward and delivered a punishing blow to his head, knocking him to the ground again, where he stayed.

At that point, Sir Hugh stepped forward and looked at the bemused King. 'Sire, I have known you since you were a young boy, and you've always been a fair man who listens to reason. William De Warenne was killed in the battle outside Pevensey Castle; I was only a horse length away and saw it happen. I assure you his sword was in his hand, and he was fighting in battle. Also, Lord Finian Ui Neill did not break the parley as he was behind me with the guards. Raynold De Warenne broke the parley by charging at us. I realise he's devastated by his father's death, and his grief has clouded his judgement, but his father would have been ashamed of him for that action or for his lies now.' He fixed Raynold with the unblinking gimlet stare that still frightened his own sons. He may be a defeated rebel lord, but he was still Sir Hugh Grandesmil, the Sheriff of Leicester and Governor of Hampshire, who rode with King William at Hastings.

Despite his clenched fists, Raynold De Warenne had the grace to drop his eyes.

King William Rufus narrowed his eyes at the Irish lord on the ground.

'That may be so, but he's still a foreign mercenary fighting against me, and he and his men deserve to be hung.' The assembled crowd cheered and stamped in approbation, as they dragged Finian to his feet and tied his hands behind his back.

There were shouts of 'B*ring a rope, and we will hang him now!*'

from the crowd.

The hope that had burned in Finian's breast for a few moments died. He could see no way out of this despite Sir Hugh's defence. As he'd foretold, it seemed he'd end his days on an English tree or gallows.

At that moment, Bishop Odo pushed his way through. The man still had an immense presence, and the muttering and shouts stopped. 'Sire, if I may, Lord Finian Ui Neill isn't a paid mercenary. Yes, he fought to defend himself, but he was sent to me as a representative of Pope Urban. Lord Finian is Chatillon's envoy. As you know, the Pope partly supported Duke Robert, but he was not sure of Robert's claim to the throne. Finian Ui Neill was sent to find any evidence, which was why he visited the Archbishop of Canterbury, Lanfranc. He has been looking for witnesses who were there when your father died. That was also why he was with me in York.'

An expression of alarm had crossed Flambard's face at the mention of Chatillon's name, and he leant and whispered in the King's ear. William Rufus was not naïve and certainly knew what Piers De Chatillon was capable of, as he'd watched him manipulate people and situations, with a smile, for most of his young life at his father's court in Caen. Chatillon was one of the few people his father had treated with wary respect, and he'd seen the apprehension on his mother's face whenever the Papal Envoy arrived.

Another person in the crowd had also gone stone-cold at the name. Raynold's elder brother, William, clamped a hand hard on Raynold's shoulder.

'Withdraw,' he rasped at him. 'Withdraw your accusations. I am now the head of this house, and that's an order. You'll not bring our name into disrepute by lying.'

CHAPTER TWENTY-SIX

Raynold looked at him in astonishment. 'What? You cannot mean this. He killed our father!'

His older brother, still ashen-faced, shook his head. 'There are things that you don't know or understand. That man they speak of, Piers De Chatillon, can wipe out our family with just a word, and Ui Neill is his envoy. Withdraw your accusation now,' he growled, gripping Raynold's upper arm so hard it hurt. Raynold had never seen his brother like this, so, gritting his teeth, he turned back to face the King.

'Sire, given Sir Hugh's interventions and Lord Bishop Odo's claim, I reluctantly withdraw my accusations.'

Flambard nodded at the young man in approval, knowing how difficult that would have been, and he mentally marked him for further favour.

'Sire, I believe that we should send Lord Finian back to his papal masters. No doubt he will report favourably on what he has discovered, and on your mercy to the rebels,' he said looking meaningfully at the King.

The King stood for a moment staring at the bleeding man on his knees in front of him. He knew when a situation was beyond his control. He didn't like it but had no choice, so he nodded at Flambard and, turning, he went back inside his pavilion, without a word.

Finian let out the breath he'd been holding while gratefully taking Bishop Odo's hand to pull him to his feet and undo the ropes around his wrists. He wiped the blood from his mouth and tenderly touched his bruised ribs. He didn't think any had been broken.

'I owe you and Sir Hugh my life, Lord Bishop.'

Odo shook his head. 'I think I probably owe you mine in Pevensey and Rochester several times over, and you kept me out of the King's hands for a month or two with your quick thinking.' They clasped arms, and then Finian strode over to Dion, who glared at the King's men behind her, daring them to lay a finger on her. He lifted her chin, and she raised her eyes to his.

'How can a mask have hidden such a pretty face as this?' he said, and leaning forward, he lightly kissed her to several cheers from his men sitting in chains on the ground behind them. 'Thank you for coming to my defence at risk to your own life. It was a dangerous thing to do and could have ended badly for you.'

She looked away. 'I couldn't let them hang you, and not after you did so much for us in Pevensey and Rochester.'

'So what now for you, Dion of Pevensey? Do you return to your father, Sir Hugh, and stay under his protection?'

'No, I cannot do that. Did you not hear? We've been banished. Or had they knocked you unconscious at that point? My archers and I need to find a new life in Normandy or wherever we can find employment.'

'I think I can help you with that, Dion. Several people will be vying for your services when I tell them what I have seen of you and your men. Meanwhile, it looks like they are moving us off to the shore. Stay close, and you can tell me on the ship why your father allowed his daughter to dress as a boy.' He smiled down at her, and she blushed, for Dion knew that she'd fallen in love with the Irish mercenary. Not that she would let him know that.

They stood quietly together for some time, each wrapped in their own thoughts before they were moved off, to be put in chains, and sent back on the King's ships to Normandy.

CHAPTER TWENTY-SIX

In Rouen, the Duke was finally sailing. Chatillon had watched in relief as Robert, and his lords rode to the wharves to take ship for England. He turned and strode back through the huge gates and towers into the bailey of Rouen castle. He had a smile on his face. Finally, in a few days, Rochester would be relieved, and hopefully, Robert would fight his way to London and Winchester to take the throne. He didn't doubt that it would inspire his supporters, who would flock to his banner once he was there.

He was entering the Great Hall when his servant caught up with him.

'Sire, a message has arrived.' Chatillon took the slip of coded paper. He hoped it was from Edvard, telling him that he and Isabella were safely ensconced on their estate outside Paris. He intended to ride out tomorrow to join them. Piers had missed them both. However, as he read, his face changed and turning, he ran down the steps to the stables to see Henry coming towards him.

'What is amiss, Chatillon?' he asked as he sprinted after him. Chatillon shouted for his horse as he turned to face Henry.

'I have had a message from Finian. Your brother Robert is about to sail, but Rochester has fallen, and the rebel lords are all prisoners!'

Henry turned a shocked face to him. 'All of them? So my brother William Rufus is triumphant! I must leave for England at all speed, as he will need his family beside him to help celebrate his victory.' So saying, he ran back towards the castle, leaving Chatillon staring after him.

That young man is a clever opportunist. It will be interesting to see what reception he gets from William Rufus, having spent all this time here with Robert, he thought.

He mounted and kicked his horse out of the gates and into a gallop, for he'd more pressing things to think about now. He had to get to the wharves to stop Robert from sailing. The Duke had left it too late, and he had lost the English throne.

Chapter Twenty-seven

September 1090 Two years later

Chatillon smiled as he watched his twin sons causing mayhem among the guests at the wedding. They had started to walk three months ago, and now there was no stopping them. Gabriel had a firm grip on the tail of one of his dogs and was giggling as it pulled him over several times. Piers met Isabella's eyes, and her face softened at him. She'd been shocked at first to discover she was having twins but had then been delighted. Knowing the dangers of childbirth and puerperal fever in childbed, Chatillon brought Ahmed to stay for a month. The Arab physician had dismissed Chatillon's fears, as Isabella was a fit and healthy young woman; he didn't expect any complications.

Now Isabella was with child again. This time, Ahmed assured them there was only one. Piers watched her as she laughed and chatted with the guests; she positively glowed. It astonished him how much he loved this woman. Chatillon had never expected to love like this again. She was everything he'd ever wanted, beautiful, clever, funny, a perfect mother and companion. She was also a consummate diplomat and assassin, with a frightening knowledge of poisons. Over the last year, she'd removed a few troublesome clerics and minor knights who had caused problems. Some were dead, and some were suffering from debilitating illnesses. She also had the knack for extracting information from men and women almost without seeming to do so. He could never remember feeling this content and happy, yet he was a realist. He knew clouds were constantly on the horizon for him and his family, as he had a dozen enemies at least.

He still remembered the physical fury he felt when Edvard gave him the details of the attempt to poison Isabella on the road to Ghent; it was clever. A week later, he'd gone to see Ahmed, related what had happened and paid him to find informers inside the homes and bases of Sheikh Ishmael, both in Spain and in north Africa. Money was no object. Since then, his family had been guarded day and night, and he received regular reports on the Sheikh's movements.

Finian, returning tired and weary from Rouen, had moved into the large sprawling fortified manor house to act as Isabella's shadow. To Chatillon's surprise, he didn't find the role tiresome or tame. This change was due to a need for normality, and the vibrant young woman he brought back from England with him. He'd been surprised to see Finian come off the boat with a woman by his side. Chatillon quickly found that she was no ordinary woman as he watched her, and the archers she led, practice each day in the castle bailey at Rouen. They had all stayed in the capital longer than expected, to deal with the fallout of the failed rebellion, and as he watched them together, it soon became clear that she loved Finian. Her eyes followed him everywhere. After she dismissed her archers every morning, Chatillon would find her standing at the fence in the paddock, watching as Finian trained his men and horses.

'You like him a lot, do you not?' he had asked her.

She had nodded, glancing shyly up at him. She was still wary of the Papal Envoy, having heard of his reputation.

'He's an exceptional warrior; any woman would be lucky to have him,' she had said, before turning away and heading back to the castle.

Finally, he had sat down in the solar with Finian and asked him if he was going to do anything about the relationship before they left Rouen. Finian had looked at him in surprise and had the grace to look abashed.

'Our friendship has indeed developed since our time here, Chatillon, but surely she cannot be interested in me in that way—I must be at least fifteen years older than her, and she has led a sheltered life with her father.'

Chatillon had looked at him in astonishment. 'You would let this chance of happiness go for what? A slight age difference? Look at Isabella and me. We have a similar age difference, and it means nothing, Finian. Or is it that you think you're too wild and worldly for this sheltered young maiden who, if you're to be believed, kills without a backward glance and would happily have murdered William Rufus for us!'

At that point, Finian had laughed; his concerns now sounded ridiculous to himself.

'We leave in two days. Go and find her and ask her. Use that renowned Irish charm of yours. She will either stay here with her men or come with us to Paris and become a welcome member of our household, because she wants to spend her life with you.'

He had seen little of either of them after that until the day they were leaving. He'd spent much of his time closeted with Duke Robert, warning him that King William Rufus may not forgive what had happened, and that he needed to be prepared for that. The next morning he had arrived at the stables, with his servants, to find a grinning Finian with Dion at his side, ready to leave.

Now they were happily ensconced on the estate; it was their home. Dion was exactly what Finian had needed; full of life and clever but with a fiery temper. When they argued, the sound of flying plates and pans echoed down the stone-flagged corridors. Isabella loved her, and Dion was now with child as well. Chatillon liked the idea of their children growing up together on the estate. Today was their wedding day, and fortunately, it had coincided with a visit from his uncle, Pope Urban II. Chatillon had ensured that Dion's father had been brought from Pevensey, where he'd been allowed to keep his post as Castellan. He was delighted with the match, as he knew this Irish lord would keep his daughter safe. He was more overwhelmed to find that the Pope would be at his daughter's wedding.

At that moment, Gironde, the older of the two twins, named after Chatillon's father, managed to pull a small table over, covering him and the rushes on the floor with wine. Isabella waved the nurse over, and the boys were whisked away to Gabriel's howls of protest. His uncle, Pope Urban, came over to join Piers, laughing at the twin's antics.

'They grow up so fast, and I am assured that your father and I were just as lively, if not worse. Wait until they are ten and old enough to get into more serious mischief.'

Chatillon laughed and searched his uncle's face as he settled into the chair beside him. He looked well, although the dark, swept-back hair was now streaked with grey. The lines on his forehead, the deeper ones down the sides of his mouth, showed Piers that the weight of responsibility of being Pope Urban II was taking its inevitable toll.

'I'm pleased you could be here. You do know that this will always be your family home as well.'

His uncle nodded and smiled. 'I might take you up on that in my dotage, Piers.'

'So, your Eminence, tell me how your tour of Europe is progressing,' he asked, raising an eyebrow.

His uncle smiled. 'Piers, I have issued a rallying call. I'm asking the kings and princes of Europe to provide an army in the next few years to liberate Jerusalem and the Holy Land, and I have to say I'm pleased with the response. I have every expectation, Piers, that the seeds of my idea have been planted in the courts of Europe.'

Chatillon was silent as he mulled this over. He was not sure about the wisdom of such a huge campaign. The logistics alone of such a journey, feeding them, finding transport, and surviving attacks in the hostile countries they would have to cross. He was not at all convinced that his uncle had thought this through. He pointed this out, but Pope Urban just shrugged it off.

'They will be soldiers of Christ, Piers, and soldiers of the cross. They will all wear a white surcoat with a large red cross.' Piers shivered and put a hand on his uncle's arm.

'We both remember who else used that phrase, and we know how it ended. Please be careful!' They grew silent as they remembered Odo's predecessor, Pope Victor, known as Dauferio. He'd established bands of ruthless killer warrior monks whom he called Warriors of Christ. Chatillon had killed his nemesis, Scaravaggi, their leader, and rescued Morvan's son, Conn, from them.

The Pope saw the alarm on Chatillon's face and tried to reassure him. 'This will be different, Piers, I promise you. I met with King Philip, as you know, last week. He has grown fatter and lazier and is obsessed with the new love of his life, Bertrade, even though it is an adulterous relationship. She's still the wife of Count Fulk of Anjou but is openly living with King Philip. He was unhappy because I wouldn't condone this relationship and annul their previous marriages. So he'd not agree to support us initially, but his younger brother Hugh the Great was very keen, and Philip will eventually agree to fund him.'

This did not allay Chatillon's fears, and he wondered how many of these knights and princes, with their entourages, would ever reach Jerusalem and return alive.

'So you travel to Normandy in a few weeks?'

'Yes, tell me, how are things with Duke Robert now?'

Chatillon sighed. 'The invasion's failure was, as you know, a major setback for Robert; he left it too long to act. More significantly, it was a triumph for King William Rufus. He was already in a strong position with land, money and power. With the banishment of Robert's supporters, he consolidated his position, gaining more land and wealth. And, his merciful treatment of the rebels brought him respect. Over the last year, he has brought his campaign to Normandy. He has now established powerful supporters north and east of the River Seine. He sends substantial bribes to win their loyalty. Philip of France did stir himself to come to Robert's aid last month, but Flambard bought him off with English gold, and King Philip retreated. We now have a stalemate. Robert is also finding that he has problems with his younger brother Henry.'

Odo frowned. 'I thought Henry had supported Robert. He lent him money in return for land on the far west coast.'

Chatillon nodded. 'He did for a while, but when Rochester fell, Henry hot-tailed it to England, to assure William Rufus that he'd taken no part in the rebellion. When he returned to Normandy, Robert imprisoned Henry for treason and took the lands of the Cotentin back. Henry found himself incarcerated with no money, having lent it all to Robert, and no land to show for it.'

Odo considered that for a while. 'So a very disgruntled and dangerous young prince who could prove very useful to us, Piers. You have said before that you were losing confidence in Robert Curthose. Perhaps we need to develop his younger brother. It isn't in our interests to let William Rufus take Normandy, as he will become far too powerful, holding all of the Anglo-Norman lands. In addition, William Rufus doesn't have much respect for, or allegiance to, the church. His relationship with the Archbishop of Canterbury, and even with the Holy See, is strained. Go to Rouen, Piers. Persuade Robert to forgive his brother, and spend some time with young Henry.'

Piers narrowed his eyes at his uncle. Could it be that Odo was discarding Duke Robert after years of money and manipulation by the Holy See, to turn him into their puppet ruler in Normandy? There was more to this. Odo laughed at his nephew's expression.

'I know what you're thinking, Piers, but there comes a time when you cut your losses. Work on Henry. There's more to that clever young man than we think.'

Piers was not naïve, and he realised what was happening. This holy crusade was his uncle's new focus, and he wanted

Duke Robert to lead it in the future, even if it meant leaving Normandy to its fate.

Isabella sat and watched the two Chatillon men. She knew by their faces that they were discussing politics and statecraft, which is inevitable when two powerful men are together. However, today was Finian's day, and she frowned at her husband and shook her head when she caught his eye. She laughed when he shrugged helplessly. She watched Finian and Dion together and smiled. She'd thought that Finian would never recover from the murder of his wife and children, but there was no doubt that Dion was healing the wounds. It would be a slow process, and inevitable that there would be scars, but they seemed happy; their new love for each other shining on their faces.

'Love heals everything, I am told,' said a deep voice beside her. She looked up to see Gervais de la Ferte smiling down at her. She rarely left the estate and hadn't seen him for several years.

'It is beautiful to see Gervais, and they have a new child on the way.'

He smiled. 'Don't tell anyone, Isabella, but I now have literally litters of grandchildren from my brood, and I often forget their names. My daughter Ette and Morvan have another boy whom I haven't seen yet. He must be at least three years old!'

She laughed aloud. Isabella had always enjoyed his company. He was still a handsome older man, an accomplished flirt and charmer, but she knew that he and Piers had a close bond.

'I hear that Ahmed will be arriving for the birth of this little one,' he said, indicating the significant swelling under her gown.

'Yes, we are lucky to have him so near, and he never seems any older. I'm convinced he has found the secret to eternal youth, Gervais.'

The French Seneschal laughed. 'If you discover it, please share, as I have a very demanding new mistress!' Isabella laughed aloud again, and heads turned in the Great Hall.

'I remember the day when Piers first met Ahmed. He was only sixteen years with a dislocated shoulder, and a grudge to repay. Ahmed has been in his life, and now yours, ever since. Do you still have the snakes?' he asked, raising an eyebrow and changing tack.

'Of course. I think Ahmed only comes here to spend time with Octavian, rather than with me. He refuses to believe that I've trained this snake. He tells me that Octavian's affection for me is abnormal.'

'That's what I wish to speak about,' he said, glancing around to ensure no one was near them. She glanced at him to see where this was going.

'Yes, they are my pets, especially Octavian, who is much bigger.' Gervais pretended to shudder, and she smiled, as he wasn't frightened of anything. He'd maintained his position as Seneschal of France, directly under the King, by a mixture of cunning and threats. Many bodies disappeared into the Seine courtesy of Gervais, and often, he'd ask Piers to remove others.

'I need Octavian's services as I have an irritating husband who is becoming a problem. I find that I'm reluctant to fight duels at my age, so I thought I would seek your help to remove him—for a price, of course.'

'Do you want Octavian to scare him to death? Or do you just need his venom?' She laughed.

Gervais leaned in closer. 'Just the venom will suffice, but as soon as possible.'

'I will give you a vial tomorrow to take with you.'

He smiled and, thanking her, kissed her hand.

'I presume there have been no further incidents with your Saracen friend as I've heard nothing from Piers,' Isabella shook her head.

'No, not for a year, although the odd servant here and there has been found with their throat cut. Piers has so many enemies, and there was nothing to attribute it to his men. We are exceptionally well guarded here and far safer than in any of our city houses.'

'Perhaps he has given up. Remember, he believes you're dead, and it has been over two years since he attacked your ship,' he suggested.

'Piers doesn't think so. He has informers in all of the Sheikh's houses. He's still very active out on the Mediterranean. Reports say he's more brutal than ever, slaughtering whole crews rather than selling them to the slave markets.'

'I know that it is pointless saying this to Piers as he enjoys meeting danger head-on, but don't let your guard down, and take care. The world would become a much darker place without your shining beauty.' She smiled and held his hand to her cheek for a moment in affection.

Glancing across the room, Chatillon watched the exchange with interest. He wondered if she had been his lover during that week in Paris, but then he dismissed the thought. Their marriage worked because they never questioned or discussed the lovers they had taken. They purely shared the information they had extracted from them. Piers couldn't imagine life without her at his side now, her fingers had wound their way around his heart. Yet he was about to leave her again to ride to

Rouen in a week or two.

He decided to leave Edvard here and take Finian with him. They would be away for a few weeks at the most. His family would be safe with Edvard here. Watching her, he concluded that they couldn't go on like this. Isabella was a star who should be shining in the courts of Europe, not hidden away on their estate. He would put plans in place to kill Sheikh Ishmael on his return from Rouen. It had to look like an accident, as he wanted to end, not exacerbate the blood feud.

28

Chapter Twenty-eight

October 1090

Duke Robert greeted Chatillon with the usual enthusiasm, although the Papal Envoy noticed that Robert's gaze slid away after a few moments. Words had been spoken by Chatillon when Rochester fell that hadn't been forgotten by either of them. Robert had blustered and objected to Chatillon's recriminations, but the guilt had been plain to see on his face. With hindsight, and now that his anger had cooled, Chatillon could see that the invasion's failure had been a combination of disasters, and a lack of communication, between the rebel groups. However, Robert's failure to be in England, to lead it seriously, contributed to its failure in the final month. Now Piers was here to repair his relationship with the Duke, and persuade him to make peace with his younger brother, Henry, whom he'd finally released, along with Belleme.

'I believe your ally, King Philip, deserted you at the battle for the fortress at Eu?' asked Chatillon.

Robert grimaced, 'Gold, Chatillon! He was bought off with chests of English gold. I cannot compete with that!'

Chatillon shrugged. 'So now we have a stalemate; the forces and supporters of William Rufus are occupying Normandy above the River Seine, and yours are occupying all below. So he holds almost a third of your land, yet Normandy is rightfully yours.'

Robert stared out of the window in the solar for a while before replying. 'My brother is flexing his muscles, Chatillon. He has also bribed and taken the garrison at St. Valery, at the mouth of the River Somme. This means he has a port for his men and horses to land. He has recently bought support from the northern lords in Normandy and the Vexin.'

'What of your brother Henry and Robert De Belleme? I hear that you released them several months ago.'

Robert could hear the censure in Chatillon's tone, and again he looked away.

'They arrived together, unchained, on a ship supplied by William Rufus. So I had them arrested and imprisoned because I suspected their loyalty. They denied the accusations, but I truly believed they were part of a plot against me.'

Chatillon shook his head in disbelief, as did Finian, who was standing by the window, adding, 'Robert Belleme fought bravely beside us at both Pevensey and Rochester, fighting in your name. I believe Belleme has always supported you in the past. You need all the support you can get, and Belleme may be an unpleasant character, but he's a powerful and wealthy lord and always loyal to you, Sire.'

Robert sighed, turned, and looked at both of them. 'Yes, you're right, Ui Neill. I made a mistake there and freely admitted it before God. I'll attempt to put it right.'

Chatillon's frustration showed on his face. 'Robert, you need your family, friends and supporters around you now. Send for them all immediately and bring them back to your court. I know that Belleme is licking his wounds on his estate in Ponthieu, but where is Henry Beauclerc?'

Robert was again silent for several moments, and Chatillon could see him biting his bottom lip. 'I removed the lands of the Cotentin from him when I suspected him. However, when I released him, he returned to his castle at Domfront and reclaimed his title as Count of the Cotentin, even though it is no longer his. They tell me he's now rebuilding and fortifying the castle there.'

Chatillon snorted in exasperation. 'Henry would have expected you to repay the five thousand in gold which he gave you in good faith, and you haven't done that. Robert, you cannot afford to be at loggerheads with both of your brothers. You don't have the capacity, or funds, to fight a war on two fronts against them. You need to swallow your pride and make amends.'

Robert stood up and paced to the window, to stand beside Finian, and stare out over the city of Rouen and the River Seine. 'I will do as you say. I'll send messages to them today and bring them both back.'

'Good, and I'll gather all information I can to find out what your older brother is up to in the north.'

So saying, Chatillon and Finian left the Duke to his thoughts and walked down into the narrow streets of Rouen. Chatillon had several informers in the city and the north, and he needed to know exactly how many forces William Rufus was bringing into Normandy. Was he planning to attack the south and depose his brother as Duke?

Finian eyed the large alehouse longingly as they passed it, and Chatillon laughed.

CHAPTER TWENTY-EIGHT

'Escort me to the house of Gerome, the printer, and you can spend an hour or two in there until I send for you.'

Finian grinned and happily strolled beside Chatillon. Both men had their cloaks thrown back over their shoulders to show they were armed, for they still took no chances. Finian left Chatillon at the printer's door and went to forget the world's cares for a few hours in jovial banter with his men.

The alehouse was a long low building that was attached to the largest inn in the city of Rouen. As he opened the door, he saw it was bustling, with almost every table occupied. As he expected, he spotted a few of his men and joined them, pulling up a stool.

'It's busy,' he commented, looking around the packed tables.

'This place is always busy, Sire; the stairs over there lead into the inn next door, and a large group arrived yesterday. The pretty, red-haired girl tells me another large party is arriving soon,' said Lazzo.

Finian was only half listening, but then he realised what had been said. 'Which girl?' he asked. She was pointed out, and he waved her over. 'How would you like to earn a goodly coin or two?' he asked her with a smile.

Her blue eyes widened. 'With a handsome man like you, Sire, gladly.' She smiled and, reaching down, squeezed his groin in anticipation. His men roared with laughter, and Finian joined in whilst gently removing her hand.

'As much as I would enjoy that, my lovely, I'm now a staid married man and all I want from you is information.' He laid two small silver coins on the table and a further two a hand's span away. 'If you bring me what I want, you'll earn all four of these.'

She nodded and licked her lips in anticipation; this was more than she'd earned in a month.

'The group who arrived yesterday, I want to know how many, where they come from, why they are here, and how long they are staying.' He placed his fingers on the second two coins and slid them closer to the first two. 'And, if you can get me the same information about the second group that's about to arrive, you can have all four of them.'

The girl nodded enthusiastically and made off with all speed for the innkeeper. After a few minutes of animated conversation, she ran up the stairs and disappeared next door to the inn.

It seemed an age before she returned, but she was grinning broadly. 'Both groups are about the same size, Sir, almost twenty men; so many that some are sleeping above the stables. They have ridden in from the north, although the innkeeper's wife has recognised a few who have stayed here before. All the talk she has heard from them has been about merchants, burghers and trading. They have booked the rooms for three days. The second group has just arrived next door, and she says several are English, and there are so many of them that some are forced to camp in the forests to the east,' she finished with a flourish and held out her hand.

Finian scooped up the coins, pouring them into her waiting hand, whilst pulling her onto his knee, and giving her a smacking kiss, which made her giggle and his men grin.

'I would do you for free if you're ever minded,' she added, stroking his face before sauntering away.

'Irish charm! It works every time,' one of his men muttered to the other.

'Don't forget to add the dark Irish good looks,' said Finian draining his tankard. He'd go to Chatillon and tell him what he'd learned, for something was amiss here. The noise behind him made him turn on his stool as several men descended the old wooden staircase. All of them seemed to be armed, and several of them were hooded. Then Finian froze and gave a sharp intake of breath, for the man at the back of the group had turned into the light from the dirty window and, even with his hood up, Finian had recognised him. He turned back to his men and gripped the edge of the table.

'Take a look at who it is, but do it calmly. Don't show that you recognise him and look down again, so that he doesn't see you staring—a casual glance now and again, no more. Watch them and tell me where they go. I cannot turn around, for he will recognise me immediately.'

His men were good at surveillance, for he'd taught them well. They still laughed, joked and swigged their ale as they watched the group make their way down.

'They have gone through the archway under the stairs, Sire. There's a small private taproom, and the innkeeper has cleared it for them. Who is it, Finian?' asked Lazzo, a long-time companion.

'Didn't you recognise him from Pevensey and Rochester? That was Raynold De Warenne, a man who hates Robert Curthose and has sworn to kill me.'

'He wanted us all hung. His men beat you on the ground at Rochester and again on the ship. Yes, I remember him, but he had his head down while he was coming down the stairs. I couldn't see his face. Why is he here so brazenly, in Rouen, in the heart of Duke Robert's city?'

Finian shrugged. 'I'm not sure Lazzo, but I intend to find out.' He got to his feet and pulled his hood up and his cloak firmly around him as he left the alehouse. He strode swiftly through the streets to find Chatillon and share what he'd seen. His only thought was that these men were there to kill, or overthrow, Duke Robert, and they had to stop them.

Piers De Chatillon was sitting opposite his long-time friend Gerome and was hearing similar disturbing news. 'I tell you, Piers, a lot of money is coming into Rouen. English gold has been making its way into the houses of the powerful merchants and burghers of the city for some time. They are using the money to buy weapons. The English haven't approached me because they know I'm the Duke's man.'

Piers put a hand on his arm. 'Do you think the burghers of Rouen would really rise against their Duke?' he asked in surprise.

'They are being led by Conan, the eldest son of Gilbert Pilatus, our richest wine trading dynasty and the most dominant faction in the city. They live in state, like lords, in their fortified houses with their own armed knights and men. They have grown far above themselves, if you know what I mean. My servants keep hearing November third being mentioned. I believe they will storm the castle and kill the Duke that day.'

Chatillon, grim-faced, listened to him in growing disbelief.

Suddenly there was a furious knocking on the door. Both men's hands went to their weapons, but they relaxed as Finian was admitted. He bowed to both men.

'Sire, there is a plot afoot. Armed men, English mercenaries, are pouring into the city. Some stay in inns, but I've discovered more men camped in the forests to the east of Rouen.'

'Yes, my friend. Gerome here has just informed me of the plot. November third is mentioned, which means we've just over a week to call for assistance for the Duke.'

Finian continued. 'That isn't all; Raynold De Warenne is

here at the inn. I'm sure that he will be leading the rebels.'

'Ah, the ever traitorous De Warenne; you should have wiped out the whole nest, Finian. We must alert the Duke to what is happening in his city. If Rouen falls, Robert will lose everything and his life. Finian, ride for Belleme and tell him that William Rufus is trying to wrest Normandy from his brother. Get him and his men here for tomorrow. I must go to the Duke.'

With that, they raced out into the night, leaving the old printer to shake his head in dismay, while he ordered his servants to arm themselves.

Chapter Twenty-nine

Almost a week later, Chatillon and Finian watched as Robert paced the floor in the Great Hall. As more information was revealed, he'd become angrier at the disloyalty of his subjects, especially having restored the city of Rouen to being his capital. He turned and faced the assembled nobles. Several lords had joined Robert, bringing their forces to Rouen, including William, Count of Evreux and William of Breteuil, an old friend who had fought for Robert at Gerberoi.

'So it seems that this Conan has made a pact with my brother William Rufus to hand my city over to him. They are committing treason and breaking their vow of allegiance to me. They will pay for this, I swear, before God!'

Chatillon was pleased to see that Henry, having made peace with his eldest brother, was equally incensed.

'It is more than that, Brother. These tradesmen have arrogantly maintained armed households without your leave and are now prepared to use them against you. They think they are our equals,' he spat.

Chatillon watched young Henry with interest as he raged

against the burghers of Rouen. Even as they spoke, the horns blew, and Henry raced to the window, shouting over his shoulder, 'It is Gilbert de L'Aigle with a huge force of men.'

Chatillon smiled and turned to Finian. 'It was never in question that it would come to a fight, but there's no doubt now who will win. Their loyalty to their Duke not only prompts these lords, but they are shocked at the betrayal of the citizens of Rouen. After all, if they are allowed to do it here, they may rise elsewhere. So retribution and punishment must be swift.' Henry standing close by, nodded enthusiastically at this.

Finian, ever a cynic, whispered into Chatillon's ear. 'Many of them will think of the large ransoms they can claim when they capture these rich burghers and merchants. I know that was why Belleme agreed to come.'

Chatillon laughed; he was in a buoyant mood. Although the delay had prevented him from getting back to Isabella, he knew she was safe in Edvard and Ahmed's hands. Yesterday she'd given birth to their third child. He had a daughter, and they had called her Annecy, after his mother.

The next day was Sunday, the third of November and the cathedral bells were ringing, calling the faithful to prayer. Unbeknownst to Robert and his followers, it was also the signal for the attack to begin. Raynold De Warenne had left the city the evening before to join his men in the forests. Now, they galloped towards the west gate to join Conan, who had arranged for the gates to be opened and the guards removed. At the same time, Gilbert de L'Aigle was bringing the other half of his troops through the south gate, where he met with fierce resistance.

The ensuing battle was chaotic as citizen fought citizen, some supporting the Duke and others supporting Conan, some just taking revenge on neighbours in ancient feuds. With Henry and his loyal knights at his side, Robert galloped out of the castle gates to confront and fight the attackers in the west. Chatillon and Finian rode in his train. The fighting was fierce in the narrow streets, with little room for the horses to manoeuvre. Some of Robert's nobles became alarmed by the numbers and violence they were facing, and, fearing for the Duke's life, they persuaded him reluctantly to leave. He was quickly taken out of the city's east gate and across the River Seine to a church.

Henry, however, remained, fighting valiantly beside Belleme and Robert's knights. Chatillon and Finian found that they were at the centre of it all.

'I fear we may be outnumbered at this gate, Sire,' shouted Finian above the ear-rending noise of battle, the clash of blades, the shouts, the screams. He turned and took on two citizens with long billhooks who seemed determined to try to gut his horse and kill him. Behind them, he could see at least another twenty of Conan's supporters, pushing their way towards them.

Chatillon grunted in agreement as he fought a large English knight, one of King William Rufus's men. The man's horse was pushed into his own in the narrow street, the man's knee pressed hard against his as they struggled, their swords straining against each other. The hilt of his sword and his hand were slippery with the blood of the men he'd slain, but his long dagger was still ready in his left hand. Suddenly there were shouts to the rear, and the mob turned to meet a new attack from behind just as Chatillon disarmed the knight beside him and thrust his dagger up through his chin. The man toppled backwards, falling to the ground to be trampled underfoot, while his horse bolted, knocking men aside in the crowded street.

Chatillon took a breath, wiped his blood-soaked hand on his horse's neck and glanced behind to see what was happening. Gilbert had finally cleared the rebels from the south gate, bringing over a hundred men to join the fray. Finian grinned and roared as he turned his horse around and rode to trample and slash at the men who had been attacking him.

The ferocious fighting continued for several hours, with all men tiring and exhausted, but the ducal forces dominated and took control. The streets of Rouen ran with blood as citizens from each faction still viciously fought each other, often trying to settle old scores. Meanwhile, Henry, Belleme, his brother Hugh and other Norman lords began to take prisoners from the surrendering or wounded men. Conan, the leader of the uprising, was captured by Henry and brutally beaten before being bound and dragged to the castle.

Finian dismounted and stood with his men at the end of one of the narrow streets leading to the cathedral. Bodies littered the area. Chatillon joined them all, and they surveyed the slaughter.

'I saw De Warenne only for a moment before he fled; he sent me a vitriolic glance and then rode for the gates to escape with his men.'

'More's the pity; these loose ends have a habit of impinging on your life if you don't cut them off, as we have learnt in the past,' he said.

Finian agreed, but Chatillon could see he was angry that the man who had ordered him beaten and gutted at Rochester, had escaped.

'However Finian, De Warenne is very young, and this will

have been his first real battle. I know we agreed that was a nest that needed emptying but let us try to move on and forget him.' He leaned against the wall and regarded the sweeping beauty of the cathedral, the autumn sky a deep blue above it. Such contrasts from the screams and moans of dying men behind them and the wailing of womenfolk searching the bloody aftermath in the streets. No doubt, many of them would have lost their husbands, sons, and livelihoods because of this foolish uprising.

'Come, Finian, let us go to the castle and celebrate the Duke's success in holding onto his capital. This failed uprising in Normandy has been a lesson for William Rufus.'

However, both men were surprised by what they found in the Great Hall. Henry was holding court and was very much in control, for Duke Robert was nowhere to be seen. Having washed his hands and face in the bowls offered, Chatillon moved to stand beside Robert De Belleme, who dripped blood from a deep cut on his chin.

'You need to get that seen to Belleme,' said Chatillon. Belleme nodded and absentmindedly wiped it on his sleeve, leaving a long streak of blood. He seemed distracted by what was happening. Henry had numerous bound prisoners on their knees and berated them for betraying their Duke.

'Where is Duke Robert?' hissed Finian.

Belleme turned and curled his lip. 'Our erstwhile leader fled, I believe. They tell me he even went over the river, not the trait we expected in our fighting Duke. Could you imagine his father, King William, doing that?'

Finian turned to Chatillon with raised eyebrows, and the Papal Envoy grimaced. This, on top of the failed invasion, would do Robert's reputation no end of harm.

Suddenly, there was a scuffle at the front. Henry had leapt down from the dais and had delivered a punishing blow to the tall, dark prisoner at the front, knocking him to the ground before dragging him back to his feet by his throat.

'It's Conan, their leader,' said Finian recognising him.

'Take him to the top of the tower,' ordered Henry. Guards stepped forward and seized the man's arms pulling him towards the far, narrow doorway. Chatillon intervened, feeling a slight apprehension about Henry's intentions.

'Sire, while I applaud your treatment of the rebels, should we not wait for the Duke?'

However, Henry was not listening. Full of rage, he shouted, 'In our family, as you know, we don't wait to deal with traitors. I'll show you what we do with them, Chatillon. Come, you must be a witness to this for the Pope.'

So saying, Henry ran for the doorway to the stone staircase through which the guards had dragged Conan moments before. Chatillon, Finian and many other lords followed to see what Henry would do.

Finian, realising what was about to happen, that Henry might hang him from the tower, hissed at Chatillon, 'You have to stop him! He should have a public trial for what he did, followed by a public execution.'

But Piers was helpless in the face of such anger from Henry Beauclerc and from the obvious support from the other lords, many of whom were grinning in anticipation. He also had to admit he had little sympathy for the rebel leader who had caused many innocent citizens in Rouen to be murdered.

There was a large open room at the top with a fireplace and several open windows that overlooked the city's streets or the sweeping wooded Norman countryside. Conan, a rough-looking man in his thirties, stood apprehensively between the two guards. His face bore numerous cuts and dark bruises from his beatings, blood still trickling from his nose and mouth. He dropped to his knees and begged for mercy from Henry, who regarded him with a slight smile but said nothing. He offered Henry Beauclerc vast sums for his life, but that didn't appease the young man, who wanted vengeance.

Henry waited for the last of the lords and knights to squeeze into the packed room before he began. He now had the audience around him that he desired.

'Do you see this man before you, this middling tradesman who thinks he's our equal and who apes our manners and clothes?'

He ripped the stained velvet tunic from Conan's body, leaving him kneeling in only his braies. His torso was a mass of bruises from the kicks and punches inflicted upon him, and he hung his head.

'He has betrayed our Duke. He's a traitor who invited foreign forces into our city and fought with them to try to capture and kill our Duke. Now he thinks that money will wipe the stain from his soul. He's mistaken.' The guards pulled the prisoner to his feet as Henry indicated to them that they should let his arms go. Conan swaying in shock and fear, begged again for forgiveness and mercy, and, for a few moments, Chatillon watching Henry's face and those of the lords around him, thought that Conan might get that mercy.

Then suddenly, without warning, Henry sprang forward and, grabbing Conan forcefully by the neck and upper arm, thrust him out of the window to fall and slam onto the cobbled street far below. Several lords shouted in shock and amazement and rushed to the window to see, but Chatillon stood stock still, as did Finian beside him, and instead, they watched Henry. Piers saw the satisfaction and pleasure on Henry's face as he folded his arms and leaned against the far windowsill. He watched the nobles exclaiming over what had happened before declaiming, 'Go down and tie his bloodied body to a horse's tail. I will have him dragged round and round the streets of Rouen so that all may see it and know that like my father, his sons will show no mercy to traitors.'

Chatillon turned away to look at Finian, who raised an eyebrow and headed back down the staircase. Meanwhile, Piers was reminded of the words he'd spoken to his uncle, the Pope, a few weeks before, *'I think we might have backed the wrong horse with Robert Curthose.'*

There was no doubt in Chatillon's mind that Henry Beauclerc was certainly his father's son in character, more so than his other brothers were. Here in Rouen, by his actions, Henry had now certainly established himself as a leader, a fighter and a ruthless young man.

Turning back, Chatillon walked over, bowed to Henry and took him to one side as the chattering nobles went down the staircase. Soon there were just the two of them left in the tower room.

'I will certainly relate to the Pope what has occurred here in Rouen today, and I congratulate you on your victory, Henry. Your brother is very lucky to have you by his side. Now I must return to my home near Paris as I have a new daughter to see. However, I will return in a few months, Sire, as Pope Urban is very interested in your plans for the future, as am I.'

Henry, unblinking, met Chatillon's dark gaze. Like everyone else, he felt apprehension and wary respect for this powerful Papal Envoy, but he had no doubt what that message meant.

He knew that Piers De Chatillon could be a very useful man on your side and a dangerous enemy otherwise.

He bowed. 'My brother and I thank you for your services, Sire, for it was you and Ui Neill who discovered and alerted us to this plot and then you fought alongside us in the streets when you too could have been away from danger in safety over the river. But I know that isn't your way, Chatillon and again, I thank you for it.'

Chatillon smiled at this clever answer and, bowing, made his way back down to join Finian. They would rest here tonight and celebrate in the hall. Hopefully, Duke Robert would return and then, at first light, they would ride for home.

A few weeks later, across the channel, King William Rufus and his favourite Flambard were dismayed and disappointed by the failure of the Rouen rebellion. However, they would continue their plan to hold what they occupied in the north of Normandy. A more pressing concern for William Rufus was the role of Henry Beauclerc in defending Rouen. The tale of Conan's death had spread like wildfire, enhancing the reputation of his younger brother, who had always been a cunning and exceptionally clever child. He'd always been in his books and tracts, and it was their father who had named him 'The Clerk'. Now Henry had changed; he had put away his books. When he was here in London recently, William had noticed that he worked with a swordsman each morning. He had filled out and put on muscle. He had a confidence and a

CHAPTER TWENTY-NINE

swagger that the ladies had certainly noticed.

'We need to watch my brother Henry, Flambard, for I think he could become a problem.' His advisor nodded his head sagely beside him.

'I've thought that for some time Sire; he left here angry with you because we refused to give him the lands in England that his mother promised him, and it strikes me that he's a young man to bear a grudge. I hear that he's becoming far too powerful and popular in the western Cotentin for Robert's liking. It may be, William, that we have to agree with your brother, Robert, and form an alliance together against Henry.'

William agreed and continued to read the reports of the battle of Rouen. He put them down and regarded the bloodied young man kneeling in front of him, who had emerged relatively unscathed apart from several cuts on his face and half a missing finger.

'How did they discover the plot, De Warenne? Were you too careless?' he asked in a soft but equally threatening voice.

'No, Sire, I swear. It was the Papal Envoy, Chatillon and that damned Irish mercenary again. They were seen everywhere in the backstreets of the city before the rising. They alerted Duke Robert, who summoned help, and his supporters came in their hundreds so that we were outnumbered and driven out.'

Flambard hissed in annoyance. 'Chatillon! That man is everywhere, ensuring the Pope's fingers are in every pie.' He waved Raynold De Warenne to his feet, and they watched him limp out of the chamber.

William shrugged. 'We will prevail, Ranulf, we hold most of the north and east of Normandy, and we have King Philip of France firmly in our pocket. It is only a matter of time before we unite Normandy and England again. As you suggest, we will play at statecraft to isolate Henry, and before long, both of my brothers will be marginalised and powerless.'

Flambard smiled, but it was not a pleasant smile as he'd be far happier if both brothers were dead or imprisoned, and he would do his best to ensure that happened.

Chapter Thirty

Piers cradled his daughter Annecy in his arms. He couldn't begin to explain the emotions in his breast as he gazed down at the swaddled bundle and then up to meet Isabella's eyes before carrying his daughter over to the window.

'She has your eyes, the beautiful doe-like shape, I mean. I know all babies' eyes are blue at first.' He handed the baby back to Isabella and watched in satisfaction as she propped her in the crook of her arm, and, unlacing her top, began to feed her.

'I'm sorry I was not here for her birth,' he murmured.

Isabella snorted with laughter. 'If you're ever here for the birth of any of our children, I'll consider myself exceptionally blessed, and from what I heard, it's a miracle you got back here at all. Your visit to Rouen was supposed to be diplomatic, not warlike.'

Finian, coming in with Dion at that moment, added, 'I promise Isabella, I will do my utmost to get him here for the next one. However, there were mitigating circumstances. We were back to back in a narrow street facing a mob of hundreds!'

Isabella sent a glance of alarm and concern at her husband, who narrowed his eyes at Finian for revealing this.

'I think you may have omitted to tell me that, Piers. I believe the words you used were, '*We were involved in a few skirmishes.*'

Finian shrugged helplessly to Piers in apology.

'It was nothing, Isabella; we came out of it with hardly a scratch, and now I anticipate a period of peace for a while. William Rufus will be licking his wounds in England. Robert will be trying to rebuild his damaged reputation by throwing himself into my uncle's crusade to Jerusalem. So Finian and I will be sitting here waiting for the birth of his child, which looks imminent. It must be huge if Dion's size is anything to go by. Meanwhile, we will start the breeding programme for these horses he wants. So saying, we will leave you and head for the stables to look at this Flemish mare he bought.'

Isabella and Dion watched them go, smiling knowingly at one another. 'I give it two months before they are off somewhere else,' said Dion.

'Five messages arrived this morning from Rome and Ghent, so I wouldn't give it that long,' added Isabella. They both laughed, for they knew the men they had married and loved. They were certainly not farmers—maybe they would be much later when they hung up their swords—if they ever did. All was well with their world for now, and they knew that Piers De Chatillon and his friends would do their utmost to keep it that way and protect their families.

CHAPTER THIRTY

Hundreds of leagues away in Zaragoza, a tall, dark-visaged man paced in the shade beside a fountain in the shape of a dolphin. His older brother sat on the carved stone bench in the courtyard against the wall and watched him.

'You need to contain that anger and frustration, Yusuf. It is doing you no good or for me watching you, for you destroy the serenity of this beautiful space.'

Yusuf Ibn Hud turned and faced his brother. 'You don't understand, Abu. It burns in here almost every day. I see the image of what they did to him in my mind, over and over again,' he said, thumping his chest.

Abu sighed. 'You've tried repeatedly to kill this man and his family, and every effort has failed. He's too clever, too powerful and too well-guarded. I truly believe that you need to let this one go, brother, for it is occupying your thoughts almost to the exclusion of everything else.'

At that moment, a servant arrived, bowed and said something quietly to Yusuf. 'Bring him in,' he answered curtly. A few moments later, a tall, bearded man appeared. He bowed and greeted the two brothers.

'Al Cazar, it is good to see you; it has been several years, has it not? I presume you've been busy about my brother's business,' said Abu.

'Indeed. I've been on board ship for six months, but I've just come from the island. Your ships are in Palma provisioned and ready for you whenever you give orders, Sayyid,' he said, bowing his head and addressing Yusuf, who didn't reply. Instead, Yusuf drew his dagger and began cleaning his fingernails while the silence hung in the courtyard, and his brother raised an eyebrow in surprise.

'Orders! You are not very good at following orders, are you,

Al Cazar, I gave you orders, and you did not fulfil them.' The man looked puzzled and even looked over at Abu in concern.

'Sayyid, I've served you faithfully for nearly twenty years. I've always done my best and, to my knowledge, have never disobeyed you or let you down,' he said in consternation.

'Ah, but you have Al Cazar. You disappointed me bitterly because you hid the truth or even lied to me. Or should I call you Don Ferdinand, the merchant from Burgos?'

Fear flickered over the man's face for a moment, and again, he glanced at Abu as if for guidance or help, but Yusuf's brother looked equally puzzled.

'What has he done, Yusuf, and who is Don Ferdinand?' he asked.

'It was a simple task, Abu. I sent him to France to kill the wife of Piers De Chatillon, as we knew she was in Paris but would be travelling north. We had a perfect plan to poison her using a rare bottle of perfume that she would not be able to resist. Al Cazar, my faithful servant, returned and told me that the plan had worked perfectly; he'd swapped the perfume bottles in her room without her knowing, and she died the next day having used the perfume. He told me that he had an informer in the inn, and they said a physician and a priest were called, and they pronounced her dead. They then buried her immediately in the local churchyard.'

'So the plan worked, and he followed your orders; he murdered Chatillon's wife for you. You have your revenge, Yusuf,' said Abu, surprised at this news but hoping this meant the end of the blood feud.

'Well, apparently, the fair Isabella, like her Christian God before her, has risen from the dead because she miraculously gave birth to twin boys last year. I've known this for several months, and I have been waiting for the return of my faithful servant Al Cazar to tell me how this was possible?' he said in a soft voice at first, but then he almost screamed, 'Twin boys! He now has twin boys, yet Chatillon murdered my eldest son Malik, my favourite son. So again, please tell me how this is possible, Al Cazar, when you promised me she was dead and buried in the graveyard of an Abbaye on the borders of France?'

The man stood dumbfounded, his mouth moving, but no sound came out as he tried to make sense of what he'd just heard. Finally, he spluttered, 'That's impossible. My man saw her buried—he saw her grave—and the rest of them rode off the following day without her. They told me she was dead. I swear I'm telling you the truth, Sayyid. You know that I have never lied to you.'

'Not dead enough, if she could give birth barely six months later!' yelled Yusuf, the anger building.

'So they tricked you then, Brother. These men of Chatillon's must have known who Al Cazar was and foiled your plot and carried out this performance. You have to applaud them. As I said before, they are very clever.'

Abu looked at his brother with a smirk that pushed Yusuf over the edge, and he waved two servants forward.

'Seize him!' he ordered, pointing to his henchman.

'You need a lesson in orders, Al Cazar, because you're now becoming slipshod, and I've no room for people like that in my retinue or on my ships.'

The man paled. He didn't want to die; he had a family, and he had served Yusuf faithfully in the past. The man pleaded for his life to both brothers, but Yusuf ignored his pleas.

At first, Abu looked away. Then he decided to intervene. 'I think it would be a waste to kill such a useful and loyal servant for one mistake, Brother,' suggested Abu while sitting back and taking a sip of chilled sherbet.

Yusuf walked close to Al Cazar, a mere hand-span from his face as he glared into Al Cazar's panicked eyes. The man was shaking. 'I will let you live, but what should I take instead in payment for your failure.' He reached for the man's groin and, grabbing his testicles, squeezed hard until Al Cazar gave a strangled scream. 'Shall I take these to teach you a lesson Al Cazar?' he asked with a smile.

The man managed to gasp, 'No, Sayyid, please. No, I beg you.' Yusuf let go and stepped back as another idea occurred to him. He walked over to the stone table and beckoned the servants to follow him with their prisoner. He pulled off Al Cazar's headdress, grabbed him by his hair and slammed his head down onto the table. 'Hold him there. I intend to give him something that will remind him to check every detail personally in future when I give him a task.' So saying, he slid the dagger up along the man's cheekbone, leaving a cut which bled. Al Cazar was wracked with anguish, and tears openly streamed down his face as he realised he was about to lose an eye. The servants held him in place. Abu thought both of them looked equally terrified, for you never knew what Sheikh Ishmael would do when he was in a fury like this.

However, at the last moment, Yusuf moved the dagger up and expertly but deeply notched the top and side of Al Cazar's ears, which then bled profusely. They held him pinned to the table as blood streamed down his face.

'Remember this lesson well, Al Cazar. Now go and tell my men we leave at noon for Palma,' he said, pushing the servants out of the way. Raising a foot, he kicked the man onto the floor. The victim scrambled to his knees. He was a shaken man, blood dripping from his ear and chin as he headed for the arched doorway.

His brother Abu regarded the blood on the table and floor tiles with distaste and waved the wary servants over. 'Clean up this mess; the women and children will be out here soon.' He took his brother by the arm and led him to the other side of the fountain. 'I suggest in future, Brother, that you conduct such business as this on your ships. Or even in one of your many bases in Palma or North Africa. You've always managed to keep your other life separate from the palace until now. Let us keep it that way. We do not want any disrespect to the family name because of your activities. And remember, servants always talk.'

Yusuf noticed the note of censure in his brother's tone and inclined his head in apology. He loved his brother and his family dearly, and Abu was right. He had let his rage cloud his judgement.

'I am sorry, Brother. I want this man Chatillon, and all of his family, wiped off the face of this earth. His twin sons will be put to the sword, and his woman—she will be mine. I'll keep her where he will never find her. I want him to know this before he dies. I want him to feel the pain of loss. I've sent more men north today, and they will try to learn every aspect of their lives.'

Abu Ja'far shook his head. 'You do know who this man is? You're trying to kill the most powerful assassin in Europe. He will see them coming, their faces, and their accents. It is almost impossible to kill this man, Brother.'

Yusuf thought about this for several moments and then smiled.

'You are right, as usual, Abu, and because of that, I will

choose several men who will be Christians. I'm a patient man, and this may take time, but I'll find slaves whom I'll rescue from the galleys and the deserts just for this task. We will feed them well, give them women and promise them gold. I will also promise more to the man who successfully gets me the woman and the children of Chatillon. I've heard a rumour of a slave we have who knows the Irish warrior, Ui Neill. He was on the galleys with him. This man was lucky—he was rescued just before the ship went down and was taken to work at the palace in Tunis, but my informer tells me he or his family bore a grudge against Ui Neill. However, when I sent to find him in Tunis, he had disappeared. He may be dead, but I am a patient man and have sent my men to search for him. If he is alive anywhere, I will find him and others.'

Abu watched his brother's face. He had to admit that this might work. He hoped so, for his brother had changed; he was eaten up with this desire for revenge.

'I'll arrange for prayers to be offered daily in the mosque for the success of this venture,' he said, standing and putting his arm around his brother's shoulders.

'Sheikh Ishmael has been absent too long from the waters of the Mediterranean. Now go and see to your ships in Palma. It will give you something else to focus on.'

Yusuf nodded, watching his brother leave, and he sat on the wide, blue, decorated tiles around the fountain while the servants cleaned up the blood and left. He sat there for some time and trailed his fingers in the water. For a few moments, Sheikh Ishmael gave himself up to the thoughts of what it would feel like when he had Chatillon's family in his hands and what he'd do to them. He could almost taste it, and a wave of euphoria swept over him at the thought.

CHAPTER THIRTY

At the far side of the palace, crouched on a roof, a servant tied a quickly scribbled message to a bird's leg. He constantly looked over his shoulder to ensure he was not followed. He was so nervous, his fingers fumbled at first, and he had to stop and take a deep breath. Every time he sent a message, he risked his life, for if he were caught, death would come, and it would not be swift. He saw what the Sheikh had done to one of his loyal friends today. He had been watching and listening to what was said as he had cleaned up the blood.

He took the bird in his hands and walked to the roof's edge but not so he could be seen from below; he took every precaution. He released her for the first leg of her journey north to Marseilles and prayed that the bird would survive the long and hazardous journey. The message contained only eight words in code, which were vitally important to Monseigneur Chatillon.

He knows she is alive with your sons

31

Character List

Fictional characters are in *italics*, and real characters are in **bold**

France – Chatillon Estate
Piers De Chatillon
Isabella De Embriaco – now his wife
Gironde, Gabriel – their twin sons
Annecy – their daughter
Edvard – Chatillon's vavasseur and friend
Finian Ui Neil – Irish lord & mercenary
Niamh – Finian's murdered wife

Genoa
Morvan De Malvais
Ette De Malvais
Marietta De Monsi
Odo De Chatillon – Piers' uncle and Pope Urban II
Gervais De La Ferte – King's Chamberlain and Seneschal of France

Conrades Di Mezerella – Archbishop of Genoa
Signori Guglielmo Embriaco - Leader of the Genoa Republic

Rouen
Robert Curthose, Duke of Normandy
Odo, Bishop of Bayeux, Earl of Kent, Robert's uncle
Count Robert de Mortain, Robert's uncle
Almodis De Mortain – his wife
Henry Beauclerc – younger brother of Robert
Roger Montgomery, Earl of Shrewsbury
Bishop Geoffrey de Coutances
Earl William de Warenne – Earl of Surrey
William Count de Evreaux
William de Breteuil
Gilbert de L'Aigle
Conan, son of Gilbert Pilatus – Wine merchant
Lazzo - Mercenary
Gerome - Printer
Father Dominic – Benedictine monk, friend and informer

Paris
King Philip of France
William De Warenne – eldest son of the Earl of Surrey
Ahmed - Physician

Ghent
Count Robert I of Flanders
Countess Gertrude of Flanders
Robert –Heir of Flanders
Viscount Philip van Loo of Flanders
Leopold - German Prince of Swabia

York
Archbishop Of Canterbury – Lanfranc
King William Rufus
Ranulph Flambard
William de St Calais – Prince Bishop of Durham
William Mallet – Sheriff of York

Pevensey
Count Robert De Belleme
Hugh De Montgomery
Sir Hugh de Chartelle
Dion de Chartelle

Rochester
Sir Hugh Grandesmil – Sheriff of Leicester & Governor of Hampshire
Yves Grandesmil – eldest son of Sir Hugh
Aubrey Grandesmil
Gilbert De Clare
Eustace de Boulogne

Zaragoza
Yusuf Ibn Hud, Sheikh Ishmael
Malik Ibn Hud – Sheikh Ishmael's son
Al Cazar – Ferdinand the Castilian merchant
Abu J'far – Head of the Hud dynasty (Berbers)

32

Glossary

Bailey - A ward or courtyard in a castle, some outer Baileys could be huge, encompassing grazing land, stables, blacksmiths and huts.

Basilica – An early Christian church or cathedral designated by the Pope and given the highest permanent designation. Once given, the title cannot be removed.

Braies - A type of trouser often used as an undergarment, often to mid-calf and made of light or heavier linen.

Castellan – An appointed official or Governor of a castle.

Chatelaine – The Lady in charge of a large establishment, holder of all the keys.

Chausses – Attached by laces to the waist of the braies, these were tighter-fitting coverings for the legs.

Citole or Vielle – An early stringed instrument similar to fiddles

Cog – Clinker-built trading ship with a single mast and a square-rigged sail. They had wide flat bottoms allowing them to load and unload in shallow harbours.

Dais – A raised platform in a hall for a throne or tables, often for nobles.

Diocese - The diocese is the territorial jurisdiction of a bishop.

Donjon – An early name for the innermost keep of a castle.

Doublet – A close-fitting jacket or jerkin often made from leather, with or without sleeves. Laced at the front and worn under or over, a chain mail hauberk.

Fealty – sworn loyalty to a lord or patron.

Give No Quarter – To give no mercy or show no clemency for the vanquished.

Gunwale – The top edge or rail of a ship's hull, previously known as the bulwark.

Holy See – The jurisdiction of the Bishop of Rome – the Pope.

Keep – A fortified tower, initially made of wood, then replaced by stone built on a mound within a medieval castle.

Largesse – Money or gifts given generously often to the local population.

Lateran Palace – The main papal residence in Rome.

League – A league is equivalent to around 3 miles in modern terms.

Leman – An illicit lover or mistress.

Mead – An alcoholic beverage made by fermenting honey, fruits, spices, grains or hops.

Monseigneur – A title and honorific in the Catholic Church.

Pallet bed – A bed made of straw or hay. Close to the ground, generally covered by a linen sheet and also known as a palliasse.

Pell – A stout wooden post for sword practice.

Pontiff – Another name for the Pope.

Pottage – A staple of the medieval diet, a thick soup made from boiling grains, vegetables, and meat or fish, if available.

Prelate – A high-ranking member of the clergy.

Prie-dieu - A kneeling bench designed for use by a person at prayer.

Prior/Prioress – A monastic, or Priory Superior, lower in rank than an Abbot.

Refectory – A dining room in a monastery.

Saracen – Members of Arab tribes who professed the religion of Islam in the middle ages.

Sayyid – Arabic word for a lord or noble person.

Seneschal – A senior position or Principal Administrator of the royal household in France.

Solar – The solar was a room in many medieval castles on a top story with windows to gain sunlight and warmth. They were usually the private quarters or chambers of the family. A room of comfort and status.

Vavasseur –manservant, a right hand man.

Vedette - An outrider or scout used by cavalry.

Vellum - Finest scraped and treated calfskin, used for writing messages.

33

Author Note

It is difficult to get a clear picture of what happened in the last days before King William the Conqueror died, mainly because several accounts by monks and priests of the period and those written later contradict each other.

During his lifetime, William promised Robert the Duchy of Normandy, seen as the prime inheritance for the eldest son and the more important of the two territories. William Rufus was sent to the English court as his father's representative. However, powerful clerics such as Lanfranc, the Archbishop of Canterbury, recorded that Robert was always William's sole heir. Many of the nobility believed this as well. Hence Robert's desire to challenge his brother, William Rufus. However, as we have seen he did not succeed in his plans.

Again there are various reasons why Robert did not sail for England, some plausible. There was no doubt the betrayal of De Warenne at York and the panic of William de St Calais sounded the death knell of the rebellion in England. The Prince Bishop, William de St Calais, did go on trial and argued his case so well that he was only banished for his betrayal of the King William

Rufus. However, he returned to favour and his post in Durham in 1091, where he finished planning and building his cathedral, one of the most splendid examples of Norman architecture.

A similar fate befell the King's uncle, Bishop Odo, who lost all of his English lands and spent the rest of his life at Robert's side in Normandy. The scene at Rochester Castle, when the prisoners of the King were cleverly rescued during the parlay, happened almost as described to the embarrassment of the King and his lords.

The riot and slaughter at Rouen in 1090, funded by William Rufus to overthrow Duke Robert, was a dark stain on the town's history, with hundreds of citizens killed, often by each other. The tower at Rouen Castle is still known to this day as Conan's leap after Henry threw the leader of the rebellion from the window. Conan begged for his life, but Henry actually replied: *'By my mother's soul, there shall be no ransom for a traitor, only swifter infliction of the death he deserves.'*

The Berber or Saracen pirates terrified the traders of the Mediterranean for hundreds of years, and North Africa became known as the notorious Barbary Coast to be avoided at all costs. Hundreds of fishermen and crews ended up in the galleys of the pirates. Although our Sheikh Ishmael used what is today called Majorca as his headquarters at Palma.

Guided by the hand of Flambard, over the following years, William Rufus made serious incursions into northern Normandy until finally, after a stalemate, both brothers came to an accord and came together to turn on Henry. He fled at first and was banished to Brittany but then he patiently waited for his opportunity to have his brutal revenge on both of his older brothers. However, that tale is for another time.

Sarah Jane Martin

34

Maps

MAPS

MAPS

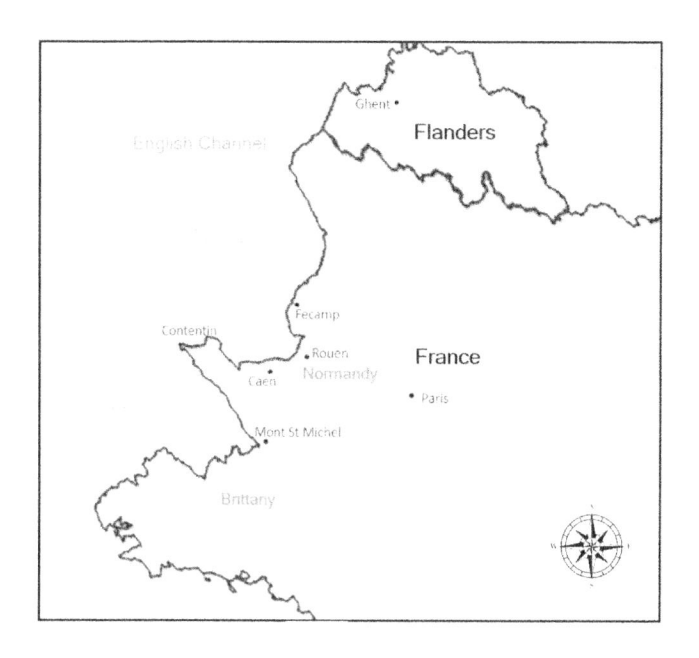

35

Read More

The Papal Assassin's Curse
Book Three in the Papal Assassin Series

Piers De Chatillon, antihero, paid assassin, wealthy and powerful, now seems to have everything. A beautiful, loving wife, thriving twin boys and the friendship of some of the most feared warriors in Europe. Nonetheless, he has made dozens of enemies along the way, and one of them is prepared to risk everything to destroy him.

Europe in 1096 was a turbulent place. Duke Robert's invasion of England has failed, and he is trying to hold on to Normandy while both of his brothers plot to take it. Piers De Chatillon, as Papal Envoy, is trying to steer a ship through these troubled waters just as his uncle, Pope Urban, calls for a crusade to liberate the Holy Land. Duke Robert foolishly leads this crusade leaving Normandy in the hands of his brother, William Rufus. At the same time, Chatillon receives an assassination request that shocks him. He is offered a fortune to kill a king!

READ MORE

Meanwhile, Yusuf Ibn Hud, known as Sheikh Ishmael, one of the most brutal and feared pirates in the Mediterranean, is launching a plan to tear the heart out of Chatillon's world. The pirate intends to snatch Pier's wife and children while Piers is on his way to Rome with the Crusaders. Will Pier's friend, Edvard, and the Irish warlord, Finian Ui Neil be able to stop them, or will Chatillon lose everything?

The Papal Assassin's Curse is available from Amazon Books

About the Author

I have had an abiding love of history from an early age. This interest not only influenced my academic choices at university but also my life choices and careers. I spent several years with my trowel in the world of archaeology before finding my forte as a storyteller in the guise of a history teacher. I wanted to encourage young people to find that same interest in history that had enlivened my life.

I always wanted to write historical fiction. The opportunity came when I left education; I then gleefully re-entered the world of engaging with the fascinating historical research into the background of some of my favourite historical periods. There are so many stories still waiting to be told, and my first series of books on 'The Breton Horse Warriors' proved to be one of them. The Breton lords, such as my fictional Luc De Malvais, played a significant role in the Battle of Hastings and helped to give William the Conqueror a decisive win. They were one of the most exciting troops of cavalry and swordmasters in Western Europe.

I hope you enjoy reading my books as much as I have enjoyed writing them.

You can connect with me on:

🌐 https://moonstormbooks.com/sjmartin
🐦 https://twitter.com/SJMarti40719548
📘 https://www.facebook.com/people/SJ-Martin-Author/100064591194374

Subscribe to my newsletter:
✉ https://moonstormbooks.com/sjmartin

Also by S.J. Martin

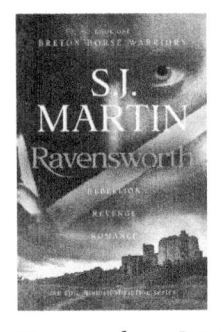

The Breton Horse Warriors (5 book series)

The Breton Horse Warriors series follows the adventures of our hero Luc De Malvais and his brother Morvan. It begins in Saxon England during the Norman Conquest and travels to war-torn Brittany and then Normandy. Luc De Malvais is a Breton lord, a master swordsman and leader of the famous horse warriors. He faces threatening rebellion, revenge and warfare as he fights to defeat the enemies of King William. However, his duty and loyalty to his king come at a price as his marriage and family is torn apart. He now has to do everything he can to save his family name, the love of his life and his banished brother...but at what price?

Book 1-**Ravensworth** - Rebellion. Revenge. Romance.
Book 2-**Rebellion** - Deceit. Desire. Defeat.
Book 3-**Betrayal** - Beguiled. Betrayed. Banished.
Book 4-**Banished** - Subterfuge. Seduction. Sacrifice.
Book 5-**Vengeance** - Passion. Perfidy. Pursuit.

Printed in Great Britain
by Amazon